Finding Thomas

Christopher J. Holcroft

OTHER TITLES BY
Christopher J. Holcroft

Only the Brave Dare
Canyon
A Rite of Passage
One Last Concert
Time Voyager

FINDING THOMAS

CHRISTOPHER J. HOLCROFT

DoctorZed
Publishing
www.doctorzed.com

This third edition published 2022 by DoctorZed Publishing.

DoctorZed Publishing books may be ordered through booksellers or by contacting:

DoctorZed Publishing
10 Vista Ave
Skye, South Australia 5072
www.doctorzed.com
61-(0)8 8431-4965

ISBN: 978-0-6455705-7-1 (sc)
ISBN: 978-0-6455705-8-8 (e)

A CIP number for this book is available at the National Library of Australia.

DoctorZed Publishing rev. date: 30/08/2022

To my wife Yvonne,
for her everlasting love.

To my brothers, Mark and Peter,
your passing was an awakening of the spirit.

To youth everywhere…
do not be worried when it comes to your time to die.
Death is a place filled with the purest of love.

*"When you were born, you cried and the world rejoiced.
Live your life in a manner so that when you die,
the world cries and you rejoice."*

Native American Proverb

Prologue

The phone rang and a familiar voice came on the line. The caller was panicking. The usual self-calm and measured delivery of the speech was now a machine gun burst of English aimed at trying to come to terms with the accident that had seemingly robbed the family of their only son.

"Daniel! Daniel, Kit's dead!" Leah yelled and sobbed through the phone in half sleep, half wake tone. It was 3 pm and Leah's afternoon sleep was over. She had woken with a jolt and had started reliving the day she found their fourteen-year-old son lying face down in the family's backyard swimming pool. The dream had a recurring theme and Daniel just had to stop work and quietly talk to his wife who had automatically rung her husband before being fully awake.

"Sweetie, it's okay. Kit's alive and doing well. He went to school today and should be home soon," Daniel said. "Leah, you've had another nightmare. It's okay. Kit is fine thanks to you. If you didn't know CPR he would be dead, but he's fine."

Leah was sobbing and slowly came to her senses with the reassuring tone of her husband. It had been a hard couple of weeks for the family as Kit regained consciousness in the hospital and re-started his life. Kit had been home with his mother during the holidays and decided to go for a dip in the pool. He walked onto the patio but tripped on a toy his five-year-old cousin Tara had left there earlier. The fall sent the lad crashing into the corner of a table and then ricocheting into the pool. He was knocked unconscious in the fall and landed face down in the water. Leah heard a commotion and came to investigate. She saw Kit floating face down in the pool with a stream of blood issuing from his head.

Without thinking, Leah jumped into the pool and turned Kit over. She dragged him to the edge of the pool and pushed and shoved him out of the water and onto the pebble-type surrounds. Leah jumped out of the pool and felt Kit's pulse. There was none. The boy was not breathing. Instinctively Leah knelt next to her son, put her lips over his and gave him several breaths. She ran her fingers down his chest to above his sternum and placed the heel of her right palm on Kit and her left palm on top of the other. Rhythmically the young mother pushed down on her son's chest. She did the count, stopped, and breathed some more into the boy. Leah watched her son's chest and then put her ear to his mouth to hear for any breathing. She continued into a second count and checked the boy's breathing. Kit's lungs re-started slowly, and he began taking in small breaths on his own. Life had returned to her son.

Blood still poured from the wound on Kit's head and the boy remained unconscious. Once Kit's breathing stabilised, Leah went to the phone and called for an ambulance. She quickly put a pad on her son's wound and bandaged his head to stem the bleeding.

Kit was taken to the hospital and within a short time was

being operated on to relieve pressure on his brain. The boy died on the operating table and was pronounced 'clinically dead' for more than five minutes. Just as the surgeon was about to call Kit's time of death, the boy's heart started beating and his lungs began breathing on their own.

The surgical staff was stunned and stood in awe before the surgeon yelled out: "He's back!"

Daniel poured himself another cup of coffee and sat down at his desk. "Leah, Kit's okay now. You did well. The medical staff helped save his life too and now our son is living a normal life."

"I'm, I'm sorry Daniel," Leah said as she fought back tears. "I had a sleep and dreamt he had died … and never came back."

"Darling it's okay. Kit should be finishing school shortly and will be on his way home. He's okay. I'll be home in a couple of hours."

"Okay. I'm sorry. I'll grab a shower and organise some afternoon tea for him."

"That's my girl. See you soon. Love you."

"Love you too."

Chapter One

Kit Green could hardly wait to talk to his mother. He had a feeling of Deja Vue after his history lesson and felt uncomfortable with the experience.

This was quite unusual for the 14-year-old hardy teenager. Kit believed he was impervious to all manner of things. However, today was different. Today, Kit's history teacher Miss Isles, walked the class through what life was like on the streets of London in the 1820s. This included clothes people wore; the gas lights used to brighten street corners, food and illnesses. Kit sat transfixed. He had lived all this and knew it backwards. The smells of old London wafted into Kit's subconscious. He started to drift off.

"Kit! Are you okay," Miss Isles asked.

"Sorry Miss. I'm back now," Kit said.

"Good. Now stay with us."

The history lesson was the last lecture period of the day. Kit felt funny about the lecture. Several times he wanted to jump into Miss Isle's descriptions of things and explain how they affected ordinary Londoners of the period. How did he know? This was the 21st Century, not the early 19th. When the school chimes rang to signal the end of the period, Kit stayed behind. He struck up a conversation with Miss Isles.

"Miss, do you believe we've improved that much since the days of Hazlitt or Thomas Hardy?"

"Kit, you tell me. You heard all the things I outlined today about life in the 1820s. Much difference to today?"

"Yeah, in a lot of ways. However, people haven't changed that much, have they? We still believe in the same sorts of things. All we have done is updated our clothes and available technology."

"Yes. You seem very passionate about the subject."

"Miss, I felt today from the descriptions, that I had lived around the time of Hazlitt and the French Revolution that you taught us earlier. I had the feeling I could almost name the streets of central London of the time."

The history teacher was stunned and studied her young charge. "Kit there has been any number of TV series depicting life in the 1800s. Maybe your mind was attracted to one of these and today's lesson reinforced what you saw."

"You're right Miss. That's it, thanks," Kit lied. His mind was like a steel trap. He had a pretty good memory and did not remember any similar TV series. No. He had lived in London in the early 1800s. Now was not the time to argue with his teacher. Kit needed something more to base his claims on. He looked at his watch, made his excuses and ran to the bus stop. Time was short if he was going to catch the early bus. Thirty minutes later Kit walked through the front door of his home.

Leah had cut up some fruit and placed it in the fridge ready for Kit. Her son loved eating cool fruit and chatting to her about his day. The front door slammed as Kit made his way into the kitchen.

"Hi, Mum."

"Hi Kit. Have a good day?"

"Yeah, but you won't believe what happened," Kit said in an excited tone.

Leah sat on a stool at the breakfast bar. She knew when Kit was excited about something he became quite passionate about it. Today seemed no different. She saw the expression on Kit's face when he came into the house. The teenager's face was lit up, his eyes widened and he was expressive with his hands.

"She took us through a typical day in London in the early 1800s, but I could have taught the class myself about what it was like."

"Whoa, big guy! Who did what and when?"

"Yeah, sorry. In history, Miss Isles took us through a typical day in London in the 1790s. I felt I had already really been there and could have told the class more about life in the homes and factories of the period than she could."

"Kit, you were born at the end of the 21st Century – not the 19th. How could you have had more intimate knowledge of the times than your teacher?"

"Well, that's the rub. I don't know. When Miss Isles got down into the nitty-gritty of life in London, I started having all these images hit my brain, like real memories. I felt the cold, smelt the coal dust, and saw the pale-looking people walk the dirt roads or cobbled pavements as they went about their business. I heard the carriages and the clip-clop of horses. I was there."

"Wow! You have a great imagination!"

Kit studied his mother's face. She was taking the same line

as Miss Isles. "Mum, I don't know how I have this knowledge. I just feel I was there. Ever since my pool accident, I have had this build-up of knowledge of life in England. I've got no idea why. But at least, if I have to write any essays on the period, I'll be okay. I can easily flood the pages with images as if I was standing looking out of my window and observing life as it was … is … whatever."

"The problem with that will be substantiating what you are writing about. You'll need to have a credible source the examiners and teachers know about and use them to tell the story."

"Like having third-party endorsement or something?"

"Yes."

Kit picked up a piece of fruit and started eating it. He thought about what his mother just said. She was right. Who was going to believe his feelings, no matter what Kit thought or remembered?

Leah discussed the rest of the school day with Kit before he finished his fruit and got up to leave.

"What about your plate?"

"Sorry, I'll put it in the dishwasher."

Kit went to his bedroom to change out of his school uniform and start his homework. Like any other teenager, Kit hated homework but knew he had to do it to score some good grades and maybe a good job at the end. His room was messy and needed a good tidy-up. When Kit took off his clothes to change, he would leave them lying around on the floor rather than in the dirty washing hamper and the usual parent-teenager arguments would ensue to clean his room.

This was not the first time Kit had had a flashback-type event in the 19th Century. The teenager had been asleep after a routine day of holidays. Daniel and Leah were asleep in bed and had their bedroom door open. A change of light conditions in her bedroom and the outside hallway walls aroused her from her sleep. She saw an eerie light moving along the hallway and nudged Daniel awake. The couple sat up and watched as Kit slowly walked past their bedroom holding a lit candle on a saucer in front of him. It was a scene straight out of Dickens. Kit walked to the kitchen, placed the saucer on the breakfast bar and opened the fridge to get a drink of cold water. He drank from the bottle and then made his way back to his bedroom with Daniel still watching him. The lad blew out the candle and snuggled up in his bed and went back to sleep. When Daniel asked Kit about the incident in the morning, the teenager did not know about the event. He couldn't explain why he had a candle in his room or why he didn't use the torch on his bedside table. What was so strange for both Daniel and Leah was the automatic response of Kit to light a candle to use as light rather than pick up a torch. Daniel joked to Leah they should buy their son a nightcap and long night dress instead of pyjamas, that way he'd be right at home. Kit's experience at school was another episode the family could not explain.

The first episode took place within a couple of hours after Kit was operated on after his accident. The teenager had been moved to the recovery ward from the operating theatre while he recovered from the effects of the anesthetic. The surgeon, Dr Liam Curry, had gone to check on his patient. Kit had slowly come round and was awake when Dr Curry visited him.

"Kit, I'm Dr Curry. How are you feeling?"

Kit studied the doctor's face and turned away from looking at him.

"What's up mate? Are you feeling nauseous or light-headed? This is normal after what you've been through."

Kit took a moment to gather his thoughts and then looked directly at his surgeon. "You gave up on me. Why?"

Dr Curry was shocked. He knew Kit had gone from the operating theatre straight to the recovery room while unconscious. He was not prepared for Kit's questioning.

"Kit, are you okay? No one gave up on you. You've had an accident and we had to operate to take the pressure off your brain. You'll be fine."

"You gave up on me during the operation and were about to send me to the morgue!" Kit looked at Dr Curry as the surgeon's eyes widened and his mouth fell open. "The nurse kept saying you should keep trying to revive me with the paddles. You gave up on me. I saw you ready to walk away."

"Kit, what the hell are you talking about?"

"Dr Curry, I saw the whole operation you performed on me. I don't know how it happened, but I was floating above the operating table. When my heart stopped beating you tried a couple of times to revive me and then gave up. You seemed to be in a hurry to go somewhere."

Tears started seeping from Kit's eyes as he watched Dr Curry. The surgeon had stood rooted to the spot as Kit questioned him and told him of his near-death experience. The lad was becoming emotional. Dr Curry walked to the side of Kit's bed and put a hand on the youth's shoulder. Dr

Curry had only experienced one other patient who had had an out-of-body experience during one of his operations.

"Kit, what you experienced is extraordinary. For whatever reason, you were given a special time that most of us will never know. What you saw was a routine operation. When your heart stopped, I tried several times to restart it. When there was no response, I thought I had lost you."

"The nurse near my head kept telling you to keep trying to save me but you wanted to give up. Why didn't you want to keep trying?"

"Kit, I thought your body had given up. Your vital signs had ceased. I believed you had died. What else did you see?"

"I saw and heard you arguing with the nurses. I tried telling you I was alive, but no one could hear me."

"Your heart had stopped, and your brain had started shutting down. Kit you were dead!"

"I wasn't. I was watching you from above the table and yelling at you …"

Dr Curry squeezed Kit's shoulder and then ran his hand down to the lad's hand and held it. "I really believed you had died. Whatever happened to you that enabled you to see and hear what was happening from above the table is very special. You are a very lucky teenager …"

Kit tried to come to grips with what his surgeon was saying and what he remembered about the operation and out-of-body experience. It was not easy as he was having problems with the effects of coming out of the operation too.

"Try to have a sleep and I'll talk to you later when you're moved to the ward."

Dr Curry gripped Kit's hand and smiled. A nurse who followed Dr Curry on his rounds had stood in the doorway to the ward and wiped tears from her eyes as she realised what Kit had been through. A miracle had happened, and the boy had been given a second chance at life. A new beginning – a nascent - had started for the boy.

Kit gripped the doctor's hand and nodded. He closed his eyes and let his body take over. He was tired and he had so much to think about – later. Now, he just needed sleep. He knew he would talk with the doctor again. Dr Curry stopped doing his rounds and headed for the staff room and made himself a cup of tea. Usually, his patients are asleep before he walked into the operating theatre. He only had to conduct his operations and then do his rounds. A routine for the doctor. Kit had thrown a spanner in the works for him. The boy not only accurately described what took place while he was under the knife and unconscious, but what was also being said. Dr Curry finished his tea and tried to make sense of what had just happened with Kit. He then made his way to the visitor's area and sought the teenager's parents to tell them of their son's experience, so they were prepared. Daniel and Leah were as stunned as Dr Curry but were quite ready to support their son. After all, it's not every day someone in the family floats around an operating theatre while being operated on and sees and hears what's happening while outside of their body!

After a few more hours of sleep, Kit slowly woke up to find his parents sitting on either side of his bed and his mother holding his right hand. He broke into a smile as his eyes engaged each of his parents. His smile was returned quickly as his parents realised their son was okay. The bandage around his head was the real giveaway and would stay on for a little while.

"How are you feeling now, son?" Daniel asked.

"Okay, I think. I have a headache, but I'm okay," the teenager said.

"We thought we had lost you," Leah said as she kissed Kit on his forehead. "You certainly gave us a fright."

"Gave you a fright?" Kit said and then thought of what he wanted to say about his out-of-body experience and his trip to heaven. "I'm okay. I've been in good hands." Kit didn't want to engage his parents now about his trip to heaven or wherever he was taken and then sent back.

Within a week of Kit being discharged from the hospital he was back to his normal routine including school. He made his way home on the bus, changed into a pair of shorts and a T-shirt and settled down at his desk to review his homework as a test was coming up. He stared at his books and drifted off in his mind. Scenes of old England filled his senses. The tick-tock of his wall clock turned into the clip-clop of horses pulling carriages along the mews. Photos of Kit and his family melted into the windows of a small bedroom in 18th Century London with images of children in peculiar clothes and their parents looking up as Kit was looking down. Two young boys were wearing three-quarter pants with coat tails; funny-looking boots and no socks, small caps and fingerless gloves. The mother had a shawl wrapped around her shoulders, a long-sleeved dress that went all the way down to her shoes and carried a small football-shaped handbag. The father had a very old top hat that was frayed, crumpled, and well worn. Like his sons, the father had a topcoat with tails and a cut-away waistline. His trousers went over his shoes, but he also wore fingerless gloves. The man began pointing up to the window. Kit pulled back from the window image and shook his head. This was not happening. The images were not real. The teenager's bedroom came quickly back into view.

"Phew. I'm back," Kit said as he quickly took in his room.

His books were still open and his pen resting in his hand. Kit was becoming concerned as the vision he just had was not a one-off. Since his pool accident, Kit had experienced several visions of old England along with scenes of ordinary day-to-day living. The visions were so strong Kit felt he could even smell the streetscapes; the sooty air from the coal fires and rain-drenched roads. At times, Kit would see the 19th Century gas lighter walking to the glass-topped poles along the street to light the various gas lights and so illuminate the road. He could even hear horse-drawn carriages as they made their way along the old wooden and stone cobbled streets.

Two other things had happened to Kit since his operation. The first was his ability to see colourful strong lights emanating from people. He learnt these were people's auras and could be used as a roadmap to how people were feeling. The second was that sometimes when he touched people, he felt how they felt. It was like opening the door into the other person's soul and feeling their fears, loves, aspirations, and anger.

Kit worried about these images and visions and was sure he was starting to develop some sort of mental condition. His real issue was trying to stop them.

Chapter Two

Daniel found it hard to concentrate on his job. Ever since Kit had been injured and operated on, the family had undergone some sort of change. Leah was not the happy-go-lucky person she used to be. Instead, she was very cautious about all Kit and Daniel did in case they injured themselves. Kit had had recurring dreams of living in England two centuries ago and sometimes prowled the house at night like a character from 19th Century books. He was also too accurate about how his parents and others felt. Sometimes, he would just look around a person as if he was enjoying a light show.

Daniel on the other hand was a pragmatist. He lived life as he saw it. The problem was some of the things Kit was saying at home had been worrisome and had started ringing alarm bells in his and Leah's minds. Their son had been able to recount dreams of everyday life in England as if he had just been there. However, today would alarm them. While Leah was having a shower and Kit was making breakfast the teenager told his father he wanted to talk to him about something important.

"Dad, you're working on a special project with Mr. Sullivan, aren't you?" Kit asked.

"Yes. It's the re-election campaign for him and his party. Why?"

"What if I told you Mr. Sullivan was looking at using you as some form of scapegoat involving the Police?"

Daniel studied Kit for a few seconds. There was no way he would know anything about his work in detail, let alone a secret report to replace the Police Commissioner if Sullivan's party won power.

"Well Kit, I'd be wondering what you know and how you found out."

Kit poured some more orange juice and tried to find the best words to use with his father. This was not going to be easy.

"Dad, since my operation a series of weird things have been happening to me. I look out my window and instead of seeing the park and kids playing ball, I see the streets of London and hear and see horse-drawn carriages being pulled up the Mall."

"Kit, that's not answering my question about my work. Has your mother spoken to you about the details of what I do at the agency?"

"No."

"Well then, how would you know anything about Mr. Sullivan and the Police?"

Kit steeled himself. "His son David came to see me last night and we talked for a while about what you were doing."

Daniel dropped his toast. He was now shocked. David Sullivan was the teenage son of Terry Sullivan, a Member of Parliament Daniel had as a client in his public relations firm. The problem was David died in a car accident when he was aged 17, and that was 10 years ago.

"Kit, David has been dead for a decade. How could you be talking with him?"

"Dad, I don't know. One moment I was trying to do my homework and the next thing I know this shimmering guy was sitting on my bed looking at me. At first, I freaked as I thought he was an intruder. Then he calmly spoke to me about you."

"Kit this can't be real. You wouldn't even know David existed or how he died. Your mother and I don't even talk about him. Anyway, what do you mean by shimmering?"

"I could sort of see through him as his image was shimmering – not whole like you and me. Dad, he told me to tell you he died in a 1990's red sedan after it hit a power pole. He had been out drinking with some mates and tried to drive home. He was the driver and was killed instantly in the accident. His two mates were thrown out of the car and lived."

Daniel was speechless. Kit had conjured a scene from a movie where a young boy talked to the dead. The issue was that this was a real scenario still playing itself out in this world and Kit had the details. Daniel sat opposite Kit at the table.

"Kit, I don't get it. You know nothing really about some of my projects at work because I haven't told you, yet you hit me with the most secret of them all. What else did this David tell you?"

"Dad, he said to be careful. David said since his death he had been watching over his father. However, things were being put in train by Mr. Sullivan that could kill him and cause grief to you too!"

"Like what?" Daniel was sitting very tense and hung off every word Kit said.

"Dad, David said if you continue on the Ratcliffe matter,

it will set in motion several things that could lead to Mr. Sullivan's murder and possibly yours!"

Daniel sat flummoxed. He had not mentioned the move by Sullivan to axe the current Police Commissioner, Todd Ratcliffe if Sullivan's party won the next State election to either Leah or Kit. And few people in the Public Relations firm where Daniel was employed knew he was working with the company's Government Relations Co-Ordinator on possible initiatives to replace the Commissioner. Daniel never took his eyes off Kit.

"Kit, how could this David tell the future? If he's that good ask him for next week's lottery numbers," he said with a marked tone of sarcasm.

Now it was Kit's turn to study his father intently. He knew he had just thrown his dad into a spin but he couldn't think of any other way to do it. Seeing the spirit of a dead teenager was only one of the issues he was personally battling and trying to come to grips with too. Kit composed himself and slowed down his racing mind.

"I asked David that as I didn't believe what he was telling me. However, you seem to have confirmed what he said to me so maybe he is real. David said spirits can't foretell the future and cannot tell you directly what is happening. When I asked why he just shrugged his shoulders."

"This doesn't quite hold water son. How come he, or this ghost, or whatever it was, has told you what he has seen so far?"

"Okay. He painted a picture like this. Imagine being in a helicopter and watching a car travel along a highway. You can see where the car has been, where it is now and where it is going. You can't see all the details about the car, who is inside, conversations people have had or what people are seeing. However, you can see the car's journey. It's the same with how the spirits see us in our everyday lives. They can't stop us because of our free will. Some try and warn us to change the courses we are on. David is one of those."

Daniel sipped his coffee and went white. He knew Kit had been having some problems since his accident and 'death' on the operating table. However, this was unbelievable. Daniel had never really believed in an afterlife and spirits, ghosts or poltergeists. Kit had turned his whole world upside down the day he was operated on and could recall everything that took place in the operating theatre while he was under the anaesthetic. Now, to hear his son had spoken with his client's dead son who had outlined a possible future was disturbing. The two sat in silence for a minute while each digested what had just transpired.

"Kit, can you call on David somehow and ask him things?"

"I don't know. I've never tried. Dad I'm just an ordinary teenager who is experiencing some heavy stuff at the moment. I don't know what to do."

Daniel got up from his side of the table and walked around to Kit. He put his arms around him and gently kissed him on the forehead.

"Kit, you just carry on being our son. Your mother and I love you very much. I'll try to find a way to help you. In the meantime, if David appears again to tell you something important let me know straight away. You can even ring me at work."

"Okay, thanks, Dad."

"Oh, Kit. Thank David for the warning."

Daniel finished his cup of coffee and walked upstairs to the shower where Leah was drying off. He opened the door and then shut it quietly behind him. Leah could tell something had happened by the strain on Daniel's face.

"What's up love?" she enquired.

Daniel closed the toilet seat lid and sat on it. He looked his wife directly in the eyes and said Kit had another issue and that it involved him this time. Leah stopped drying herself and sat on the edge of the bath, wrapped the towel around herself and listened intently to her husband. Daniel only detailed the gist of what Kit had said so he didn't over-concern his wife. In the end, Leah looked as dumbfounded as Daniel had earlier. Both had no idea where to go or how to help their son with his sightings and visions. Their religion had dealt with Jesus Christ and his apostles driving unclean spirits from people who were tormented. Kit was becoming concerned but was not tormented. Anyway, what was an unclean spirit the couple asked themselves? What did a spirit look like? Do they really exist? If so, how can they communicate with some people and not others?

Daniel went back downstairs and saw Kit dressed for school and ready to go out the door.

"Kit thanks for telling me what you did earlier. I'm glad you have remained as calm as you have and taken a grip on the situation, but I wouldn't be telling anyone else about our discussion as it could jeopardise what David has told you. Okay?"

"Okay Dad," Kit said and broke into a huge smile. "I guess what's happening to me is just another part of my personality and I have to learn to live with it."

Daniel winced when he heard Kit. "Yes, for the moment. Your mother and I will try and get someone to help you. In the meantime, don't mention anything to your friends."

"No probs. See you, dad." Kit then walked up the hallway and yelled goodbye to his mother before he ran out of the front door on his way to school.

Daniel went back upstairs and finished dressing. Again, he and Leah spoke about Kit and the boy's visions. The couple was determined to help their son, but each agreed it would be hard to find the right person to help Kit.

The drive across town seemed to take forever for Daniel as his mind kept returning to what Kit had said about the plan, he was working on with Terry Sullivan to oust the current Police Commissioner if Sullivan's party won the elections. Commissioner Ratcliffe had come under the notice of the Opposition several times by people who had claimed the top cop had intervened in criminal activities and was supposedly in the pay of organised crime bosses. Too many times the Commissioner was linked with both the Government and crime. He had to go so confidence could be restored in the Police Force as an independent arm of justice. Daniel's Government Relations Co-Ordinator at his firm was Reg Clementson. He was a hard-nosed political person who worked long hours talking with party members about various issues. His main drive was to ensure the public relations firm was the preferred company to deliver the party's messages if fortunes changed in the next election and the Opposition party won government.

Daniel wasn't sure where to go with Kit's 'spiritual insight' as to what was happening. When he entered the company building, he went straight to his office and closed the door. He asked the receptionist to hold all calls for 30 minutes. Maybe this would give him a head start. Daniel pulled out the Ratcliffe file and started poring over it. Somewhere in the file, there may be a lead as to why Sullivan was becoming a target, never mind himself.

A tall wide figure with a flat top haircut in the guise of Reg Clementson filled the glass frame of Daniel's office door and tapped on the glass. He walked straight in without bothering to be asked to enter.

"Mate, you, okay?" Reg asked as he made his way into Daniel's office. "I saw you walk in and tried to ring but the receptionist said you weren't taking calls for half an hour."

"Sorry, Reg. Sit down, please," Daniel said as he closed the Ratcliffe file and looked directly at his guest. "You know when you have one of those nights when you wake up and something you were doing either at work or home is niggling you and you can't work out why? Well, I had one of those nights."

"So, what's bothering you about Ratcliffe?"

Daniel was about to say something Kit had said. Instead, he changed tack. "Well, this is only the first file I am about to go over. I want to ensure everything is right on track and where we want to go."

"Mate, of course, it is. Terry has had it confirmed by the party leader that Ratcliffe will be replaced the day after the election win. We'll have his Deputy Commissioner; Ken McRae take over until we can advertise the position. It can't be clearer than that."

There was something in the way Clementson spoke that didn't sit well with Daniel. He made small talk with his offsider until the first phone call came through. A voice broke in over the intercom. "Mr. Green, Mr. Sullivan called and wants to discuss the upcoming fundraiser with you."

"Jenny, I thought you were holding calls for me for 30 minutes," Daniel said.

"I did Mr. Green. I have a list of four calls to be returned. It's now been 35 minutes since you arrived."

Daniel was surprised. "Thanks, Jenny."

"Okay, Daniel I better get back to work too and leave you to Terry," Clementson said. "He probably wants to see your latest designs on the flyers for the major sponsors."

"Thanks, Reg. I appreciate your help. I'll give Terry a ring and see if he's happy with my first drafts."

Clementson looked at Daniel and then the Ratcliffe file on his desk as he stood up to leave. "Daniel don't get too wrapped over the axles with Ratcliffe. He's only one of a clutch of front-line Government appointees we're looking at replacing. The Opposition feels they can't work with the man as he's too well connected with thugs and crooks. Don't worry; his going is all part of the game."

"Thanks, Reg. I just want to ensure we have the right answers for the right time once the announcements are made."

The two men shook hands and Clementson left the office. Daniel sat back down and mentally went over what had just taken place. He knew he was on the right track. The question was which one? He also wanted to arrange drinks with Terry Sullivan away from his office so he could discuss his son David but there was no way he was going to reveal Kit had said he had spoken to David. That would be so hard to prove and could upset Sullivan enough to move his business away from Daniel's firm.

Also, he wanted more information on Ratcliffe.

Chapter Three

Leah mulled over what Daniel had said to her earlier about Kit. Within her circle of friends, there must be someone who could give her some insight as to who to contact to help her son. She arranged to meet Sarah Kaplan, one of her old school friends, for lunch. The two women had attended different schools but had met on the sports field running against each other. They were pretty evenly matched for speed as teenagers and results see-sawed in each of their favours depending on the day. The pair decided to meet at a café within a shopping complex so they could check out the shops afterwards.

Leah was first to arrive at Café Central and ordered a pot of tea for two. She knew Sarah was quite diligent about being on time and the tea would serve as an ice breaker while they decided on what meal to order. No sooner had the waitress left after taking her order than a tall, stocky woman with a thick gold necklace started to approach. Sarah was still reasonably fit and played tennis and scuba dived. She was a strong woman both in character and physique. The two women kissed each other on the cheeks before Sarah sat down. They exchanged the usual pleasantries of enquiring into each other's family's health.

"Kit's doing well, but he is starting to worry Daniel and me about some of the things he comes out with," Leah said.

"Like what?" Sarah asked as she got more comfortable.

"I told you he says he has these visions of scenes straight out of 19th Century London. You know, horse-drawn carriages up the cobblestone streets and gas lighters lighting each of the corner gas lights – that sort of thing."

Sarah took in what Leah was saying. She had been a drug and alcohol counsellor for a decade and tuned in quickly to what people were saying and how they said it. "Maybe he's watched too much TV lately or has read books at school on the subject and they're playing in his mind."

"Could be. Daniel and I quizzed Kit over his schoolwork and the closest we came was his study of the history of life in the late 19th Century. It seemed he had been taking too much to heart over what he was studying."

"Either that or he has a wild imagination, or the study just ignited something inside him about the period forcing him to think he was seeing scenes of that period."

"Mmm, could be. He seemed to describe things as if he had just opened his bedroom window and saw London in the early 1800s."

"What else is happening with him?" Sarah asked as she finished her cup of tea.

Leah wasn't sure how Sarah would react to the latest news, and took her time before answering. "He told Daniel today he was visited by the ghost of a boy who sat on his bed and spoke to him."

Sarah's eyes lit up and she became spellbound. She leaned

forward to listen more intently to what Leah was saying. "Did this dead boy visit Kit for a reason? Was he also from the 19th Century?"

"No. The strange thing is that the boy supposedly died a decade ago and is the son of one of Daniel's clients."

"Did Kit know the boy or his family?"

"No. That is what is so strange. The boy said he wanted to tell Kit about some of the work Daniel was involved in."

"Is Kit concerned about his father's work or any impacts it is having on the family?"

"No, I don't think so. Daniel is working on the re-election strategies for the Opposition and rarely discusses his work with Kit – especially in detail."

"Leah, do you think Kit saw a ghost?"

"Well, he sounded pretty convincing."

"You know our two religions differ on ghosts and spirits. Yours won't talk about them except in general about unclean spirits driven out of people by Christ and his followers. In mine, we don't talk about spirits much at all."

"Why not? Don't they exist for all religions?"

Sarah sipped her tea and put the cup down. She looked Leah in the eyes. "We teach the story of the witch of Endor in the Jewish Bible – your Old Testament in the Christian Bible. Are you familiar with it?"

"No."

"This is another area where our two religions sort of meet. Check out 1 Samuel 28 where it talks about King Saul ruling over Israel with God's help and how he often spoke directly with God or had helpful dreams. Saul had issues with spirit

Mediums and had most of them killed, supposedly on the say-so of the Lord. There came a time when Saul's enemy the Amalekites threatened Israel and the Lord told Saul to kill every one of them including their animals. Saul instead captured the opposing king, and the Israelites kept the good animals of the Amalekites without killing them."

"So, Saul disobeyed God?"

"Yes. Therefore, God didn't speak to Saul anymore. The prophet Samuel was the one who told Saul what to do with the Amalekites. When Saul didn't do what he was told, Samuel told him that God had left him."

"Where does this bring our religions together?"

"Ah you see, Saul wanted someone to tell him what to do. He was used to dealing with the head spirit of us all, God. However, God ignored Saul after he disobeyed him. Anyway, after Samuel died, the Philistines started rising against Saul and Israel. Saul became worried as he had no one to spiritually advise and guide him. He posed as an ordinary man and went to see the witch of Endor and ask her to speak with the spirit of the dead Samuel. The witch supposedly conjured up the spirit of Samuel who told Saul he was soon to be defeated and would be joining him. Shortly afterwards the Philistines overthrew Saul and God's favour moved to a young boy called David."

"Is this the David of Goliath fame?"

"Yes. David beat the champion of the Philistines by using a slingshot. So began what you call the Jesse tree whose lineage reached down to include Jesus Christ."

Leah had slowly finished her cup of tea. She took in what Sarah had said but it was like a riddle.

"Okay, so your religion believes in the witch of Endor. How can that help me?"

"Well, since the days of Saul my religion has had nothing really to do with beliefs in the spirits of the dead. This has always caused a lot of discussion in our various communities and several people seeking the services of Mediums for advice. Leah, I can't help you but I know someone who can."

Sarah detailed a woman who lived near her and was believed to have the gift of speaking to the dead.

"You mean she's a Medium?" Leah asked.

"Yes. She's quite good and hard to get into to see."

"Why?"

"Leah, she's in heavy demand. I know her well and will speak with her this afternoon to see if she can see you and Kit. He'll need to go along and meet her too."

"Do you think it's wise to take Kit to see her with all the things happening to him?"

"That's exactly why you need to take him. Also, she will quickly see if what is happening to Kit is real or not."

Leah felt satisfied. She and Daniel had not wanted Kit to go to a psychologist and have endless sessions about his experiences. Seeing a Medium had not entered her head, but Leah believed deep down this mystery woman may hold a key to helping Kit come to terms with himself. The two former school friends finished their lunch and went shopping, with each picking up some good bargains.

Once the two women parted ways, Leah rang Daniel at his work and told him what Sarah had said. Daniel was initially taken aback at the thought of taking his son to a Medium.

However, the more he thought about it, the more he began to believe this could be a way forward for Kit and the rest of the family.

"You don't think this will screw him up any further, do you?" Daniel asked Leah.

"No. If we take him to see the local priest, we'll only be told that dealing with spirits is unhealthy and could lead Kit into all sorts of problems. I'm betting we'd be told to take him to a psychologist anyway and let him deal with Kit and any mental issues."

"Okay. But if this woman starts any mumbo jumbo stuff that looks like it could play on Kit's mind, you must promise me to leave straight away."

"Yes. Sarah seems to have pretty good faith in this woman as do several her friends."

"What? Have they all had a séance with her or something?"

"No. It's not like that. Apparently, they see her individually and the woman either tells them what's happening or uses her tarot cards to read for them."

"Well, that's certainly hedging your bets."

"What do you mean?"

Daniel paused for a moment. He didn't want this conversation now; he had too many things to do at work.

"I guess if the woman can't see what is happening directly with people, she resorts to tarot to help."

"Yes. The cards help confirm what she has felt or seen about a person. Anyway, I'll talk with you tonight about it."

"Alright, my love. See you soon."

The couple rang off and Leah drove home.

Chapter Four

Some of Kit's teachers had noticed changes in the teenager since his accident. The lad used to love playing football and roughing it with the other boys on the playing field. Now he stopped playing outdoor games and complained of sensitivity to sunlight. Kit was also on the school's debating team. Each member would wear portable microphones attached to their waist belts with the leads fed under their jackets to their lapels and a clip microphone – like television reporters. Now, Kit would only debate using his natural voice. He had found some intolerance to electrical devices close to his body. Also, more students would engage Kit at school as his personality seemed to be more charismatic and his wit increased. Some teachers put all the signs down to puberty and the sudden onset of extra hormones in the boy's body.

The science master, Mr. Nelson had also noticed the change in Kit but took a different view. Mr. Nelson had been teaching high school students for more than 30 years and had seen some interesting teenagers in his classrooms. Kit had started to stand out for him and come under his notice. Barry Nelson had worked closely with Kit before the boy's pool accident and found him meek and mild. He was a teenager undergoing normal growth spurts and was slightly awkward on his feet at times. The science master observed how Kit was very wary of the class bully and sat two rows away from him. Since Kit's pool accident, the lad had been more tolerant of the bully and more engaging with students from other cultures. His charm had seemed to increase, and more students were now interacting with Kit.

Mr. Nelson looked at his watch. Time was up. The unannounced test should now finish, and he would see who had been studying and who had not. He was about to call 'Pens down' when he looked at Kit. The teenager had been hard at work on the test but was now just looking at the students in front of him almost in awe in a sort of daydream mode.

"Okay pens down," Mr. Nelson said. Twenty-nine pens made noises as they were placed on the tables. The thirtieth belonged to Kit, and it was already down.

"I'm going to be holding some more impromptu tests as a lead-up to your final examinations, so get used to it. The best way to deal with them is to do your homework and some nightly study ..."

Before Mr. Nelson could go too far the electronic chimes sounded for the end of the period. The students packed their bags and started filing out of the classroom to their next subject.

"Kit, got a sec?" Mr. Nelson asked.

"Sir, always for you."

"You finished the test pretty quickly, is everything okay?"

"Yeah, I think so. You got me on some of the properties about the gases, but I think I did alright."

Kit studied Mr. Nelson. A strange feeling came over Kit as he looked at his teacher. "Is there a problem?"

"I noticed that when you finished your paper you sat looking at the boys in front of you as if you were seeing things for the first time. Is everything okay?"

Kit then realised what Mr. Nelson had observed. He had watched him take in the various coloured lights shimmering around the boys sitting in front of him. When the boys moved, so did their light emissions. The light show had captivated Kit.

"Sir, I'm okay. Thanks for asking."

"Kit, my brother had a near-death experience when he was a bit older than you, so I've lived with someone who probably had a similar journey to you. If ever, you want to talk about things, just let me know, okay?"

Kit was taken aback. He quickly focused.

"I'm fine. Thanks for the offer, though."

"Okay, Kit. Hurry to your next class."

Kit smiled and quickly walked out of the classroom and along the corridor towards his next lesson. He didn't realise Mr. Nelson had been observing him as he sat and watched all the beautiful, coloured lights around the other students. Seeing auras around people had only started after Kit had recovered from his pool accident. There were times when Kit was on the school bus or walking through the playground when he would see various coloured light emissions around people. It fascinated him but he didn't tell anyone for fear of being labelled a nut case. He found when some people walked into a room, they seemed to give off a very strong glow while others had subdued emissions. Kit was slowly trying to read the differences and what they meant. He realised this was a fantastic opportunity to have an insight into people even before he had met them. The rest of the day dragged on for Kit as he sat through his various subjects. He was hoping to meet David again so he could talk more about life on the other side.

Funny how a whole new style of seeing life ... and death ... had opened for me since my accident. I never asked for it. The window just sort of opened for me, he thought to himself. *The only connection I have is the sights and smells of old London coming into my brain around the same time. I give up.*

Leah was preparing some afternoon tea for Kit when the phone rang. Sarah was on the line to tell her friend she had contacted the Medium and had made a tentative booking for the Greens to see her. The call made Leah quite happy, and she was keen to tell Daniel and then discuss it with Kit. Sarah made a point of saying that although an appointment had been made; the Medium knew nothing of Kit or what had happened to him. The back door opened, and Kit made his way into the kitchen.

"Hi, mum. Have a good day?"

"Hi, love. Yeah. Sarah and I went shopping and had lunch."

"Great. Buy anything interesting?"

"No, but I saw some beaut summer clothes starting to come into the stores for you. We'll have to check your wardrobe and see what needs throwing."

Kit started laughing. "Hang on. What about you? Shouldn't you be throwing out a lot of things too? Like, maybe last winter's collection?"

"Ah. Well, I'm not the one still growing. I can keep mine a little longer."

"Okay. Thanks."

Kit grabbed a glass then went to the fridge and picked up a cold-water container and started drinking out of it. He felt there was something his mother should be telling him but couldn't work out what. He gave her some quiet time while he slowly drank the water, waiting for her to re-start the conversation.

"That's gross, Kit."

"What do you mean?"

"You know exactly what I mean – drinking directly from the top of the same container everyone else shares."

Kit went red and closed the top of the container. He was about to put it back in the fridge when he noticed the frown on his mother. He put the container on the sink and wiped down the lid before replacing it in the fridge. Leah smiled and pulled the cover off a batch of scones she had made and asked Kit to take the fresh cream and strawberry jam from the fridge.

"Mmm, smells and looks nice. Are we expecting guests?" Kit asked.

"No. I thought you may like a treat before you hit the books this afternoon," Leah said with a large smile.

Kit thought about it for a moment. He was keen to just zone out and listen to music on his bed for a while. However, he saw what his mother had done for him and broke into a smile too. "Thank you … these will help me replace some of my energy before I get changed and start my homework. Phew, I'll be glad when I finish school."

"You know love, you never stop learning. School is only the key to your immediate future. What you do after that will determine your future."

Kit was hungry and quickly scoffed two scones with jam and cream. He then kissed his mum on the forehead and thanked her for the scones. Quickly Kit made his way upstairs to his bedroom and closed the door. He undressed and put on a pair of shorts and then lay on his bed to think. He was about to reach for his earphones and then shook his head and put his hands beside himself. Without realising it he slept until his father arrived home. Leah told Daniel about her day with Sarah and explained what she had said about the Medium.

"The good news is, Sarah, rang back while I was cooking the scones to say she had managed to book us into seeing this Mrs. Bishop," Leah said.

"Yeah, I bet she told this woman all about Kit too."

"No. Sarah made a point of saying she only told Mrs. Bishop it was important to see us. She gave no other information except to say there would be the three of us."

"Okay. That's great. Have you told Kit yet?"

"No. I wanted to talk with you first. He's upstairs doing his homework."

"Okay. Come on, we'll see him now before dinner. It may be easier."

"Alright."

The couple made their way upstairs to their son's bedroom. Daniel quietly knocked on the door. When he heard no answer he opened the door, turned on the light and saw Kit sound asleep on his bed. Daniel went over to his son and gently shook him awake.

"Hi mate. Time to get up. Looks like you've had a busy day."

Kit focused his eyes on his father. "Hi, Dad. Oh sorry, I must have dozed off."

"You've probably done too much sport at school today."

Kit sat up and rubbed his eyes. "No, I think it's the volume of learning. Also, nothing physically active to do."

"Mate, your mum and I want to talk with you."

"About homework?"

"No not tonight. But it still needs to be done."

Kit realised his parents were about to say something important. He guessed this was what his mother had stalled about in the kitchen earlier.

"What's up?"

"Kit, when I was out with Sarah today, we talked about some of the things that are happening," Leah said. "You know how you saw David sitting on the bed; how you believe you lived in the 1800s and even the auras you see around people?"

Kit started fuming. It sounded like he had some sort of mental problem, and his mother was airing it publicly with one of her friends. Before he could say anything, his father put a hand on his shoulder and spoke.

"Kit, Sarah has put us in touch with a lady who is a Medium. This woman can speak with the dead and can also read auras. We thought you may like to meet her."

Kit calmed as quick as he had started to fume. He could see where his parents were coming from and what they were trying to do. His hormones settled.

"Is she a witch or anything?" Kit asked.

Leah smiled. "No. She is an ordinary woman with extraordinary abilities, apparently – much like you."

"Does anyone have to know we are going to see her?"

"No. This is a private family business," Daniel said.

"Okay. She may have some answers for me."

"Kit, your mother and I have been helpless in trying to assist you with the sorts of things that have been happening to you. Hopefully, this Mrs. Bishop will give us all an insight as to where to go."

Kit realised what his parents were trying to do for him and stood up. He placed his arms around his parents and gave each of them a hug and kiss.

"Thank you. I appreciate what you're trying to do for me."

Kit grabbed a T-shirt and the three went downstairs for dinner. They talked over the sorts of attributes Kit had developed since his near-death experience.

"Kit, you have always been a loving boy to us but since the pool accident your acceptance of everyone, regardless of belief or persuasion, has increased manyfold," Leah said. "I've also been watching how you are more sensitive to light and electrical things, and I believe all this has come about as a result of your accident."

Kit broke into a knowing smile. What his mother was saying was quite true. The lad had not mentioned a lot of things about his trip to heaven. For instance, he had not gone into a lot of detail with his parents as to how he left his body; or what he fully experienced hovering around the operating theatre above the doctors and nursing staff. Also, what happened to him before he re-entered his body. He never spoke about seeing spirits on the other side and what he went through.

These were all things for another time.

Chapter Five

Daniel was driving to work when he looked into his rear vision mirror and noticed a car change lanes behind him.

The car moved into position directly behind Daniel. It had two men in the front seat wearing casual clothes. As the traffic came to a standstill at a set of traffic lights Daniel saw one of the men in the car pick up a hand-held radio microphone and start talking into it. Once traffic started flowing again the car behind started sounding a police siren and turned intermittent flashing lights on. Daniel moved to the side of the road and stopped to let the unmarked police car pass. Instead, its two occupants got out of their vehicle, drew their handguns, and walked toward Daniel.

"Keep your hands where I can see them," one officer said as he pointed his handgun directly at Daniel's head.

"What's the problem? Who are you?" Daniel shouted out as the second officer appeared around the passenger door also pointing his weapon at Daniel.

"Okay, get out of the car and kneel on the footpath," the officer next to Daniel ordered.

Daniel slowly got out of the car, walked around the front of it to the kerb, and knelt on the grass verge next to the footpath. He was ordered to put his hands behind his back. One of the officers handcuffed him while the other still pointed his weapon at him. Daniel was then ordered to lay face down where he was pat searched back and front. His wallet was retrieved by the search officer and his identification was verified. The officer then took the wallet to the police car and made a call on his mobile phone. Daniel protested several times and was fuming with the indignity of being searched by the police near his home and being forced to lay on the grass in his well-pressed shirt and dry-cleaned pants in front of the constant stream of cars. He was being treated like a criminal, yet he had done nothing wrong. The second officer returned from his car, knelt down and undid Daniel's handcuffs. The first officer slowly put his weapon away.

"Sorry Mr. Green, you check out," the officer said. "We had a report of a sighting of an offender we were after driving a similar car to yours. Unfortunately, he also looked similar to you."

"Who are you and what section of the police are you with?" Daniel asked as he fought for control of his voice.

"I'm Constable Michael Squire and this is Senior Constable Jeff Harris. We're from the armed hold-up squad. We've been after a specific bank robber and thought we had him in you. Our apologies. Have a good day."

Daniel knew not to harangue the officers as they were just doing their jobs. The damage had been done and he now had to return home and change before going to work. The officers returned to their car and made a radio call before driving off. Daniel found it hard to stop shaking. He got back in his car and sat there. Being pulled over by police wearing shorts and T-shirts and brandishing handguns was one thing but being handcuffed and made to lie on the ground was quite embarrassing. Daniel was sure his pseudo-arrest would have been seen by many of his neighbours. He returned home and found Kit had already gone to school and Leah out shopping. Daniel pressed another shirt and changed into a clean suit. Before returning to his car, he made a coffee and took it with him to drink on the way to work. He rang his secretary and said he would be late. It took Daniel quite some time to calm down and restart his day.

Reg Clementson was the first to meet Daniel in the office. He had a worried look on his face and followed Daniel into his office, closed the door and sat down uninvited.

"Mate you look like crap," Clementson said. "Are you okay?"

"Yes. Now. This morning I wasn't."

"So, I heard."

Daniel was flummoxed. How the hell would Clementson know anything of his personal life – never mind the fact he had been pseudo-arrested by police. Daniel suddenly became very suspicious and tense.

"Reg, what did you hear? How would you know what's happened to me today? I've told no one yet."

Clementson studied his offsider for a few moments.

"Daniel, I have a friend in the police. Your arrest was noted by a police headquarters radio operator who I know. Do you have any idea why they stopped you?"

"No! There were two plain-clothes cops and they pulled me over in their car just a few blocks from home. They made me get out of the car before handcuffing me and forcing me to lie down. They then searched me, found my wallet, and checked my driver's license. It was all embarrassing; I can tell you."

"Daniel I'm doing a quiet check to ensure there is no connection with what we're working on."

"Connection? Jeez Reg, if there was a connection, we could have the Commissioner himself arrested today and charged."

"Yes. You'll have to go quiet on this for a little while. Let me do some more ferreting and see what I can come up with. In the meantime, I suggest you write down what happened today as best as you can remember it with as many details as you can about the cops, their names, car etc and then put the info in a safe area."

"Okay. If you are right, then this means this office could be compromised."

"I'll meet you later and talk again."

Clementson left the office and Daniel started soul searching. Kit had warned him of the dangers associated with his current projects. Was this the first of the signs coming to fruition? Would the meeting with Mrs. Bishop tonight shed any more light on what Kit said? Daniel got stuck into writing down all that happened with his pseudo-arrest and saved it on a memory stick to take home. He then opened a series of folders on his desk and ploughed them into some real work. Daniel's phone rang.

"Daniel, it's Terry. All going well?" Terry Sullivan asked.

"Yeah, Terry. All is fine. What about yourself?"

"Mate couldn't be better. What are your family plans for this Friday night?"

"Let me check my computer diary. Yep, we're free. Why, what's on?"

"Betty and I are having a barbecue and would like you all to come over. Bring your swimmers as it's time for a swim."

"Sure, Terry. What time do you want my horde there and what do you want us to bring?"

"Mate just bring your family and come over about 7 pm – it will be good to see you all."

"Okay, Terry, see you then."

The moment the two rang off Daniel couldn't help but think something was circling him. First, Reg Clementson tells him he knew of him being pulled over and now Sullivan was inviting the family for tea. Coincidences don't always occur; they can be orchestrated. Daniel ploughed into his work and went to a series of meetings. Before too long he had the usual afternoon phone call from Leah. This one was to remind him of the meeting with the Medium and not to be late. Daniel looked at the clock and saw it was after 5 pm. Where had the day gone? He cleaned up his desk and made his way to the office car park and his car. The trip home was uneventful. However, Daniel kept searching his car's side and rear-view mirrors for any suspicious cars.

Kit had arrived home buoyant about the meeting with the Medium. He had started to write down some questions he wanted to ask and then stopped. An overpowering feeling of comfort and ease filled him and he remembered he had partly felt this after his swimming pool accident. He stopped writing and instead forced his mind to start remembering what he wanted to know. This was going to be a great opportunity – if this Mrs. Bishop was what Sarah said she was supposed to be. Kit was keen for dinner to be over so he could meet the woman. Daniel and Leah decided to have tea out at a fast-food restaurant so they could talk more about the Medium. Kit also enjoyed the occasional fast-food burgers.

"We need to ask her directly about what is happening with Kit and whether the things that are happening differently to him will wear off," Leah said.

"Come on mum, the things I can do and see are fantastic," Kit said as he finished a bite of burger. "I look around this place now and I can see virtually everyone's auras. It's wonderful. Also, I met David and I hope to meet him again."

"Kit, that's one thing I'd be very keen for you to do," Daniel said. "I think whatever he tried to warn me about maybe starting."

Kit looked at his dad. It was as if the lad was trying to look inside his father rather than at his face.

"Dad, you had some trouble today, didn't you?"

"Yes, sort of."

"It had something to do with the police, yes?"

"Yes."

"Whatever it was is part of what David was telling us about. Do you want to tell me what happened?"

Daniel had already spoken with Leah and told her the story. Now he told Kit. The lad could have made a lucky guess in line with what David had suggested, Daniel thought. He looked at his watch.

"Time to saddle up team, our Medium awaits," Daniel said as he took the last sip of his coffee.

The family drove to Mrs. Bishop's home a few suburbs away. Daniel was the first to be shocked at the woman's home as he was used to living in a suburb full of double brick dwellings. Mrs. Bishop's home was a blue fibro house built in the middle of the last century and was on a corner block. The house itself stood on what looked like a high mound as the lawns were very steep. The Greens made their way to the door and Daniel rapped the knocker three times. Mrs. Bishop opened the door and asked the Green trio to enter her lounge room.

"Hello Daniel, I'm Niva," Mrs. Bishop said as she shook hands with Daniel. "Hi, Leah. Sarah holds you in very high regard." Mrs. Bishop waivered for a second then reached out for Kit's hand with her right. She took his right hand in hers, placed her left hand on top and slowly shook the youth's hand. "Hello Kit, I'm glad you could make it tonight."

"Thank you, so am I."

Kit felt an electrical pulse emanating from Mrs. Bishop as he shook hands. This was the first time this had ever happened to him. He studied the woman and saw a very colourful aura brightly flashing around her. She smiled knowingly.

The Greens went into Mrs. Bishop's lounge room and sat down. Daniel was amazed. He expected some gipsy sort of wall hangings, a crystal ball or even a darkened room. There was none of it. The lounge room was just the same as in any other home. It had a lounge, lounge chairs, a coffee table and an entertainment unit with a television in the corner. Photos of Mrs. Bishop and her family hung on the walls.

"Daniel, there's nothing to worry about," Mrs. Bishop said.

"My family and I are much the same as yours. The difference is I have a few gifts other people seek that may assist them."

Daniel smiled, sat back more on the lounge and relaxed.

"Mrs. Bishop …" Daniel started to say.

"Please call me Niva."

"Niva, it's hard to know what to expect when seeing a Medium for the first time," Daniel said.

"It's okay. We should start with what I can offer you. I can sometimes see what is happening with people in their lives. I guess you would call it intuition. I can also sometimes see what possible futures lay ahead for people if they continue the path they are on. Lastly, I can communicate with those who have already passed over."

Leah slowly slid her hand into Daniel's and Kit sat more upright as Mrs. Bishop spoke.

"Daniel, Leah, I know Sarah asked me to talk specifically with Kit and I will shortly. For now, I can see I need to tell you a few things about what is happening with you."

Mrs. Bishop was sitting in a lounge chair opposite Daniel and Leah and looked and talked in easy conversational tones. She looked directly at Daniel.

"Daniel, I have the feeling you are involved with the law in some way now. You are not a police officer, but have been in contact with them very recently."

Daniel squeezed Leah's hand and sat riveted, hanging off every word Mrs. Bishop was saying.

"Be wary. The people you spoke with today are part of a special group of people who know about you and what you are trying to do in your business. Be careful who you trust."

"Niva, these people I spoke with today were police officers who pulled me over in my car, made me lie on the ground and handcuffed me."

Kit swung his head around quickly to his father. "This is the beginning of what David told me would happen."

Mrs. Bishop put her hand up to her mouth and looked at Kit. "Kit, we'll get onto you shortly. Daniel, these police are working on a mission that could have dire consequences for you," she said.

"Are you saying I should give up the project I am working on as my life may be threatened?"

"No. Many circumstances can still come into play to change the course you are on. You must evaluate what you are trying to achieve and think about several ways in which you can still reach the same result."

"Thank you, Niva," Daniel said as he started some serious soul searching.

"Leah, your grandmother has passed over, hasn't she?"

"Yes," Leah said as she squeezed Daniel's hand.

"Her name is Gwyneth … no … its Gwendolyn, yes?"

"Yes."

"Well, she's with you now. She says the answer to your question about the flowers, is no."

Leah started crying as she heard about her grandmother.

"Gran always loved flowers," Leah said between sobs. "When she died, I kept some flowers from her cortege and planted them in my garden. I always hoped she never minded."

Mrs. Bishop continued after Leah had wiped her eyes using tissues on the coffee table near the lounge.

"Your gran is with your uncle Stan and a young woman. This woman is connected to your father. Yes. Her name is Eileen. Do you know of her?"

Leah worked through what Mrs. Bishop had said. "The only person Eileen could be is my father's sister – my aunty."

"Yes. She says your middle name was given after her. It starts with a J – it's Joy!"

"Oh my God. Yes, it is. My aunty Joy died of a heart attack. She was my favourite aunty."

"Leah, she acknowledges that because she is patting her heart. She says you used to make her cups of tea from your plastic tea set as a little girl."

"Hell. I had forgotten that … you are right."

Mrs. Bishop looked at Kit and Leah who sat back and wiped their eyes. Kit braced for what this lady would do with him. He was not so much apprehensive as impatient for her to tell him things. She smiled at him.

"Kit, let me assure you that I have known nothing about your family until you walked in the door tonight," Mrs. Bishop said. "When Sarah rang to discuss you, all coming to see me she never told me background about any of you. However, it is a pleasure to meet you and to have shaken your hand.

"Kit, I can see from your aura you have been where all will go but only a few will return. I know you have died and come back to life. I know from shaking your hand tonight you have been in the presence of spirits …"

"How do you know?" Kit asked.

"I know you are a person of special abilities because I can see beautiful energy patterns around you. Also, when we shook hands, I had a feeling of a small electric current running through me. Something I last felt when I died on the … sorry, I'm not supposed to say, am I?"

Mrs. Bishop smiled. "Kit, you are a treasure. You want to know how I know about you and how to help you. Around each of us is an aura, an emission of light as you said earlier. These auras tell others what has or is happening to them. There are several different light emissions and each one has a particular meaning. I know from yours you have been in the presence of spirits and that you have already died and returned. You felt a trickle of electric current from me to you and back again as we shook hands – this was why I clasped my second hand over yours to confirm what I was feeling. Rest assured Kit, no one has told me anything about your background."

"Are there other spirits here with us now?"

"Yes. You mentioned a boy before called David when I was speaking to your father. He's here."

"What can you tell me of him?"

"Kit, he is the son of a person who has a close connection to your father. He says he has come to you to help his father and yours."

"Why can't I see him now?"

"David and other spirits can't be seen all the time and so they choose when their energy is sufficient to allow them to be seen by someone who can see them. Not everyone is receptive enough to see them. You can because you have been where he is now and you have returned to complete a journey."

"Are there others here?"

"Oh, yes. Each of us has a spirit guide and yours is with you."

"Can you tell me who it is, please?"

Mrs. Bishop seemed to look through Kit as she studied the teenager in front of her.

"Leah, this is unusual as normally I would see someone like maybe a Red Indian as a spirit guide for someone. Here I'm seeing a young man who says he is a distant relative of Kit's on your mother's side. Has your grandfather passed over?"

"Yes. Both Daniel's and my grandparents have died."

"Leah, this sounds confusing, but he is your great grandfather's grandfather. I'm getting the name Tom … no, Thomas. He is very particular about his name. Do you know a Thomas in your family line?"

Leah was no longer surprised at what Mrs. Bishop was saying. She was enthralled by what she had seen and heard. She had to think back to family names she had heard.

"Yes. Yes, there was a Thomas, but that was in the 1800s. We think he died in a boating accident. I know because my mum had done some family history research. Niva, you said Kit's spirit guide was a teenager. Is this the same person?"

Now it was time for Mrs. Bishop to work harder. She closed her eyes, nodded a few times and raised her right hand as if motioning to someone she now had the message right. Mrs. Bishop looked at Leah and Daniel and then settled on Kit.

"Thomas said he passed over when he was six years older than Kit in a carriage accident not in a boating mishap, so he wasn't a teenager either."

Kit jumped in. "A horse and carriage accident?"

"Yes. But it didn't happen here. It happened …"

"In England during the 1820s," Kit finished.

Both Daniel and Leah looked at Daniel and then Mrs. Bishop. They were surprised. It was like watching a slow-motion tennis match. Mrs. Bishop smiled. She realised Kit was reaching out with his extra sensory perception to grasp the answer. Kit's ESP had improved substantially since his accident. He had also started to listen to the voice in his head which sometimes told him answers or gave warnings.

"Niva, this Thomas may have been my great grandfather's grandfather. It all seems to fit. Strange he would attach himself to Kit," Leah said.

"Thomas says Kit has very similar looks and personality to himself. He also says Kit is an old soul," Mrs. Bishop said.

"What do you mean?"

"Kit has walked on this Earth several times before."

"Like I've been alive and died before?" Kit asked.

"Yes – that's what Thomas is saying."

Kit was slightly amused at the revelation about his spirit guide and what Thomas was saying about him. However, it possibly explained a lot. It could complete the picture of why he thought he had been born in the mid-1800s and why he could so vividly 'remember' scenes and even sounds and smells.

"Mrs. Bishop, will you ask Thomas if he has been giving me images and thoughts of living in the 1800s. This has been something I've been trying to come to grips with recently that I lived in this period. I keep having images of the period come into my head along with sounds and smells."

Every time a question was asked, Mrs. Bishop would take a few seconds to answer. She would nod or raise her hands as if to make a silent point. In reality, Mrs. Bishop was communicating with the spirits she could, to define the answers required. She made a point several times that spirits only come into a communication mode at certain times.

"Kit, Thomas has been trying to give you those images as a way of letting you know he was there and helping to guide you. The problem has been your ability to understand how those images, smells and sounds got into your head."

"So how come I can feel his presence at times and see and hear the images and sounds he sends me?"

"When you had your accident, you opened a sort of doorway or portal to the spirit world. Thomas has always been with you, but you couldn't feel, hear, see or smell the sorts of things he was sending you. We all have spirit guides, but your parents can't experience the strong bond you have developed with yours as they have not been where you have. There is a lot of learning to do and you should come back and see me to understand more about yourself."

"Thank you, Mrs. Bishop. Thank you, Thomas and David, too. I appreciate your help," Kit said with a cheesy smile as he looked around the room.

The session was over, and the Greens and Mrs. Bishop all stood up. The Medium walked over to Kit and took his hand once more.

"Kit you are on a difficult path and adventure. Listen more to your feelings as Thomas tries to advise you about what's happening and possible ways forward. You will always have free will but listen to your spirit guide as he is trying to help you achieve your life's purpose."

"Thank you for your help," Kit said. "I'm sure mum will speak with you and work something out about seeing you some more."

Mrs. Bishop moved over to Daniel and shook his hand. She placed her left hand on top of his and his eyes seemed to widen as he felt a surge of energy through her hands.

"Daniel, be careful. You will come through this project of yours but like Kit, you need to listen to your gut reaction."

"Niva, this has been a most eye-opening time. Thanks for your support," Daniel said as he withdrew his hand. While Mrs. Bishop moved next to Leah, Kit noticed his father feel his right hand as if he had experienced a small shock. The lad smiled knowingly.

"Leah, please ring. We need to make some times for Kit so I can help him develop his gifts if you like."

"Will do. Thanks," Leah said as she kissed Mrs. Bishop goodbye.

The Greens went back to their car and drove home. Daniel was the first to break the silence.

"Kit, are you okay with what we just experienced with Mrs. Bishop?"

"Yeah, I think so. She gave me some insights I was looking for and explained some of the things I have been experiencing," Kit said as he looked out of the car window. "Would you both be comfortable if I saw Mrs. Bishop some more?"

"I don't mind Kit," Daniel said.

"I don't have a problem with it Kit," Leah said. "However, I think we need to talk some more about tonight, so we confirm what we all got out of it. Also, we have to work out where we think Mrs. Bishop can further help you."

"Okay. Do you have any photos of Thomas?"

"No, but I bet your grandmother does."

Chapter Six

Terry Sullivan was shaken when his secretary announced the Police wanted to speak with him.

The last time the police had been in contact with him and his wife was over the death of David and the subsequent Coronial inquest.

"Mr. Sullivan?" a male voice on the phone said.

"Yes. Who's this?"

"Sir, it's Detective Sergeant Garry Hart from the Fraud Squad."

Sullivan's jaw dropped. He suddenly became anxious. His mind raced. Sullivan's office had been in charge of running several activities for his political party. How would these have caused issues with the police?

"Detective Hart, what can I do for you"

"Mr. Sullivan, I understand you and your wife Betty recently travelled to Hawaii as part of a fact-finding mission. Is this right?"

"Yes. Why what's the problem with that? It was all approved by the Parliament?"

"Mr. Sullivan you will need to come into Police Headquarters and talk with me. I have received a complaint about your trip, and we need to discuss it face to face."

"Can you tell me anymore?"

"No, not at this stage."

"Detective I'll have my solicitor ring and arrange a time."

"If you wish to involve a solicitor, by all means."

Detective Hart gave Sullivan his telephone number and office address. Sullivan was rattled. He had gone on a business trip to attend a meeting of economic agencies and had taken his wife Betty. While he was attending business forums, Betty went shopping and sightseeing. At night the two would meet and privately dine together or visit some of the landmarks. Sullivan believed his financial affairs were in order and had submitted his expenses and receipts to the public accounts section of Parliament. He had heard nothing of any impropriety. Sullivan rang his solicitor Gregory Hinton and arranged to see him mid-afternoon. He then went to see his political leader Graham Moon. This week Parliament was sitting and both men were in their parliamentary offices, a level apart.

The Opposition Leader was a bear of a man. He was tall as he was wide. Moon was powerfully built with little fat for a person in his 50s. He was a busy man orchestrating a myriad of opportunities to score points off the government and so raise the popularity of his party for the next election. Sullivan was announced by Moon's secretary.

"Graham, thanks for seeing me," Sullivan said.

"What's up, Terry? Unusual for you to see me like this."

"Do you remember the trip I did to Hawaii a couple of months ago?"

"Yes. You went to the economic forum, and I think Betty went with you, privately of course."

“Correct. I thought all my accounts were right. However, I’ve just had a phone call from the Fraud Squad about the trip.”

“Jeez, Terry. What did they say?”

“I spoke with Detective Sergeant Garry Hart, who said he had received some kind of complaint about the trip. Graham, Betty may have come on the trip with me, but I checked I had paid whatever I had to for her.”

The Opposition Leader sat in his chair and thought for a moment. Sullivan went to speak, and Moon lifted up his right index finger in a motion to silence him.

“Terry, you’re working on the razor list of who we could or should cut from departments when we gain office. Yes?”

“Yes.”

“I’ll lay odds Todd Ratcliffe has found out somehow, he’s on our list. If your accounts are correct, then all roads lead to Ratcliffe. You better have your accountant double-check your paperwork from the Hawaii trip. In the meantime, have you started to organise legal representation?”

“Yes. I’ll be seeing my solicitor this afternoon and arranging a time to go to the Fraud Squad.”

“Ensure it’s after hours, outside news cycles. We don’t need this going anywhere. Terry, I’ll start making some private enquiries too. Keep me informed every step. I don’t need to tell you what could happen if they charge you with fraud.”

“I understand. If that happens, then I’ll have to step aside.”

“Yes. Sorry, Terry. Let’s start getting some answers.”

Sullivan stood up and shook Moon’s hand and left the office. He had some work to do. If Ratcliffe was up to no good, then there had to be a way of proving it. If the Fraud Squad had something on himself, it would mean the end of his political career. He made his way back to his office.

"Mr. Sullivan, Daniel Green rang," Cindy, his secretary, said.

"What did he want?"

"He was just confirming the barbecue at your home tomorrow night with his family."

"Thanks, Cindy. Ring him back and tell him it's definitely on. No, wait. I'll do it, thanks."

Sullivan walked into his office and rang Daniel. He wanted some other insurance.

"Hi mate. Can you come and see me now, by any chance?"

"Terry, what's up?" Daniel asked.

"Mate, I need your professional guidance. I can't talk to you now but need to see you face to face."

Daniel picked up the nervousness in Sullivan's voice and knew he had some sort of problem.

"I'm on my way. Do I need anyone else?"

"Yes. I think you'd better get a hold of Reg."

"Okay, Terry. We'll link up and ring you on the way."

"Cheers."

The two rang off. Daniel rang Reg Clementson and relayed what Sullivan had said. Clementson was just as astounded.

"Mate, something is going down I bet," Clementson said. "It will be interesting to see if whatever it is, is connected in any way to your little adventure the other day."

"I started having that feeling the moment Terry rang. It must be important for him not to give us a burst on the phone as to what it's about."

"I think you're right. See you at Terry's office."

The two men rang off. Both had pretty busy schedules. However, when one of their main clients rang and said he needed help, both men agreed to reschedule events to assist.

Daniel was wondering if maybe Sullivan had been pulled over and searched. No, that can't happen, he thought. Sullivan doesn't drive. Anywhere Sullivan needs to go, he either takes taxis or Betty drives him because of his heavy drinking. Daniel switched his thoughts to Betty. It would be a pretty low act by the police to target the MP's wife. No, if the police were involved, they would target the man, not the wife.

"Mr. Sullivan. Mr. Green and Mr. Clementson have arrived," Cindy announced on a desk intercom.

"Thank you, Cindy. Please show them in," Sullivan said.

Sullivan stood up and walked to the front of his desk as Daniel and Clementson entered the room. He ushered them to a lounge, and he sat opposite in a lounge chair.

"Gents, thanks for coming in at such short notice," Sullivan said. "If it wasn't important, I wouldn't have made the calls."

"No problems, Terry," Daniel said.

Clementson nodded his head.

"I had a call from the cops this morning, so I'll be going to see my solicitor shortly," Sullivan said slowly, trying to add import to his words. "A Detective Sergeant from the Fraud Squad has called to say he needs to speak with me about my last overseas trip."

"Mate, you fixed all your accounts, and nothing is outstanding, is it?" Clementson asked.

"Yeah. As far as I know, I submitted all the receipts and paid for everything correctly."

"So why does the Fraud Squad want to talk with you?" Daniel asked.

"The cop wouldn't say over the phone. He just wants me to go to Police Headquarters and meet him there."

Reg Clementson was uneasy about the latest developments. He shook his head in thought and then looked up at Sullivan.

"Are you connecting Daniel being pulled over with this fraud enquiry and the work you are doing to replace Ratcliffe?"

Sullivan looked at both men and bit down on his lower lip. He eased the pressure and then spoke.

"If you don't believe in coincidence then it all seems to make sense. Somehow, Ratcliffe must have found out Daniel's company is working on the proposal and that I'm the main instigator. If my party is elected to Government and I'm re-elected, then I'll possibly be Minister for Police and Emergency Services."

"Sounds like Ratcliffe is getting in first," Clementson said. "First, he publicly humiliates Daniel by having him pulled over and seemingly arrested on the side of the road, and now he's gunning for you, Terry."

Daniel felt uneasy. It was fine to work on political campaigns in an office, but when the people they affect strike back physically, it was a different matter.

"Have you been to see Graham Moon yet?" Daniel asked.

"Yes. As soon as I received the call from the Police I went and saw the Leader ..."

Daniel started chuckling. "Don't you call Moon by his first or second name as Opposition MPs?"

Sullivan was slightly taken aback and then laughed. "It's

just a term I use for my boss – sorry. Anyway, I'll be seeing my solicitor shortly and then will visit the Fraud Squad after the evening news deadline."

"Good move, Terry," Clementson said. "This will cut down on who will be waiting for you from the Media."

"Yes."

"I'll sniff around and see if anyone is onto the story as yet. Let us both know what happens tonight and whether you need us there, okay?"

"Reg, you'll be the second person I'll call. The first will be the Leader."

The three men stood up and shook hands. Both Daniel and Clementson made their way out of Parliament House and onto the main street.

"Reg don't sniff too hard with any news organisations in case they get onto you," Daniel said.

"She'll be right mate. Just watch your back from now on and keep in touch if anything untoward happens."

"Okay, no probs. You do the same. Cheers."

Both men made their separate ways to their offices while Sullivan travelled to see his lawyer.

Terry Sullivan was worried. He believed he had served his party well and was now within a short grasp of becoming a state minister. Sullivan had decided on a political career early after leaving school and became elected on his local Council. Within a short time, he had the support of his fellow Councilors, and he became Mayor – a position he held for three terms. After securing positive support from his party's State leader, Sullivan was nominated for a seat in State Parliament and was successful in the first election he contested. Sullivan spoke up on any issue he could that affected his electorate and soon became well known throughout the Media and among his Parliamentary colleagues. He served three years as a backbencher before being promoted by his boss, the Opposition Leader Graham Moon, to Shadow Minister for Government Affairs. A Shadow Minister was like an opponent on a football field who had to cover off against their government opposites and keep track of what they were doing.

Sullivan had proven exceptional at this and often had the Government on the wrong foot about issues in the Media. Moon had given him the job of drawing up a list of who their party would axe or move from the top positions within the Public Service, if and when they won government. The trip to his solicitor's office didn't take long as it was within walking distance of Parliament.

"Mr. Sullivan, good to see you," the receptionist said as Sullivan approached her desk from the lift. "Mr. Hinton will see you straight away. Please go in."

"Thank you," Sullivan said as he made his way past the large reception desk in the lift foyer. He knew his way to Gregory Hinton's office quite well. The two had been to school together and Hinton had assisted Sullivan in several legal matters over the years. This had included organising the legal paperwork for Sullivan's first home; advice on several large electoral issues, and finally helping him draft some amendments to Government bills before the Parliament. Sullivan opened the door to his friend's office.

“Terry, great to see you,” Gregory Hinton said as he was met halfway across the office floor by Sullivan.

“Gregory, it’s been too long. I’m sorry we have to meet like this rather than over a wine or beer somewhere.”

“Terry, grab a seat, we have to cover a lot of ground this afternoon.”

The two men sat at a coffee table which had some files marked “Sullivan – Terry” on top. Hinton listened intently to Sullivan and took notes in earnest. Sullivan produced copies of the paperwork and receipts he had given to the Clerk of the House at Parliament. The two men went over each of the receipts, with Sullivan trying to remember what each was for. Hinton split the receipts into “his” and “hers” columns to cover Sullivan and his wife Betty. He double-checked each one.

“Terry, I can’t see a problem with these accounts. Your rationale as to why you paid for some things and the Government paid for the others seems to gel quite well,” Hinton said. “It will be interesting to see what this cop thinks he has on you.”

Sullivan explained to his friend what he was currently working on for the Opposition Leader. He then told him of Daniel being pulled over.

“All roads seem to lead to Ratcliffe but, then again, these could be two distinct incidents that are not linked. Terry, don’t jump to conclusions yet.”

“Greg, I believe Ratcliffe has organised some minor demonstrations to prove he is the top cop.”

“Maybe. If he has, he is holding the cards until we can prove otherwise. For the moment we must play the game as you, my dear Member of Parliament, are under Police investigation. This is still pretty serious."

Hinton's last comments re-set the tone and Sullivan became nervous. The lawyer rang Detective Sergeant Garry Hart and arranged a time to see him … after the main evening news bulletins. Sullivan believed he had done nothing wrong. Even his lawyer couldn't find anything wrong. The two men had some coffee and sandwiches brought in as they went back over the accounts for a final time before going to Police Headquarters. Sullivan's phone rang. It was Daniel.

"Hi mate. I've prepared a Media Release and had Reg go over it for me just in case any Media are lurking at Police Headquarters," Daniel said.

"Thanks Daniel."

"Both Reg and I will be outside Police Headquarters if you need us."

"Mate, I'd appreciate that, thanks."

The two men rang off. Daniel faxed a copy of the final version of his Media Release to Clementson and Hinton before driving to Police Headquarters. If Media were around when Sullivan left the building, the release would be used as a talking point by the politician or his lawyer and then handed out by Daniel. Clementson arrived by taxi and joined Daniel in his car.

"Daniel, seen any reporters around?" Clementson asked.

"Nope. I went around the block a couple of times before parking to ensure no hacks were around.

"Okay, the wait begins."

Sullivan and Hinton spent more than an hour with Detective

Sergeant Hart deep in the bowels of Police Headquarters. The pair had brought a box of files with copies of all the necessary receipts for the overseas trip and the sign-off by the Clerk of the House.

"Mr. Sullivan, who paid for the airfares for you and your wife?" Detective Sergeant Hart asked.

"I paid for the fares and then reimbursed the Parliament for my wife's share," Sullivan replied.

"Did you pay taxes for each of you?"

"Of course, I did. The receipt is here."

"Well, you see Mr. Sullivan; you seem to have paid the taxes for both you and your wife. You also seem to have been reimbursed by the Parliament for you and your wife. Therefore, your wife's taxes were not paid by you and that's called fraud!"

Sullivan turned a deep scarlet. He suddenly became deeply embarrassed as he thought all payments had been made correctly. Even Gregory Hinton didn't see where the detective was going to come from with his investigation.

"There's another problem too," Detective Sergeant Hart said.

"What's that?" Hinton asked.

"Who organised affairs for you and your wife while you were in Hawaii?" Detective Sergeant Hart asked.

"Do you mean on a day-to-day basis?" Hinton asked.

"Yes. The day-by-day organisation of where to go, what to see and how to get there, type of things."

Sullivan looked at Hinton and saw through the question.

"Sergeant, my itinerary was organised by my staff. What

Betty did was organised by her and that included all you said," Sullivan said.

"Mmm. That's interesting," the detective said as he flipped through a file on his lap. "My understanding is that your staff organised the tour itinerary for Mrs. Sullivan."

Hinton was quick to answer. "No. Mrs. Sullivan organised her own itinerary. No public servants were involved in organising Mrs. Sullivan's itinerary. I take it, that's where you're going?"

"Yes. My understanding was that Public Servants had been involved. If that's the case that could also be construed as a form of fraud."

"Detective, no fraud has been committed here. Mr. Sullivan's staff was only involved in organising for their boss – not his wife. The matter of airport taxes will be resolved simply tomorrow by the reimbursement of those monies to the Clerk of the House. This is the normal type of affairs for any MP who travels overseas with his spouse or family and then conducts official business. Do you have anything else for us?"

"No, Mr. Hinton, I think the matters seem to have been explained."

"I'll send you a copy of Mr. Sullivan's reimbursement of airport taxes to the Clerk of the House tomorrow. When that's done, this matter should be resolved."

"I think so. Once I receive the copy of the receipt that should solve these issues."

Sullivan and Hinton made their way out of Police Headquarters. They refrained from making any comments to each other about the interview until they were well clear of the building. Sullivan rang Daniel as he waited in a corridor leading to the main foyer of the building to see if any Media turned up. The answer was 'no' so Hinton and Sullivan exited the building.

Daniel and Reg were already out of their car and heading to the front steps of the building. They kept scanning the approaches to ensure no photographers were around.

"Terry, Gregory, our car is over here," Daniel said as he pointed to his sedan.

The four men said nothing else until they were in Daniel's car and driving off. Clementson was the first to speak.

"Terry, Greg, what happened? Are you okay?" Clementson asked.

"Reg, someone seems to have set me up. The cop thought he had me on a fraud technicality, but it is truly nothing," Sullivan said.

"What do you mean?" asked Daniel as he drove off and headed towards Parliament House.

"Terry had paid Betty's airport taxes and claimed them back along with his," Hinton said. "It's just a technicality as Terry can pay the money tomorrow to Parliament and this is over."

"The rotten animals," Clementson said. "So, this was a frame-up to have it look like you are being investigated on something bigger, yet it is only a piddling matter."

"Yes," Sullivan blustered. "Gregory was able to prove I had done everything correctly except this one oversight. I'm pretty brassed off with Ratcliffe if he set this in motion."

Daniel told Sullivan no Media had been seen while the pair were being interviewed.

"Gents, I'm really thankful to the three of you for your help and support today and tonight. I know it was a big ask to drop everything for me," Sullivan said.

"What's your next move?" Clementson asked.

"I've got to see the Leader and give him an update, so he knows the heat is off me …"

"For the moment," Clementson finished. "We'll all have to be on our guards from now on, particularly when we discuss any moves surrounding Ratcliffe."

"Why?" Hinton asked.

"Just in case he pulls another one of these stunts. Think about it, Terry. He's picking us off one by one. By my reckoning, I must be next on the list."

Chapter Seven

Kit had searched around the house looking for old photographs. He was on a mission. Not everyone knew the identity of their spirit guide. Kit wanted to take it further and try and identify Thomas through a photograph. He had seen David and knew what he looked like, now it was time to find Thomas.

Leah spoke with her mother Jessica and explained Kit was looking to identify Thomas. It was a long conversation on the phone, only interrupted when Kit arrived home from school.

"G'day mum," Kit said as he went to the sink and got himself a drink of water. "Everything alright?"

"Hi, love. Yes, all is fine. That was your grandmother on the phone. She thinks she has a photo or picture of her relative Thomas for you and is now looking for it."

"Thanks, mum." Kit went to walk away when he stopped and looked at his mother. "A picture? What sort of picture?"

"You're talking about the middle 1800s. Instant cameras weren't around when Thomas was growing up. The camera had been invented but few people had had their photos taken."

"Okay, I'll bite," Kit said as he knew his mother had steered him to a set answer. "You're about to say there could be a painting of him somewhere. Yes?"

"Yes. There could be, but your grandmother is not sure. She remembers seeing a painting or something similar of a teenage boy from when she was a little girl. The painting had been in the family for a while. She's now looking for it for you."

"Thanks, mum. I'm pretty keen to find out what I can about Thomas."

"I know."

Kit picked up his bag and headed to his bedroom to get changed. He felt a small cold chill and a tingling come over him as he climbed the last stairs. His awareness became magnified and the teenager slowed his pace. It was not a feeling of doom or danger but a feeling he had felt before … recently. He opened the door and standing near his bed was the shimmering spirit of a teenager. Kit broke out a huge smile and then closed the door.

"Hi Kit, I'm David – Terry Sullivan's son."

"Hi. How are you?"

David seemed to hover just off the floor and returned Kit's smile.

"I'm always fine. There's no change for me where I am."

Kit put his bag down and went and sat on his computer chair. David sat on the edge of Kit's bed. The two teenagers looked at each other for a few seconds without a word being spoken. David broke the silence.

"I'm glad you went to the Medium's home," David said.

"Yeah, so am I."

"Were you surprised to know I was there with you too?"

"Yes. We have so much to talk about. I didn't know where you were. Are you able to tell me?"

"Kit, when you died on the operating table do you remember what happened to you?"

"Yes. I floated for a while above the doctors and my body then went through a dark tunnel to a place of the purest light."

"I'm in the place of purest light as you called it."

Kit started to ask a lot of questions, but David said he couldn't answer them. Instead, he had come to ask Kit a favour. He knew he and his family were going to his father's home for a barbecue.

"Please tell my mum I'm okay and to stop worrying," David said.

"Can't you tell her yourself?"

"No. Not everyone is receptive to our presence – especially adults"

Kit was taken aback by David's answer. "Are you saying children can't see you and adults can?"

"No. Children are more open and receptive to our presence. Somehow, adults close their minds. It takes special people for us to appear to and talk with."

"So, I'm special?"

"Yeah. You are now."

"You mean now that I have come back from where you are?"

"Yes. Your mind has been opened to communicate with us."

Kit thought for a few moments.

"David what can I say to your mum so she will know I am telling the truth about you?"

David seemed to beam a smile.

"Do these actions like me and she will know."

David then closed his right hand and used his index finger to point at his chest. He opened his hand over his heart and then pointed at Kit.

"What does that mean?" Kit asked as he emulated David's actions.

David smiled.

"Tell her I said *I love you* when you do the actions. She will know it's from me. We used to do it to each other all the time."

Kit agreed and then asked David why he couldn't see Thomas and talk directly to him. David laughed and said Thomas was standing next to Kit. David then disappeared. Kit got changed out of his school uniform and laid on his bed to think over what David had said to him when there was a knock at his bedroom door.

"Come in, it's open," Kit said.

Leah opened the door and entered her son's room. "Don't forget we're going to the Sullivan's place for tea tonight."

"I know. I just spoke with David."

Leah studied her son's face. "What did he want?"

"He asked me to do him a favour and tell his mum he's okay."

"That's nice of him. Did he say anything else about your father?"

"No. He only wanted to talk about his mum."

"Okay. Your father should be home early so we can get to the Sullivan's place by 7 pm."

"No probs."

"Kit, it might be better if I was with you when you told Mrs. Sullivan of David. We don't want her to have any problems."

"Alright. I'll lay odds Dad will find a quiet corner with Mr. Sullivan to have a drink anyway. That should be our time."

Leah nodded and walked over to Kit. The boy sat up and his mother kissed him on the forehead.

"I love you, Kit. Always remember it."

"Love you too, Mum. Watch this!" Kit then made the gesture David had just taught him.

"What's that?"

"This is what David and Mrs. Sullivan used to do to each other to say I love you."

Leah smiled and nodded. She left Kit and went back downstairs. Kit sat at his computer and for the next hour started researching his great grandfather's grandfather in his search engine. He typed in Thomas Brown and was surprised to find so many people who shared the same name as his spirit guide. The word search didn't take him anywhere as he had insufficient information. Kit went to the image section and narrowed his search to Thomas Brown in the 1800s.

"What the …." Kit said aloud as he saw a photo of what looked like him in fancy clothes.

He called up the image and saw it was one of the paintings held by the National Portrait Gallery in London. Kit sat staring at the image in disbelief. It was virtually himself to a tee. Change the period clothes and this Thomas could pass for him and vice versa. Kit was stunned by the resemblance. A scent of burning coal and a feeling of mustiness crept over him. In his mind's eye, he saw the 18th Century family in London he had seen earlier as he looked out his window. One of the two boys looked at Kit and waved. Kit shook his head and refocused. This was the 21st Century and he was in his bedroom. He printed out the photo and took it downstairs to his mother.

"Hey mum, what do you think of this?" Kit asked as he handed his mother Thomas's image.

"I'd say you've been working too hard on your computer programs. Pretty clever though, I can't tell where you have cut and pasted your head onto the teenager's body," Leah said with a smile as she went to hand back the printout.

"Mum, I think you are holding an image of your great grandfather's grandfather. I think I found Thomas!"

"You're joking! This is a photo of you cut and pasted onto someone else, surely."

"No. Mum, look at the writing next to the image. It says it was painted by Reuben Barlow in 1820. I found the image by using an internet search engine to check for Thomas's name."

"Kit, this is remarkable. The resemblance is extremely uncanny. Even so, there is no guarantee it is your Thomas ... our Thomas. It could be a teenager who looks very similar to you from that period."

"Mum, I feel convinced its Thomas. When I was staring at the photo on my computer, I saw the image of an English family from the 18th Century walking by. It was as if I was looking down at them. There was a set of parents and two young boys. One of the boys looked up and waved at me. I can't quite communicate with my Thomas directly, but I bet it was him. I think I know how to find out."

"How? Your grandmother has been going through all the family papers in the garage for you. She can't go any faster."

"Who said anything about my grandmother? Next time I see David, I'll ask him. He'll know."

Leah went to say something but stopped. She nodded knowingly and looked at the image again.

"Can you show me where you found the image on the computer so I can bookmark it, please?

"Sure. Open your computer and I'll send you the link from upstairs."

Kit returned to his bedroom and sent his mother an electronic link to the image he found. He then saved the image on his computer as a screensaver before printing a second copy. He was chuffed. If the print he found was actually Thomas, then he had achieved something most people never could. He would have sourced an image of his own spirit guide.

Daniel arrived home and smiled when Leah showed him an image of Kit in period clothes. Like Leah, Daniel believed Kit had cut and pasted an image of him onto an old English portrait and wanted to know the joke. When Leah explained to Daniel where Kit had found the image and then showed him the link he was flabbergasted.

"This is unbelievable," Daniel said. "The likeness is so uncanny. If I didn't know this image was from a real National Portrait Gallery, I'd be wondering why Kit was playing around. Even the smile is his. Wow."

"I'll be taking Kit to see mum tomorrow, so we'll see how she has gone in her search."

"Now that should be interesting. I'd love to see her face when you show her the printout."

"You may even be able to compare images."

"Yes. Either way, it should be fun."

Kit finished surfing the net and made his way downstairs. He joined his parents.

"That's an uncanny image you've come across," Daniel said.

"G'day Dad. Yeah … especially if the person in the image is the same Thomas I am looking for."

Daniel held up the image and put it near Kit's face. Leah joined her husband as the pair looked hard at the image and their son. Both flicked their eyes from the image to Kit and back again as they took in both teenager's images.

"Come on. I give up. What do you think?"

"Well mate, it's the best similar-looking likeness I've seen of you," Daniel said. "I'll be interested to know the story behind the painting."

"Yeah, me too."

"Okay team let's saddle up and head to the Sullivan's. A barbecue awaits," Daniel said.

The Greens drove for around 30 minutes and came into a leafy suburb. The power poles stood tall and freshly painted with a wood preserver; most of the homes were double storey and some had balconies around the upper level. The Sullivan's home was set back from a tall protective brick fence. It had a special double gate that quickly rolled open and closed for visitors once they were recognised by a security camera. Past the gates, the lawns sprawled and a fountain with the statue of a little boy in the centre was floodlit.

"Dad are you sure this is the Sullivans?" Kit asked as he slowly took in all the home's surroundings. "It looks like something out of Hollywood."

"I think this was originally owned by a man who was involved in the gaming industry – that's why the security," Daniel answered.

Daniel parked the car in a car park built for four cars. The front door to the Sullivan mansion opened and Terry Sullivan exited wearing a Hawaiian shirt, shorts and sandals. Kit smiled as this was not the usual image he had seen of Terry Sullivan. Gone was the sartorial elegance of the pin-striped suit, double French cuffed shirt, large Windsor knotted tie and bright shiny shoes. The figure now before Kit was more pedestrian. Sullivan made his way over to Daniel and shook hands. He then gave Leah a peck on the cheek and walked toward Kit.

"Mate you've grown quite a lot since the last time I saw you," Sullivan said as he shook Kit's hand.

"Hi, Mr. Sullivan. I love your home. Should I smile for the cameras?"

Sullivan was amused. He laughed and put his arm around Kit as they walked towards the front door.

"I don't know if they work, but they seem to only allow in the nice people Betty, and I love to have over. Welcome aboard. I hope you're hungry?"

"You bet. It's been a long day at school and I'm famished. My mum wouldn't feed me."

Sullivan ruffled Kit's hair and laughed along with Leah and Daniel.

"Don't worry mate, you'll never get through what's on offer at Chez Sullivan's."

The four went inside the home and were met by Betty

Sullivan, Reg Clementson, and his wife Janice. While the adults were talking amongst themselves Kit had a walk around the lounge room looking at the family photos. His face changed colour when he saw a photo of David with Mr. Sullivan. Kit looked hard at the photo and saw the more defined features of the spirit he had become friends with.

"That's our son David with his dad a month before his accident," Betty Sullivan told Kit as she sidled up to him.

"What was he like?" Kit asked.

"He was always the one I could rely on. David had a lovely wit and sense of humour."

Kit looked at Betty and chose his words carefully.

"Mrs. Sullivan, I need to speak with you and my mum privately, if that's alright?"

"Sure Kit. Problems?"

"No. I have something you need to hear."

Betty looked at Kit's face and saw the heavy concentration. She realised this was going to be a special time. She followed Kit's eyes as they strayed onto the photo of David. Her heart seemed to miss a beat, but she couldn't work out a connection. She was intrigued as the scent of David's favourite cologne wafted in the air.

"Come on you two, the barbie's calling," Sullivan said when he saw Kit and his wife looking at David's photo. "Betty, Kit's pretty hungry so we need to fill him up."

"Alright love, we're coming."

Kit and Betty walked through the lounge room and out to the back yard where the others were gathered around a huge electric barbecue. Reg and Daniel were talking to Terry Sullivan about their adventure with the Fraud Squad. Betty, Leah, and Janice quickly became engrossed in their own conversation. Kit drifted to where his father was sitting and pulled up a chair. All the men had beers in their hands while the women were drinking wine. The men loved wine too but started the night with a beer. Terry got Kit a soft drink and asked him if he'd like to start cooking the meat. Kit looked at his Dad and then at Sullivan.

"I can't," Kit said with a wince.

"What's wrong mate? Don't worry about what to cook – the lot must be eaten," Sullivan said.

"That's not it," Kit started to say. Daniel saw the worry on his son's face and finished the boy's reply.

"Ever since Kit's accident he has had problems working with electrical items with metal surrounds."

"That's pretty interesting. How do you go with computers and TV?"

"I'm okay with most computers as they have some sort of anti-shock mechanisms built in. When it comes to big metal surfaces like the barbecue, and it has electricity running through it I feel little shocks go up and down my body if I get too close."

"Kit, I'm sorry. I didn't know," Sullivan said.

"It's okay. I don't tell a lot of people as it becomes too hard to explain sometimes."

"So, this electrical problem was a result of falling into the pool?" Reg asked.

"Yes and no," Kit said as he sipped his soft drink. "Yes, the problem was caused because of hitting my head and falling into the pool. However, the real issue was dying on the operating table and then coming back to life. This has meant a few changes for me."

"Mate, no probs. You'd be good as a crook. You could find where the electrical security beams were in buildings," Reg quipped.

"I can tell you Mr. Sullivan has an infrared light pointing at us from his roof right now."

Sullivan dropped his beer. The rest of the men turned their heads towards the eaves and searched for the light. Sullivan picked up his beer and looked at Kit.

"Sorry folks. I've still got fat on my hands from the sausages. Kit's right though," Sullivan admitted.

Reg and Daniel shook their heads. They couldn't see any protruding light.

"Kit where is it?" Daniel asked.

Kit pointed to a mossy patch on the eaves and said it was camouflaged. Sullivan was impressed.

"Well done, mate. The previous owner was very worried about security, and he had it installed in case anyone broke into his backyard," Sullivan said.

Reg and Daniel stood up and moved closer. They then nodded and pointed to the moss and could work out the shape of the light.

"I'm stuffed if I could have seen it," Reg said. "Yet, I'm pretty good at finding media crews and their hidden cameras. You're amazing Kit. What else can you do?"

Kit was embarrassed. He didn't want to let on too much.

"Not much really."

Leah had noticed Kit was struggling. She knew he hated to be the centre of attention concerning his accident. Leah stood up and said she'd give Betty a hand preparing the salads and asked Kit to join them. Janice joined the men as they moved on to discuss the upcoming election.

"Thanks, Mum," Kit said as he sidled up to her as she walked into the kitchen with Betty. Leah put her arm around him and kissed him. Nothing more had to be said.

While the ladies were preparing the salad Kit walked into the lounge room and retrieved the photo of David and his father Terry. He showed Betty and then dropped another bombshell.

"Mrs. Sullivan, do you still have the photo of David and his dad fishing?"

Betty kept cutting the carrots. "No love, it went missing some time ago," she said. Betty then stopped in her tracks. "Kit, how did you know about that photo, you've never been here before?"

"Mrs. Sullivan, I have something to tell you that you'll find hard to believe."

"What is it?"

"First, let me show you something."

Kit closed his right hand and used his index finger to point at his chest. He opened his hand over his heart and then pointed at Betty. Her eyes opened in disbelief and shock.

"Do you know what those hand movements mean Kit?"

"Yes. David taught me. He said you two used to do it together often."

Leah moved closer to Betty to support her if needed. Betty

looked at Kit and then at Leah and started to cry. Kit walked closer to her and put his arm around her. Leah organised some tissues.

"When I had the accident in the pool, I sort of died on the operating table and the doctors brought me back."

"Yes," Betty said. "I'm sorry. I haven't had someone give me the *I love you* motions like you did since David died."

"That's okay. Well, one of the things I can do now is sometimes I see spirits."

"Do you mean ghosts?" Betty asked.

"Yeah."

"Don't be silly Kit. There's no such thing as ghosts or spirits."

"If I told you David has come to see me, would you believe me?"

"What? My David? He's been dead for a long time Kit."

"I know. It was him that showed me the love message that only you two did."

"This is unbelievable … it is truly unbelievable."

"I now have two things to tell you from David if you're up to it."

"Leah, what's he going on about?" Betty asked.

"Betty, I know this is hard, please hear Kit out."

Betty turned from looking at Leah and looked directly at Kit and began to shake.

"I have seen David a couple of times in my bedroom. I don't know why he chose me, but we've had some long talks about things."

"Kit, this is preposterous."

"Mrs. Sullivan, remember earlier we were talking about the missing photo of David?"

"Yes."

"If you look behind your dressing table you should find it," Kit said slowly and with a very sincere voice. "Mr. Sullivan threw it there not long after David died."

"Oh, come on Kit, how on earth would you know that? This is silly. You have never been in this house before. This can't be true. We've looked everywhere for that photo including under the dresser. What else do you need to tell me?"

Kit looked at Leah and then Betty.

"David is here tonight and wants you to know he really loves you. He wants you to know he's okay and to stop worrying … that's why he showed me the hand gestures so you would believe me."

Betty started crying and Leah put her arm around her friend.

"Betty, several things have happened to Kit since his operation. Daniel and I believe him," Leah said.

"How can you talk with David, he's gone, he's no longer here?" Betty sobbed. "And the photo, you've got no idea what you're talking about."

Terry Sullivan walked into the kitchen to get some more beers and saw his wife upset.

"What's up, honey? Is everything alright?" Sullivan said as he scanned the faces of Kit and Leah.

"Terry, what happened to the photo of you and David fishing?" Betty asked as she wiped her eyes.

"Darling, it went missing some time after he died. Why? What's going on?"

Kit took the initiative and told Sullivan of David visiting him and the dead teenager's wish for Kit to speak with his mother. He then detailed what he knew of the missing photo.

"Mr. Sullivan, did you take the photo upstairs to your bedroom when you were upset over David's death?" Kit asked.

"I've got no idea Kit. What has this got to do with anything?"

"You know I have never been to your home before, so I know this is a shock to you. Could you please just have look behind your dressing table for the photo?"

Terry put the three beers down and walked upstairs to his bedroom. He looked underneath it and saw nothing there. He pulled the dressing table away from the wall and a metal 'clunk' could be heard. Slowly he bent down and looked under the table for what fell. He pushed his hand into a crevice and felt a metal object. When he withdrew his hand the object, he saw was the dusty photo that had been lost for years. It was his favourite photo of him and David fishing on a wharf. The photo was taken shortly before David died in the car accident and was the one, he liked most. Sullivan wiped away the dust from the photo and started to cry.

A familiar hand rubbed his shoulders, and he knew it was Betty. He showed her the photo and buried his head in her lap. Betty too shed a tear when she saw her husband so overcome with emotion. Kit entered the room with Leah and put his hand on Terry's shoulder.

The teenager stepped forward and put his arms around both the Sullivans and gave them a large hug. He gently pulled away and stood in front of them.

"What was that for mate?" Sullivan asked.

"David said you two always liked group hugs and to give you one."

Sullivan was past being astonished by Kit. He drew closer and gave him a hug of his own. Kit felt a tear drop onto his neck as his spiritual friend's father held him tightly. Sullivan released Kit and composed himself. He took the photo back from Betty and looked at it again.

"Come on everyone, we best get downstairs I smell a wonderful barbecue being cooked by Daniel and Reg," Sullivan said as he wiped tears from his eyes.

The women led the push downstairs leaving Sullivan and Kit slightly behind. Kit put his hand on Sullivan's arm and then put his right index finger to his own mouth as a symbol of 'quiet'.

"I need to talk to you very soon," Kit said in a hushed tone.

"What about?" Sullivan replied quietly.

"Ratcliffe."

Sullivan stopped in his tracks. He looked like a deer being caught in the lights of a car. "What has your dad told you about Ratcliffe?"

"Nothing."

"Hrrmph. Then what could you tell me about him?"

Sullivan was ready again to dismiss Kit. The boy wouldn't have a clue what was going on within the political party room or with discussions between Daniel and himself over the Police Commissioner. Sullivan started walking down the stairs again when Kit dropped a verbal hand grenade.

"I know he is out to get you and events may lead to you and my father being killed."

Sullivan stopped in mid-step. His face turned an ashen colour as he leaned against the wall. This teenage boy seemed to be a force to be reckoned with, yet he had been told nothing about current events.

"How would you know what's going on with Ratcliffe if your father hasn't told you?"

"Through David, and he has a special message for you."

"Kit, this can't be true. There's no way you would know anything about this. This can't be happening. David died ten years ago. He's gone. He's no longer here."

"How would I have known about the missing photo, who lost it and where it was hidden? I suppose I really knew nothing about the group hugs you and Mrs. Sullivan and David used to have of a night before he went to bed or out with his friends?"

Sullivan opened his mouth as if about to sing opera and then closed it as he composed himself once again.

"Terry, come on, this meat will be burnt if you don't eat it now," Daniel yelled up the stairs as he saw Kit talking to his client. "Kit, come on down mate, we need some help please."

Kit looked at Sullivan and then down to his father.

"Coming, dad."

"Kit we better join the others," Sullivan said.

Kit looked slightly dazed for a moment and then nodded. He refocused and smiled.

"One last thing, Mr. Sullivan. Check who is supporting the Police Minister as they are at the centre of your problem."

"Sure Kit. Thanks," Sullivan said in a way to placate Kit.

The politician felt he had been lectured by a teenager. What would this boy know about anything with regards to Ratcliffe and his removal from power? What would he know about the Police Minister and any connecting political support to the Commissioner? No, this boy was lucky tonight with David's photo. He was stepping outside the normal bounds of conversation about politics. Kit was just a teenager. The pair finished walking down the stairs. Daniel was waiting with a beer for Sullivan and looked at Kit.

"Come on mate, we need a hand to get the gas heater started."

"Alright, Dad."

Kit went past his father and Sullivan and joined the women and Reg on the back lawn. He saw the mobile gas heater and started to play with its dials. A click could be heard and then a low humming as the light came to life and emanated its warm heat with an instant effect.

"Mmm," Kit thought to himself. "This was easier to start than the light poles of Thomas's era."

"Thanks, Kit," Betty said as she put some salad on the table. "It makes all the difference with the heater on it just takes the chill out of the air."

"No probs Mrs. Sullivan," Kit said.

Janice Clementson joined the other women as they started work on the salads and other side dishes in the kitchen.

"Are you two okay? You've been gone for a while. The boys and I were getting worried," Janice said.

Leah looked at her friend and put her hand on her arm.

"Sorry, Janice we got side-tracked on a photo hunting expedition."

"A photo hunt? Did you find what you were looking for?"

"Yes. A photo of David and Terry that has been missing for nearly a decade."

"What made you look for it now? Is there a special occasion coming up or something?"

Betty took a couple of deep breaths and then answered.

"Years ago, we lost a photo of Terry and David fishing. Kit suggested where it could be, and Terry found it. Quite remarkable!"

"Where was it? Surely you would have searched the house over the years looking for it?"

"Oh yes. We searched but never found it. Tonight, Kit was able to detail exactly where it was stuck behind the dresser in the bedroom. Terry checked it out and there it was – just waiting to be found."

Janice smiled knowingly and put her arm on Betty's shoulder. The pair had been good friends for many years.

"Where's the photo now?"

"Where else? Terry has it. I bet it won't be far from him all night."

"That's great news then. I'm glad Leah and Daniel brought Kit along tonight. He seems to have brought a mixed bag of delight with him."

Betty nodded and turned to Leah.

"You know Leah, Janice is right. It makes all the difference having Kit here tonight. I'm glad you brought him, even though he had me reaching for my tissues."

"He's a good kid and loves his family. Daniel and I are not looking forward to the day he moves out of home I can tell you."

"Leah, you have several years ahead of you yet before that happens. Enjoy him while you can. He's a lovely boy, but seems a bit, well, I don't know, into things none of us ever talk about."

"You mean spirits and dead people?"

"Yes."

"Do you believe he has met and spoken to David's spirit?"

Janice couldn't hold back on hearing Leah's question.

"Is Kit turning out to be a Medium or something?"

"No," Leah said. "Since his accident Kit says he is being visited by David and it was him who told Kit where the missing photo could be found."

Janice went quiet as she mulled this over and took another drink of her wine.

"I don't know what to believe," Betty said. "I had a feeling come over me tonight I have not felt for a very long time. Terry and I don't believe in the spirits of the dead talking to the living. Yet tonight your son gave us things no one else knew."

"You mean the photo?"

"Yes, and the group hug – that was our special family embrace we all loved. It's one of those things you don't talk to others about so you and Daniel would not have known. In fact, Janice wouldn't have known either."

"I know what you mean," Leah said. "I enjoy organising afternoon tea for Kit for when he arrives home from school. It can be a time when he and I discuss anything and everything. For Daniel, it's being with Kit whenever he can. He dotes on him."

Janice picked up on the vibes and decided it was time to move on with the night.

"Come on you two let's get this food on the table before the men start a rebellion," Janice said.

The three women picked up the various side dishes and bread and placed them on the table. Kit joined in by retrieving any remaining dishes. He noticed Sullivan had placed David's photo on a ledge of the barbecue and as he turned the meat, he would glance at it. Kit nodded knowingly. He never knew how emotional events would turn out tonight but was glad to help the spirit of the teenager who had sought him out and became his friend.

"Okay guys, this meat is done. Let's get it onto the table before we all die of starvation," Sullivan said.

"Amen," Daniel said. "I'm famished."

"Ah, you two have gas-bagged enough tonight," Reg said as the three men all laughed.

"Never mind you too," Sullivan chimed in.

Kit laughed as he watched and listened to the antics of his father and his friends. It was good to see them in such fine spirits. Sullivan and Clementson moved the meat and fried onions to the table while his father scraped down the barbecue plate to clean it. Kit looked at the teamwork. It was so coordinated it was as if the moves were rehearsed. He then watched Sullivan return to the barbecue and retrieve David's photo and place it on the table in front of where he was going to sit.

"Terry, you seem to be guarding the photo of David," Janice said.

"Well, it's been missing for ten years and I won't let it go missing again in hurry."

Everyone around the table looked at Sullivan and nodded quietly. They all knew how much David meant to his father. It was like the pair were reunited again.

"Let's propose a toast," Reg said. He picked up his glass of wine and lifted it up. "To good friends."

The group picked up their glasses and chimed in: "To good friends" before quaffing their drinks.

Sullivan picked up his glass again. "A new toast, everyone. To all our loved ones – wherever they may be."

Sullivan looked at David's photo and then at Kit as the group joined in the toast. Kit knew he had struck a rich chord with David's father. The problem was, how much would Sullivan listen to him if David told him things that would affect his future, maybe his life. Kit internalised the conundrum and hoed into the barbecue. After the main course, he helped take the plates to the kitchen with Janice.

"You seem to have brought a lot of joy to the Sullivans tonight, Kit," Janice said.

"I was just helping out I suppose."

Janice started unpeeling the plastic cover sheets from the various sweet dishes on the kitchen bench.

"Betty and your mum were saying you had a visit from the spirit of David. That must have been exciting?"

Kit wasn't sure where to go with this conversation. "Yeah. Since my operation, I've had a couple of visits from David."

"Did you ever see ghosts before?"

Kit's eyes narrowed as tried to work out where Janice was trying to lead him.

"No. But it's okay."

Kit picked up a sponge cake and custard sweet and was about to walk away.

"I knew when I saw you tonight you were different," she said slowly in a bid to hold his attention.

"How?"

"Your aura compared to the others is brighter and different. It's more electric in its shimmer."

Kit had been told the same by Mrs. Bishop. He stopped moving and looked at her.

"Can you also see spirits?"

"No. I can see people's auras and sometimes have an inkling of the future, but I can't see those who have passed over. It must be exciting."

"It's a bit disturbing at first – but when you get used to it it's like talking to anyone else."

"Was it David who told you where the photo was tonight?"

"Yes."

"Well, you certainly made the Sullivans very happy by doing so."

"Thanks."

Kit took the dessert out to the table and noticed his mother following him in. She looked at Janice and then at Kit. The boy winked at her to acknowledge her look and placed the sweet on the table. He returned to the kitchen to pick up a second dessert which Janice had organised.

"You're here tonight to do something else aren't you?" she asked Kit.

"What do you mean?"

"I get the feeling you found the photo as a vehicle for something else."

Kit smiled. "David was very keen for me to show his parents where the photo was hiding."

"Nothing else?"

"Mrs. Clementson, I bet you don't tell everyone you can read auras, do you?" Kit asked as a way of changing the subject.

"No, most people don't understand."

"David is very keen to let his parents know he is okay and for them to stop worrying about him."

Janice had listened carefully and was about to ask Kit some more questions when Leah entered the kitchen.

"Now that homemade fruit salad and cream looks absolutely delicious," Leah said.

Kit smiled. He knew what his mother was doing – ensuring he was not bailed up by Janice.

"Thank you. I know Daniel and Reg both love fruit salad, never mind Terry."

"Ah, but then Terry loves the fresh cream."

"Don't we all."

The women laughed and walked with Kit out to the rest of the group. Kit placed the dessert down and followed his mother's movements with his head, then nodded when they made eye contact. Leah smiled at him and nodded before reaching for her glass of wine.

The group continued with their second course with Kit enjoying the adventure. Kit was a firm believer in God but didn't think this was why he hadn't died in his pool accident. He knew there was a place for people's spirits to go to after they had died as he had been there when he was being operated on. Mrs. Bishop had told him he has things yet to set in motion and accomplish in this life before returning to the sphere of the dead. He also believed his spirit guide Thomas had helped open his "third eye" to communicate with those who had died. This had been an emotional night for the Sullivans and Kit.

The teenager knew he had to deliver the message for David, but Kit didn't realise what the effect would be on Mr. Sullivan. The photo of David and his father sat comfortably in front of Sullivan as he swung the conversation round to politics and the upcoming election.

"Kit, will you give me a hand to clear these dishes please?" Betty asked.

"Sure, Mrs. Sullivan."

Kit and Betty picked up several empty plates and took them into the kitchen.

"Kit I want to thank you for helping us to find the photo of Terry and David. This will help calm Terry down some. He … we, both really miss our son. He was a good kid."

"Mrs. Sullivan, I want you to know I don't go talking to spirits everywhere. Since my accident, I seem to have had this ability open to me. You know I have never been here before so I wouldn't know anything about the photo. I'm glad you found it."

"Why us Kit? Why come to us about David?"

"I don't know why I was chosen but David had visited me a few times. He was very keen to have me tell you a few things."

"It's just been an unbelievable evening, Kit."

The teenager went quiet for a few moments and then smiled as he eyed Betty Sullivan directly.

"Mrs. Sullivan on your house keys you carry the tiny surfboard David used to carry on his keys. David is very glad you do this."

Betty dropped a plate on the kitchen bench as she tried to lift it. She went red and then began to cry and sniffle again. Kit reached out and hugged her.

"Be happy for him Mrs. Sullivan, as he is with you. David will always be near you and will always love you."

"How did you know about the surfboard? I know, David told you. Right?" she sobbed.

"Yes. He said it was a special message to you."

Betty released Kit and reached for a tissue in the kitchen. She wiped her eyes and took Kit's hand.

"Come with me for a few moments. I want to show you something," Betty said as she regained her poise.

She took Kit into her study and picked up her handbag. Her right hand rummaged through the bag's contents and retrieved a set of keys. Attached was a tiny red and white foam surfboard.

"David had this on his key ring the night he died. I decided to keep the board and put it on my keys as a way of constantly reminding myself about David. Only a few people know my keys have David's board attached."

"Mrs. Sullivan, I know David was a joyful person from the way he has spoken about you and Mr. Sullivan and the family. I'm lucky I guess, to know him as he is and to have brought you some joy tonight on his behalf."

"Kit, you don't know what you have done. You have re-connected Terry and me with our son in a way we could never have imagined. If there's anything Terry and I can do for you, let us know. Okay?"

Kit shook his head.

"Mrs. Sullivan what I did tonight, I did for you because of David. Nothing else. Thanks."

Betty replaced her keys in her handbag and then placed an arm around Kit as the pair returned to the kitchen. She turned on the electric jug of water ready to make coffees and tea. Kit helped set up the cups on a tray ready to take outside. Janice and Leah entered the kitchen carrying more plates for the dishwasher.

"How's the tea and coffee coming Betty?" Janice said as she looked at her friend and then Kit. Janice reached over to the tissue box and took a couple of tissues out. She quietly gave Betty the tissues before looking at Kit. "Kit, will you see who's up for coffee and who's up for tea outside?"

"Sure, no probs," Kit replied. He was glad to leave the women and re-join the men.

"Betty are you okay?" Leah asked.

"Yes. Kit was just helping me to stack the plates. He's a good boy."

"Yes," Leah said. "But he can be full of surprises at times."

"Thank you, Janice," Betty said as she wiped her eyes.

“You’ve been crying again. Did Kit help you find another photo?” Janice asked.

“No. He told me something even you two don’t know.”

“What?” Janice pushed.

“The night David was killed he had a small foam surfboard on his key ring. Afterwards, I took the board and put it on my house keys. There’s no way Kit would have known that.”

“So, what did Kit say?” Leah asked.

“He told me David was very glad I still carried his surfboard on my keys. I took him into the study and showed him my house keys with the board attached. Hardly anyone knew I had the board or why I carried it.”

“Leah, your son is amazing. His accident has certainly opened doors most of us can only hope to see, never mind enter,” Janice said.

“Yes. I’m sorry Betty if he’s caused you and Terry any heartache tonight. He wouldn’t have meant it.”

“No, no Leah. On the contrary, he has said and given us things tonight we could never imagine we would hear or have happened. It’s just that what has happened has touched some pretty emotional spots. He wouldn’t know that – he’s too young to see it.”

“I’ll talk to him quietly to be more considerate with others and their feelings.”

“No, please don’t say anything. Just love him for the beautiful young man he is … Kit’s a treasure.”

The three friends moved closer and had a group hug.

Daniel followed Kit with his eyes as his son walked out to the rear lawn. He seemed unsettled.

"Everything alright mate?" Daniel asked.

"Yeah. All's well. Mrs. Sullivan is putting on tea and coffee. What would you gents like?" Kit asked the group.

Reg and Sullivan stopped their conversation, and both signalled they preferred coffee. Daniel said the same.

"After you tell Mrs. Sullivan the men's order, come back and join us, okay."

"Alright, dad."

Kit was now truly a messenger boy. First, it was delivering messages from David to the Sullivans and now the coffee order. He didn't mind. He felt useful and knew the adults appreciated him. Kit told Janice that all the males would love a coffee.

"Typical isn't it," Janice said. "They like tea in the morning and coffee at night."

"I think most of us do," Leah said. "Something light to get you going in the morning and then something heavier to give you a buzz at night."

"Thanks, Kit," Betty said.

"No probs," Kit replied as he returned to the men.

Daniel put his arm around Kit and hugged him when the teenager sat down. Kit smiled and seemed to lighten up.

"Kit, Terry was just saying you're invited to stay here anytime you like – especially if you're at a loose end on weekends," Daniel said.

Kit looked at his father and then Sullivan.

"Thanks, Mr. Sullivan."

"Mate, we have plenty of room here and if you want to go for a swim or just sit back in the cinema room and watch films, let me know," Sullivan said.

"Thanks. Do you have your own cinema set up?" Kit asked.

"No, not quite. Betty and I turned the family room into a home cinema area where we have a large TV and DVD playback system. It's good for me when I'm reviewing films of the government in action or just enjoying good movies with Betty."

"Sounds great Mr. Sullivan. Thanks for the offer."

Janice, Leah, and Betty brought out the teas and coffees and handed them out. The group settled back to enjoy the final phase of the evening together. Kit sipped slowly on his coffee and watched the Sullivans. Betty had moved the photo of David and Terry to face her. It was her time to enjoy the special framed image. Terry was trying to talk to Daniel but kept looking every so often at the photo. Janice was talking to Reg and the group but kept looking at Kit. Daniel and Reg swung the conversation away from politics to the upcoming long weekend and what each of the families would be doing. Leah noticed Kit had gone quiet and seemed to be just observing the group. He must be bored, she thought. Kit had delivered his messages and was now zoning out. The teenager looked at his mum with a quizzical look. Somehow, he had picked up on Leah's vibes.

"Daniel, I think we better start to make a move to go home," Leah said. "It's getting late."

"Okay love," Daniel said. "Terry, Betty, I think it's time we let you lovely people get to bed."

"Reg, I think we better head off as well," Janice said as she squeezed her husband's arm. "It's been another lovely evening but it's time to help clean up and hit the sack."

"Ah, now you've got my attention," Reg said.

"You haven't changed since I married you," Janice said with a huge smile. "Come on, give me a hand."

Betty made slight protestations about leaving everything where it was on the table. Both Leah and Janice ignored Betty and started to pick up the cutlery and crockery. Kit joined in after his father looked at him and nodded his head in the direction of Leah.

"Okay ladies, we know when we're beaten," Sullivan said as he and Betty started to help pick up things. "This has been an evening I'll always remember."

"Terry, I think your luck has started to change," Reg said.

"What makes you think that?" Daniel said.

"I think a teenage boy brought along a change tonight no one expected."

"Gents, Kit had an accident, and it created a change in him none of us could imagine … never mind know how to handle," Daniel said.

Sullivan picked up the photo of David and himself and put an arm on Daniel's shoulder.

"I hate to say it mate, but I'm glad Kit had that accident. It has helped solve a few problems for us."

Daniel stopped walking and held Sullivan and Reg back.

"Gents, I know Kit is different in some ways, but please give him some space. The kid has had some issues at school and within himself since his accident. It will take some time to work through it."

"No probs Daniel," Sullivan said. "My offer for him to stay here is still on the table."

"Thanks."

"Daniel, if Janice and I can be of any assistance, don't hesitate to call us," Reg said.

"Same here," Sullivan said.

"Thanks, team, I appreciate your support," Daniel said.

The Greens were the first to leave the Sullivan's home. Betty and Terry ensured they gave Kit a group hug and thanked him for what he had done for them.

"Don't forget our offer to stay here," Betty said.

"Thanks for the great find," Sullivan said as he held up the photo of him and David.

"No probs and I won't, thank you," Kit said. He then farewelled the Clementsons and got into the rear of his family's car.

The Clementsons said their farewells and exited after the Greens. In all three families, Kit was the topic of conversation.

"Betty, I'm so glad Kit found this photo," Terry said. "All I can remember is that sometime after David died, I'd had some drinks and was holding the photo and crying. The next thing I remember is you putting me to bed. The following day the photo was gone. Now tonight, we supposedly not only receive messages from David saying he's okay and not to worry, but we also find the photo no one could find in a decade."

"Terry, Kit was amazing tonight. I felt so shocked when he told me David was glad I was still carrying his surfboard. That really rocked me. But you know I'm pretty glad he did."

"Surfboard? Kit even knew about your keys and David's surfboard. I'm really surprised by all this."

"We're lucky he came along. Hopefully he'll take us up on the offer to stay here on weekends as a sort of break. It would be nice to have a teenager around again."

"Yes."

The Clementsons were also abuzz about Kit. Janice had never seen people from the other side – those that had died – communicating through someone so young before.

"You know, Reg, we'll have to keep an eye on young Kit," Janice said. "I think he's headed for an interesting time."

"But what's the kid got to do with us?" Reg asked.

"Who knows? Tonight, he showed Terry where a missing photo had been hidden for ten years. He also told Betty that David was very happy she carried his little key ring surfboard on her house keys."

"The point that got Terry, Daniel, and I was the comment he made about a possible murder threat against the other two. I don't know. If you believe in this hocus pocus the kid may have a lot to offer. To me, the photo and surfboard were just lucky guesses."

"Hmm, I don't know about that. This kid has something special about him. This much I can tell you."

"Come on, let's get home – it's late."

The Greens were just as inquisitive as the other couples about their son too. Leah started the quizzing.

"Kit, how did you know where the photo was in Mr. Sullivan's bedroom?"

"David sort of showed me," Kit said.

"Did he appear and talk to you or something?"

"No. Every time I have been visited by him, I have this

strange feeling at the back of my neck. Sometimes I have seen him in my bedroom. Tonight, was different."

"How mate?" Daniel asked.

"I had the tingling, and I knew it was David. When I saw the family photos of the Sullivans I started seeing in the back of my mind the dressing table and the photo wedged behind it."

"Was that just like a thought?" Leah asked.

"No. You know when you have been somewhere, and you remember the places by the images you see in your mind? Well, it was like that."

"How come you were so sure the missing photo was there?" Daniel pushed.

"When Mrs. Sullivan mentioned the missing photo the tingling in my neck really increased. I kept seeing images of Mr. Sullivan upset and throwing the photo against the wall. It landed behind the dresser and became wedged. David must have seen all this and was showing me images of what happened. It was as if I had been in the room at the time."

"Wow, that's fantastic," Daniel said. "David must really like you to let you in on his family's secrets."

"I don't think it works like that dad. I think I must have some strong receptivity to him or something and he is using me like a tool."

"Kit, don't be too uptight over David. So far all he has done is show you things to help you and his family. We'll see Mrs. Bishop again this week and start getting you some lessons in what's happening and how to work with it," Leah said.

"Thanks. I'd like to see her again. I'm starting to build up a bank of questions for her."

"Kit, you told Terry that David had some information that could possibly stop his and my murders. What was that all about? Daniel asked.

"Remember we talked about the Police Commissioner, and I said David told me stuff about him?"

"Yes."

"Well, tonight David added a bit more by saying Mr. Sullivan should check who is supporting the Commissioner."

"Did he give you any names or more detail?" Daniel asked. Kit shook his head. "Okay, let me tell you it's a bit disconcerting someone from beyond the grave says you're the subject of a possible murder but he may have the answer for you."

"Dad, if I didn't tell you and something happened, you'd probably never forgive me … would you?"

"No, you're probably right there. Kit, just know your mother and I love you very much no matter what life throws at us."

"I know thanks. I'm very lucky to have parents like you two. I love you both too."

Chapter Eight

Terry Sullivan found it hard to sleep. He had placed the photo of David and himself back on the dressing table so he could view it from his bed. In his mind, he had already organised to take the photo to work, and have it scanned so he could make a poster of it and a computer screen image. He wasn't going to lose it again.

"Are you awake, love?" Terry asked as he raised himself on one elbow.

"Yes. Do you really think I could sleep much after tonight?" Betty replied.

"I can't get over what Kit did and said tonight. First, he tells me he has information from David and then calmly sits in the backyard and tells me where our infrared scanners are positioned. I forgot about those."

"You probably forgot because of all the moss covering them."

"Well, it didn't worry Kit. He still found them."

"You know the hand signals David and I used to make to each other?"

"Yeah."

"Well, Kit did those as well tonight. He said David said we wouldn't believe him unless he did them."

"How the hell would he know?"

"I don't know. When Kit did the hand signs and later told me about David's key ring surfboard all I could think about was that David was in the same room. I could even smell his aftershave."

"Then it wasn't just me then. I also smelt his aftershave when Kit showed me where the photo was wedged. I thought I was imagining it."

The Sullivans continued to dissect the evening with most comments involving Kit.

Janice was in a similar position to the Sullivans. She couldn't sleep as her mind kept going over what Kit had said to Betty; how he found the missing photo and how he knew about David's key ring surfboard.

All her life Janice had wanted to be a Medium. She believed she could predict the future with reasonable certainty. When people walked into a room Janice could sometimes see their auras and had started working out what the various shimmers and colours meant. Last night was a strong validation of her ability with auras. The moment she saw Kit, Janice saw a bright light shimmering all around the boy. He stood out as if his body was a human handheld torch. The others at the dinner had the usual low-intensity auras which almost looked like ordinary shadows. Janice had been taken aback by Kit and made a mental note to watch his progress.

Daniel and Leah had also found it hard to sleep. Their son had taken his swimming pool accident and its after-effects to new heights. Daniel had been sceptical of Kit talking about spirits and being 'visited' by David. He couldn't explain the photo Kit had found of Thomas … that was still mentally on hold. What rattled Daniel was Kit finding Sullivan's lost photo and reducing the man to tears. He also found it hard to fathom how Kit knew about the security sensors around the property.

Leah had known Kit was going to deliver a message to Betty from David. She believed Kit could speak with the dead and after talking and visiting with Mrs. Bishop, Leah was comfortable that Kit had a grip on what he was doing. Leah was still amazed at how Kit had found the photo for Sullivan and was pleased with the maturity he had shown when he did. She was also pleased that Kit had spoken to Betty about David's key ring surfboard. Her friend had never been so emotionally moved in all the time she had known the woman.

Kit had felt reasonably in control of events surrounding him at dinner. The usual neck tingling had occurred and he knew David was with him. He felt comfortable when images of the missing photo were flashed in his mind followed by Terry Sullivan throwing it at the wall, wedging it behind the dresser. Kit was okay with knowing about the cameras and security sensors. However, he felt David had pushed him when it came to the surfboard key ring. It was as if David was trying overly hard to connect with his mother and had come on a bit strong with Kit. The teenager made a mental note to bring this up with Mrs. Bishop to see how he could better control what David wanted. He also wanted to spend more time researching the image of Thomas and find out from his grandmother if it was the same one she had hidden away.

Terry Sullivan had a recurring thought being played out in his mind and that was Kit saying to him to check who is controlling the Police Commissioner. Obviously, the Police Minister and Premier controlled Ratcliffe, but was this scenario too obvious? Did Kit know what he was talking about? He did some great party tricks at dinner, but did he know anything about his political work? Maybe he did. Surely for Kit to be talking politics he must have been speaking with Daniel and got a feel of the situation. He was only trying to show his maturity to the adults. Sullivan wrestled with the thought for a while before slipping out of bed. He instinctively picked up the photo of him and David and took it downstairs to the kitchen. The first rays of sunshine were breaking into the backyard. Sullivan made a pot of tea and looked at the photo. He held an imaginary conversation with David.

"Kit did not know about you, the missing photo, or your key ring surfboard. So where did he get it from son? Did you tell him in some way? I have spoken to Daniel and Leah about you but never in personal detail. Are you really trying to connect with your mother and me through Kit? Are you really a spirit now? As a family we've never really believed in an afterlife or spirits. Are you trying to prove us wrong through this boy? I wonder."

Sullivan sipped his tea and mulled over his questions. He thought about the Police Minister and then how the Minister's office would function. The Minister controls what he wants to be carried out in his portfolio after discussions with the Premier; the Secretary of the Premier's Department and sometimes the Premier's Chief of Staff. The Minister tells his Chief of Staff what he wants, and the Chief makes it happen.

"Ahh. Is this the road I should be travelling," Sullivan said to the photo. "It may not be the Minister at all, but a rogue Chief of Staff who is pulling Ratcliffe's strings. Mmm, that's worth pursuing."

Sullivan looked at the photo and smiled. A new beginning had begun. He put his cup down and picked up the photo.

"Thank you, David," he said as he kissed the photo. "I think I have a lead." He placed the photo on his dresser and showered and got dressed. Sullivan then went to his study and pulled out a file on the Police Minister. Although he had read the file many times, he had been looking for different things on each occasion. This time, he wanted information about the power behind the Minister.

Kit woke up lying on his back. He flexed and stiffened all his muscles and then relaxed them. This was his way of brushing out the cobwebs in his body. He put his hands behind his head and thought about what the weekend would hold for him. A small amount of homework had to be completed and a beginning made on a history assignment. Kit figured he could do the schoolwork that afternoon leaving him the day free to investigate Thomas.

Strangely Kit felt invigorated. He had worked with David to help the Sullivans and bring some joy to them. By doing so he had also assisted a spirit who showed great love for his parents. Kit had felt the presence of security cameras and backyard sensors before seeing them. This was a new sensation to him. If Sullivan hadn't said anything about the sensors, he would not have known what the sensation was hitting his body. The cameras he saw as his father's car approached Sullivan's mansion. It was exciting to know his body had changed since his accident and he had a new way of looking at life … and with the advent of Thomas's images and David's appearances, death.

Kit clambered out of bed and checked the image of Thomas he had found. It was like looking at a painted image of himself wearing clothes from another century. He turned on his computer and checked the scribble he made on a notebook next to his mouse pad. Reuben Barlow painted Thomas's image in 1820. The teenager called up his computer's search engine and interrogated it for more information about Barlow.

> "*Reuben Barlow – 1790 to 1850. Born in London to a Cobbler and daughter of a Squire. Barlow is best remembered for paintings of everyday life in London. He held several exhibitions in London and Paris in the 1830s. One of his most famous paintings is of the Laughing Lad painted in 1820 and now hanging in the National Portrait Gallery of London.*"

"*Laughing Lad*, eh Thomas?" Kit said aloud. "I have an idea about Barlow. What I really need is information about you and how you came to be painted."

The teenager closed down his computer and went and had a shower and got dressed. He was joined at the breakfast bar by his mother who had heard him showering.

"Don't forget we're going to your grandmother's today. She might have found her image of Thomas for you."

"I found out the image I showed you was painted by an artist called Reuben Barlow in 1820 and was called the *Laughing Lad*."

Leah poured them both some orange juice.

"How did you find that out?"

"I went searching on the internet and found some info on Barlow. What I'd like to find is information about the person he painted."

"Well, I don't think your grandmother would have that."

"No, but the art section of a major library may."

The pair sat on the breakfast stools and sipped their juice.

"I've got nothing on today as far as ladies' meetings or club sports. How about we visit the city library after seeing your grandmother?"

"Are you sure? It could take a while and we may not find anything anyway."

"Kit, we haven't been to the library together for a long time. However, to make it more worth our while, do you have any assignments you need to research for school?"

"Yeah. I have a history assignment I was going to work on this afternoon anyway."

"Okay. How about you get some breakfast, and we go to your grandmother's first thing? I'll ring her to let her know we're on the way."

"That'd be awesome. Thanks, mum," Kit said as he poured some cereal into a plate. He looked at his mother and smiled. Not every mum would offer what she just did to their teenage kids. Kit was luckier than most, but then again, he had no brothers and sisters to share with his parents.

Leah poured a cup of tea for herself and rang her mother. She knew once she started a conversation with her mother she'd be on the phone for a while and wanted to enjoy her early morning tea.

Chapter Nine

Todd Ratcliffe was becoming concerned. The warning salvos he had fired at Terry Sullivan and his team had all but backfired. Sure, a scare had been put into Sullivan and the Opposition party, but he had the information they were still planning to replace him after the election. It was virtually a certainty the Government would be voted out of office. The Government had been in power for 16 years and the State was crumbling from major mismanagement. The Opposition had only to continue looking good and it would fall over the line and win the election with a resounding landslide.

Ratcliffe lived in an old double-storey, late 19th Century home with huge ceilings and rooms. He had converted two large rooms at the rear of the house into a board room where he held special executive meetings with his inner circle of Police Commanders and officers. Slowly he walked around the room checking he had enough cups, coffee, tea and mugs. Today was an update meeting where his senior officers would report on what was happening around the State. Ratcliffe often held these meetings at his home on Saturday mornings rather than at Police Headquarters. After the meetings, a select few officers would remain and Ratcliffe would entertain them at lunch while they discussed any politics concerning the police.

The large car park on the grounds of the Ratcliffe home soon filled as police officers arrived in civilian and police cars – depending on whether they were on duty or not. Among the group today was Adrian Elliott, the Chief of Staff in the Police Minister's office. Elliott was a short man with a large stomach and a well-pronounced receding hairline. He earned the nickname of 'Penguin' for the way he looked and sometimes seemed to waddle. Elliott had been involved in politics for some years and had helped in the re-election of his boss Paul Scully who became Police Minister. Scully appointed Elliott as his Chief of Staff as he had proved to be a very loyal worker who would stop at virtually nothing to protect his boss.

Both Ratcliffe and Elliott got on well with each other. They knew they could use each other for their own purposes if they wanted. Elliott used the meeting as a sounding board to hear and see what the State senior Police thought of their Minister. He would also advise the Police on what the Minister would require with certain investigations or Media issues if they came under political view. Today's meeting centred on the use of speed cameras and whether more were needed to catch speeding drivers or whether more Highway Patrol officers should be employed. Elliott explained the Government had reached a ceiling with Police numbers and was looking for a more lucrative way of enforcing the law and raising much-wanted revenue. Most of the senior Police agreed with Elliott as the cameras would take some of the load off the busy Highway Patrol Officers. The junior officers disagreed but didn't pursue the arguments too aggressively. They would wait until a change of government and then push their demands through meetings of their union and the new government.

The meeting was over within two hours. Discussion had been light as issues surrounding Police were off the boil with the Media who were focusing more of their time on the Premier. A small clique of Ministers had let it be known to the Media they were not happy with the way the Premier was running the State. However, they were not ready to run against him at this time as they didn't have the numbers within the party room to depose him. This gave the Media another side story every time the Government was challenged from within, whether it was the public servants, other Ministers or department heads that came under the spotlight; the Media would always defer to the breakaway group of Ministers to see if the issue was enough to cause a political spill. There was also no major crime to report at present. The throng of police departed leaving just Elliott and Ratcliffe together.

"Well, that was short," Ratcliffe said to Elliott.

"Yeah. The Government knows it is sitting on a time bomb concerning employment across the board." Elliott said.

"What do you mean?"

"We should have more Highway Police on the roads patrolling the traffic. The Government can't afford the wages and other monies to employ more Police."

"What time bomb?"

"Todd, this Government is going broke. We know if the unions start a rolling strike campaign so close to the election it will signal the end of us."

Ratcliffe picked up his coffee and motioned for Elliott to

do the same. The pair went to the rear verandah and seated themselves at a coffee table in the warm sun.

"You know Adrian, I'm still hearing that Terry Sullivan is drawing up plans to replace me if there is a change of government."

"I thought the fraud issue and the police shakedown of his staff would unsettle him somewhat."

"So did I, but he seems unflappable."

"Hmm. I'll have the Parliamentary Accounts Committee re-check his claims."

"Okay. If you need some muscle in blue, let me know."

"Alright."

The meeting was over, and Elliott departed. Ratcliffe went for a walk around his garden while he thought about the meeting he had just had with Elliott. He stopped to look at his roses. His wife Ellen had planted them a month before she died of cancer in their home. It had been a long battle with the dreaded disease. Todd had brought Ellen home from the hospice so she could die with dignity in her own familiar surroundings. The woman never knew her husband had been involved in any corruption or bribery. She doted on her policeman husband who had loved her since they were teenagers together. Her ashes were now buried in the garden so she would continue to be part of Ratcliffe's home.

"Honey, I miss you," Ratcliffe said quietly as he touched the petals of his red roses. "You helped provide so much light for me when you were alive. Now, all I see is enveloping darkness. This government is crazy with power and will stop at nothing to stay elected. If the government wins another term of office I could have up to three more years at the top. If they go, so do I. Once I'm out of uniform the Media will have a field day with anything they can find on me as I won't have any protectors in the new government. The question is: what do I do?"

Ratcliffe accidentally pricked his fingers as he grabbed the stem of a rose too hard. The shock of the pain caused by the thorn piercing his fingers stopped him from talking to his garden and his dead wife. He made his way back into the house and placed a phone call with a Police Inspector in an undercover squad.

"Joe, I want you to have a look into the background of Adrian Elliott," Ratcliffe said.

"Mate, isn't he the Minister's Chief Of Staff?" Joe asked.

"Yeah. I just want to check out how squeaky clean he is."

"Not feeling too comfortable with the way he's running things, huh?"

"No. So I want to ensure we have a good bargaining chip if ever we need it."

"Consider it done. I'm on the case."

"Thanks, mate."

The two men rang off. Joe West and Ratcliffe had been police officers together and had once made a lucrative living by collaring drug dealers and keeping a lot of the money gained through their illicit deals. Joe was now an Inspector in charge of an undercover squad who reported directly to Ratcliffe.

Chapter Ten

Leah was on tenterhooks as she drove to her mother's home. She knew her mother had found the photo of the portrait Kit was after. Kit was more apprehensive as to whether the portrait his grandmother had was the same as the printed copy of Thomas he had found on the internet. Leah was following Daniel's instructions to the letter by watching her speed and driving exactly to the speed limit. Daniel was still worried his family may be under some sort of police scrutiny because of the work he had been doing for Sullivan. Finally, Leah and Kit drove up beside Leah's mother's home. It was a two-bedroom weatherboard cottage with a rickety wooden fence and a rusting gate. This had been her family home where she had grown up and shared so many memories with her brothers and sisters. Being home always meant feeling good. Leah tooted the horn as she and Kit exited her car. Within moments the front door opened, and Leah's mother Catherine stood there with open arms. Kit quickened his pace and gave his grandmother a strong hug and kiss when the pair met. Leah did the same and all three went into the cottage, down a hallway and into the kitchen.

"Leah you're looking so well," Catherine said. "And Kit, look how tall and big you've grown."

"Thanks, mum. I'm doing okay. Yes, Kit has had a growth spurt and started filling out. Before you know it he'll be leaving school and starting a job."

"Oh Leah, don't make him grow up too quickly. Enjoy him as a boy while you can. He'll be a man soon enough."

Catherine noticed the folder Kit was carrying and changed tack with her conversation.

"Okay young man, you certainly led me on a merry chase this week looking for that print."

"Nan, I really appreciate what you've done," Kit said.

"He always knows how to butter people up, doesn't he?" Catherine asked Leah as the pair of them laughed.

"Kit follows his father when it comes to people skills. He knows how to work a room and say the right things."

"Come on mum, we're not here to boost my ego," Kit said.

Catherine noted the hint of anxiety in her grandson's voice.

"Leah put the kettle on and let's have a cup of tea while I get the portrait, I think you're after. It's in the lounge room."

Kit played with the edges of his folder while his mother filled an old kettle with water and put it on the gas stove. She found the gas lighter and lit the gas jets before going to the cupboards to get some cups and saucers. Her mother returned with a postcard size copy of a portrait.

"Kit here it is. Pass me my glasses, will you?"

Kit passed his grandmother her reading glasses as she studied the portrait. She was halfway to reaching out to Kit to give him the copy when she stopped.

"My, my, will you look at that?" Catherine asked. "I hadn't seen any resemblance before but now I do."

Catherine studied the portrait of Thomas and then Kit's face a couple of times. Before she could say anything, else Kit opened his folder.

"Nan, does it look like this?" Kit asked.

Catherine was gobsmacked as Kit placed an A4-size copy of Thomas on the table. She placed her copy of the same portrait down and shook her head.

"Kit, if you already had a copy of this portrait why did you have me searching my house from top to bottom for you?"

"Nan, I came across this image on my computer, and I had to know whether it was the same one you had," Kit said.

Catherine studied both images and raised her head to speak but refrained. She looked carefully at the images and then at Kit. The resemblance was remarkable. It was as if Kit had posed for the painting himself.

"How did you get such a large print of the portrait?"

"Nan, I was playing around with the internet when I came across the image. What mum and I saw you just do is exactly what my parents did when I showed them the image."

"Kit this is pretty unbelievable. This image has been in my family for several generations now and is pretty special."

Leah had finished making the teas and put the cups on the table."Mum what's on the back of the portrait?" she asked.

Catherine turned over her image and smiled. Written in old handwriting was a message from her own grandfather to her.

"To my dear Katy, here is an image of my grandfather Thomas that hangs in the National Portrait Gallery in London. Love, Granddad."

"Nan, how did your grandfather get the image?" Kit asked.

Catherine slowly drank some of her tea before answering. For a few moments, she had been transported back in time when she was a little girl and she was savouring the experience. When she placed her cup back on her saucer, she looked a couple of more times at the portrait and then Kit.

"Well, I was just a little girl and my grandfather was very old. He and my grandmother had gone on a steamboat to England and been away for a long time. When they came back, they brought us presents. Mine was this image."

"Mum, I don't remember seeing it when I was growing up?" Leah asked.

"Well, maybe not. I only ever brought it out at family gatherings if someone wanted to see it. This was my treasure which was in a special box your grandfather made for me after we were married."

"What else is in the box?"

"Oh, it has our marriage certificate, both my parent's death certificates and other papers. I also kept some trinkets from when I was growing up. You have seen them, but a long time ago I think."

Kit thought it amusing how his mother was now a child along with him.

"I'll have to have a look at the box and your papers so if we do any family research I know where the source documents are located."

"Leah, the box is in my wardrobe. I had it in the old shed down the back yard and after your telephone call, I went looking for it. It took me a while to find it, I can tell you. I can't believe the resemblance between Kit and Thomas. Either they are twins or it's Kit dressed up in old clothes."

Kit had been reading the inscription on the back of his grandmother's image. "You know, maybe I'm Thomas revisited."

"What do you mean?"

"Well, maybe when my mum and dad had me, Thomas was re-born."

Catherine stopped sipping her tea and took in what Kit said. "Well, I don't believe God would re-use people this way. No, I think you have a lot of genes from my family in you and it took a couple of generations to come out."

"Like the same way some people have red hair or are bald?

"Yes. My father had a good head of hair when he died yet my grandfather went bald early. Maybe it's your turn to have a good mop of hair."

"Phew, I hope so. I don't want to go bald early, or at all."

Catherine found it hard to talk with Leah and not look down at the image on the table and then at Kit. The similarity was too uncanny. She also sensed a strong spirituality with Kit and special awareness.

"So, Kit, what was it like seeing a Medium?" Catherine asked as she studied her grandson's face.

"It was a bit odd Nan," Kit said. "One of mum's friends had organised the visit and didn't tell her anything about me or mum and dad. Yet, after meeting us all she told us things only we would know."

"Mmm," Catherine said as she sipped more tea. "Are you sure your mum's friend didn't tell her about you all in other conversations?"

Kit looked at his mother and then his grandmother. "I'm pretty sure she wouldn't do that."

Leah picked up on where her mother was going with the conversation. "Mum, you remember Sarah Kaplan?"

"Sarah … no."

"Yes, you do. We went to school together and used to play tennis."

"Ah, yes. Sarah. Sorry, it's been a while since you spoke of her."

"Sarah and I talked about Kit and some of the things he's been doing and saying since his accident. She recommended we see a Medium she knew."

"Was she a gipsy or something?"

Leah laughed. "No. She's just like you and me. Anyway, Sarah said she only recommended us to the woman, a Niva Bishop. She didn't tell her anything about us, yet when we met her, Niva was able to tell us personal things even Sarah didn't know."

"Like what?"

"Oh, the sorts of things Daniel is working on, what Kit has been going through since his accident. That sort of thing."

"Did she work with a crystal ball, or did you have to hold a séance or anything?"

Kit was amused at his grandmother and her old-style way of thinking. "Nan, when we went to her home, we didn't have to tell her much as she either knew about us or was being told by spirits what she needed to know."

"So, if this woman was being told things by spirits, are you sure you weren't in some sort of séance?"

"Nan, all we did was shake hands with Mrs. Bishop and talk with her as a group and individually. There was no sitting around a table and holding hands while she called on spirits to visit us."

Kit finished his tea and picked up the image his grandmother had found for him. In the back of his mind, he saw a young girl with long plaits sitting on a much older man's lap while he smoked a pipe.

"It sounds like a lot of fun to have been with this Mrs. Bishop."

Kit looked at Leah and then his grandmother with a small frown. "Nan did you used to have light brown hair and long plaits?"

"Yes, when I was around five or six, I think, why?"

"Did your grandfather used to sit you on his lap and smoke a pipe when he visited?"

Catherine went white. Her face drained of colour, and her fingers trembled as she fought to control the fine China teacup in her fingers. Leah noticed the change and reached out to her mother and placed her hand on her arm.

"Mum, are you okay?" Leah asked.

Catherine settled and took a couple of deep breaths as she studied Kit intently.

"Yes, yes, I'm fine thanks. Before you arrived today, I was sitting here having a cup of tea and looking at this portrait and thinking back to my grandfather. It was the same image as Kit just asked about. My mother used to always plait my hair before guests would arrive. I had beautiful long brown hair, and the plaits saved the hair from getting into my face."

Catherine asked for more tea and Kit poured her another cup.

"My grandfather used to smoke a pipe and he would sit me on his lap and tell me stories of his adventures. It used to really fascinate me. Kit, what made you ask that question?"

"Nan, I sometimes get images in my head as if they are memories and yet, I know they can't be as they are from different eras and about different people. When I picked up this image of Thomas, I had this memory fill my mind about you."

Catherine was stunned. "Go on, what else?"

"You used to like wearing a blue and white check dress, small white socks and black sandals like shoes with buckles."

Leah felt a small tremor in her mother and looked to see her mother's eyes starting to well up with tears. Kit continued.

"You had a special doll your grandmother had bought … no she made for you … which you kept for a long time."

"Yes, it was my Narna," Catherine said.

"Something was odd about the doll's face," Kit said as he groped for words to describe what he was seeing. "It's not like dolls of today have, it was special."

Catherine put her hand on top of Leah's and gripped tight. "Kit, when I was a little girl, dolls used to have faces made of China."

"China? Like this teacup?"

"Yes, sort of. The faces were all thin porcelain and were painted. Did your mum tell you about my doll?"

Leah wiped a tear from her eye. "No mum, that's the first I've heard of Narna in a very long time. You told me you used to play with dolls and always ensured I had one … but I never knew yours was called Narna."

"Well, here's another family secret then."

Kit rubbed his fingers around the portrait and continued his story: "Nan, I bet you called your doll after your grandmother."

Catherine winced and gripped Leah's hand again. "I don't know. I can't remember how I got the name."

"Nan, you used to really love your grandmother, didn't you?"

"Yes, of course, why?"

"I think you named the doll after her when you couldn't pronounce the word Nanna."

Tears streamed down Catherine's face as she thought about her favourite grandmother and the many games and fun she had with her. Leah had started crying too when she saw and felt how emotional her mother had become.

"How did you know that?"

"I don't know. It just sort of came to me."

"I haven't thought about my own grandmother, God rest her soul, for a long time. Now that I do think back, I believe you're right. I either couldn't say Nanna, or it was just my special way of saying her name."

Catherine wiped her eyes and looked at her daughter. "Will you do your mum a favour?"

"Sure."

"Go to my bedroom and bring me what's on the bed."

"Okay."

Leah got up and looked quizzically at Kit. The boy smiled knowingly. He knew he had opened a memory box from decades ago for his grandmother. Kit also knew what was about to happen, so he reached across to his grandmother and held her hand. Leah returned to the kitchen with a little doll dressed in a blue and white check dress and bonnet. The doll's painted porcelain face had faded with time but was quite discernable.

"Mum, is this Narna?" Leah asked.

"Yes. When I was rummaging around for Kit the other day, I found her in an old suitcase. The clothes are the same as I used to wear."

"Nan, did your grandmother make the clothes for the doll and the ones I told you about too?"

"Yes. My parents and grandparents used to make a lot of clothes in the old days. My Nanna made me a dress and with what was left over she made Narna a set of clothes too."

Leah sat down at her seat and kept feeling and playing with Narna. She looked at Kit.

"Kit, how did you know about Narna?" Leah asked.

"Mum, I didn't until I picked up the image of Thomas and started feeling it. Then I had a lot of images flood my mind including Nan dressed as a little girl sitting on her grandfather's lap. I also saw the doll and that the clothes were the same. When Nan asked you to go to her bedroom, I knew you'd walk back in with Narna. It's like I was told it was all going to happen."

Both Leah and Catherine sat back quite amazed at seeing Kit's talents in operation. However, Kit wasn't finished yet. He lifted the teapot and noticed it was empty.

"Nan, mum, would you like some more tea?" Kit asked.

"Well, I think I could go another round Kit after all this," Catherine replied. "What about you love?"

"Yes mum, I'm certainly feeling like I need another cup after all this. Thanks Kit."

Kit took the pot to the sink and rinsed out the tea leaves. He filled the kettle, placed it on the gas stove and lit the gas jet. His gaze went to the kitchen floorboards, and he thought about them for a few moments before sitting back in his chair.

"Nan, tell me about this kitchen. Was it always like this?"

"Yes, it's been like this for many years? Why?"

"Mum, tell Kit how you used to help make dinner here and the work you would do before school," Leah said. "He might be intrigued to know how slow progress has been."

Catherine was about to speak but stopped with her mouth open as she remembered being a young schoolgirl in her parents' home … this home. When her parents died, she stayed in the house and continued to live in it, bringing up Leah and her brothers and sisters. The memories of the home being filled with children playing, singing, and fighting came flooding back to her with vivid clarity. The images of the children growing up kept coming into her mind so fast, but so clear.

"Mum, Mum," Leah said as she rubbed her hand on her mother's wrist. "Are you okay?"

Catherine blinked hard, gripped Leah's hand and looked her directly in the face. "Yes."

"You looked like you were off with the pixies or something."

The kettle started emitting a shrill whistle, so Kit stood up and waited for it to boil properly before he took it off the stove. He poured the water into the pot after putting some tea into it and replaced the teapot's lid. Just as he was about to lift the pot and take it to the kitchen table Catherine stopped him.

"Ahh, no you don't," Catherine said. "Turn the pot around in circles three times before bringing it to the table."

Kit was slightly amused. "Why is that, Nan? Is it some sort of superstition?"

"No, it helps settle the tea before you pour it."

Kit smiled and turned the pot slowly clockwise three times as if he was winding some imaginary gear. The teenager was about the pour the tea for his grandmother and mother but was stopped again in mid-tracks, this time by his mother.

"Kit, let it settle first," Leah said as she got up to look in the cupboards for some chocolate biscuits.

"They're in the left cupboard," Catherine said. "I'm sorry, I forgot to put them out."

"That's okay. Ahh, there they are," Leah said as she took out a packet of double-layered chocolate biscuits. "Kit, mum's been buying these for me since I was your age. See, some things don't change."

Kit put his hand on his grandmother's arm and asked his last question again about the kitchen. "Nan, this kitchen never always looked like this, did it?"

Catherine took a deep breath and looked at her grandson with very focused eyes. "No. Before the gas arrived, we used to cook our meals on a fire – that's why the stove is set so far back into the wall. It's where the fireplace used to be."

"Nan, what about the floor?" Kit asked.

"Well, when I was growing up, this floor used to have a clay-like surface. My parents couldn't afford floorboards for years."

"And did you ..."

"Hang on, Kit," Catherine said as she got up a full head of steam as the memories crystallised in her mind. "I had to pack the kitchen floor before I went to school."

Now it was Kit's turn to be dumbfounded. "Nan, I don't get what you mean. How did you pack the floor?"

"Well, it was my job to use a small spade-like tool to gently flatten the earth in the kitchen and stop the dust from rising and getting into the food."

The teenager was amazed to hear about his grandmother growing up and the hard work she had to perform as part of her daily routines.

"My job was also to clean out the fireplace and re-set the fire ready for my mother," Catherine said.

"Do you mean a dustpan and broom?" Kit tried to clarify.

Leah had poured the fresh teas and opened the biscuits and began sharing them around. "No, your grandmother was right. The fire used to leave a residue of ash and coke from the coal that was burnt so the place we used to sweep it to was called the ash pan. Today I use a dustpan to clean the dust from around the house as we don't have any open fires to cook on."

"Mum, I thought the days of open fires and clay floors were the era of the convicts and pioneers. You know, generations before Nan," Kit said.

"No. Progress came slow, and it's certainly in your grandmother's living memory of how times have changed, but slowly."

Kit chewed on a biscuit and sipped his tea. The history lesson was amazing. He listened intently while his mother and grandmother talked about the various dolls they had while they were growing up and how the house had changed over the decades. Now only the grandmother was left living in the house. All the time Catherine was talking to Leah she would slip a look at Kit to take in his features. Kit finished his tea and pushed his cup away.

"Kit, turn your cup upside down on the saucer for me," Catherine said as she put on a serious face.

"What for Nan, it's empty?" Kit askcd.

A smile raced across Leah's face as she took in what her mother was doing. She had seen this scene played out numerous times in the kitchen with her mother and grandmother. Now it was her son's time.

"I just want to have a look at your tea leaves," Catherine said.

"But Nan …" Kit started to say when his mother broke in.

"Kit, your grandmother's going to read your tea leaves for you, not spill your leftovers."

Kit was amused and intrigued. The afternoon tea in his grandmother's kitchen had turned into a fortune-telling session.

"Kit, turn your cup three times clockwise and then hand it to me," Catherine said. "Who knows, we might be able to see what's happening in your world."

Kit turned his teacup around three times clockwise and gave it to his grandmother. Catherine looked all around inside the cup, pulled it away from her face to have a different perspective and then smiled.

"You have lots of writing coming up," Catherine said without taking her eyes off the cup. "Are you doing lots of assignments at school?"

"No, but my exams start next week, and they go for a whole week," Kit said. "That will involve lots of writing."

"Mmm. I can see a boy and a woman having lots to do with you. You must have a special friend at school you do lots of things with."

"No, not really. I hang out with several guys, not any special ones. Is the woman my mum?"

Catherine turned the cup in her hands and viewed the leaves from different angles and shook her head.

"This doesn't make sense, Kit," Catherine said. "It's as if the boy and woman don't exist, but they do."

Leah picked up on what her mother was saying straight away. "Mum, Kit has been visited several times by the spirit of a dead teenage boy. Could that be him?" she asked.

Catherine frowned when she looked up from Kit's cup. She had a vacant stare as she tried to work out what she had seen in the leaves.

"This doesn't quite make sense," Catherine said as she stared into space. "You definitely are having some sort of contact with another lad. However, he isn't fully in view."

"Mum, what about the woman?" Leah asked.

"Leah, she's the same as the boy. She will soon come into Kit's life, but she's not quite there. This is so strange."

Kit tried to ease the way for his grandmother. "Nan, mum told you I have been occasionally seeing the spirit of a dead teenager called David," Kit said. "He comes to see me at all odd times. However, the only woman I may have anything to do with is Mrs. Bishop, a Medium I have started seeing."

"No Kit. I think you're going to be visited by a woman

who has something to do with this David. They seem to be connected in something. Whatever the purpose is, the outcome is good."

Catherine started to replace Kit's teacup on his saucer when the youth reached out and took it. Kit looked inside the cup and around the bottom wall, he saw two clumps of leaves stuck to the china.

Catherine leaned over and pointed to the clump on the left. "Can you see the face of a boy here?" she asked her grandson.

Kit looked again and saw the outline of what could have been a boy's head. He nodded and raised his eyes to look at his grandmother. Catherine then pointed to the second clump and explained she saw a woman. Kit closed his eyes and then opened them. He looked again at the leaves and this time he could make out the shape of a woman's head and shoulders.

"Okay, now I see the shapes of people," Kit said. "What about the writing part?"

Catherine pointed out a long-pointed stem and a small rectangular leaf underneath it. "This is the pen and that's the paper," she said.

Kit could easily see the shape and laughed. Leah put her hand on Kit and smiled.

"Don't worry, Mum used to do it to us all the time," Leah said. "It was her way of finding out what was going on in our lives without us telling her."

"Nan, that's the first time you've ever read my tea leaves. What made you do it now?"

"I don't know Kit. Sometimes something inside me takes hold and I just do it."

"Well, I'm impressed. Now I'll be looking to see who the mystery woman is that comes into my life."

Leah stood up and started gathering the teacups and saucers.

"Come on Kit, it's time we made a move and let your grandmother rest," Leah said.

"Alright, mum. Thanks, Nan, I appreciate you looking for the image your grandfather gave you and the afternoon tea," Kit said as he helped clear the kitchen table.

"Kit, I have known your father since before you were born and you are very much like him," Catherine said.

"What do you mean Nan?"

"He always was looking for some kind of adventure or another. Enjoy the moment and don't keep looking for tomorrow."

"Thanks Nan. I love adventure like any other boy my age, but I also enjoy the time I have with people as I know what it's like on the other side."

"Do you mean when you die?"

"Yes. It's a great and beautiful feeling being a spirit, but nothing beats living and all it has to offer."

Catherine nodded and her eyes moistened as she reflected on how Leah and Daniel had coped with Kit and his accident. The boy had definitely changed and had an understanding of life beyond his age.

Leah had rinsed the cups and saucers and left them to drain in the sink. She dried her hands and picked up her handbag and Kit's image of Thomas.

"Come on Kit, we better keep moving or your father will wonder where we are," Leah said.

"Okay mum," Kit said as he hugged his grandmother and kissed her. "Thanks again for everything."

"No problem love. Don't leave the visits too long next time," Catherine said.

"I won't."

Leah gave her mother a hug and kiss and walked out of the house with Kit. The pair gave Catherine a wave before they drove off.

Leah's mind had been racing all afternoon while she was at her mother's place. She was fascinated when Kit asked her mother about her childhood and her doll Narna. She was now intrigued to find out how her mother's reading of Kit's tea leaves would play out. Kit didn't speak for the first part of the journey to the library as he reassembled in his mind what happened at his grandmother's place. He was surprised he had the images of his grandmother as a child with her grandfather. The doll with the painted face was also interesting. However, the icing on the cake was that he had indeed found an image of his spirit guide.

Now he had to find a way of communicating with him and not just through David.

Chapter Eleven

Terry Sullivan decided it was time for a two-pronged attack on the Government. He sought advice from his political leader to leak a news report about some of the department heads who may lose their jobs if the Opposition won power in the upcoming elections. Opposition Leader Graham Moon wanted to know why Sullivan was prepared to tip his hand so early.

"I really believe Ratcliffe is behind the Police harassment of Daniel Green," Sullivan said. "One of the ways to put our Commissioner on notice is to leak a list of possible department heads we may want to roll and include him on it."

"Don't you think this will push him even harder to try and reach you in some way?" Moon asked.

"No. If Ratcliffe is included in a list of possible axings then he can't say he is being specifically targeted. If he tries harder to intimidate us and we catch him out, then he has set the scene for his own political demise. Also, the paper is keen to run some stories of power abuse by some of the department heads. The paper wants a list of who we could be considering so they can run a sort of exposé on a number of these people."

"Well, this would certainly sow more seeds of discontent among the voters and put another nail in the Government's coffin. What about the unions? Are they on our side?"

"Yes. I have spoken to some of the senior Union organisers representing the department heads. They say several departmental heads put their hands up for redundancy but were turned down. The organisers indicated that various Ministers said the Government could not afford their payouts as there were too many of them wanting to leave."

"Terry, we might just have another look at the list before you leak it, in case there are a few adjustments to make."

"Alright. Also, I want to name Adrian Elliott in Parliament."

Moon looked up from his desk and studied Sullivan for a few seconds. This was an unexpected turn.

"Ratcliffe, I understand, but why Elliott?" Moon asked.

"I believe Elliott is the one pushing Ratcliffe about my expenses through the accounts committee. I've spoken to a couple of members of the committee, and they keep indicating there have been several requests from the Police Minister's office."

"Yes, but that doesn't tie in Elliott."

"The only one empowered to direct staff to make those enquiries is the Minister's Chief Of Staff. Therefore, I'd like to accuse him of hatching a smear campaign against me and then detail what has happened with the Police. This way, it clears the air and puts Ratcliffe on the back foot and names Elliott in the Parliament."

"Good move Terry. Once Elliott is named, his position will be untenable for any Minister to employ him if indeed you can prove the allegations. Go for it. Just ensure you can back it up with evidence if pushed."

Sullivan returned to his office and started getting his notes organised. He was pleased with the meeting's outcome and now he was the one empowered to start reaching out to his critics and start taking action. Parliament sat again in four days. This allowed Sullivan time to 'leak' his information to the newspaper and for the articles to appear on the weekend. On Monday he could champion the Opposition by replying to the leak and naming Elliott as the power behind a failed plot to implement him in fraud. Sullivan picked up the phone and rang Daniel to tell him what he was doing.

"Terry, that's great news," Daniel said. "I've been trying to tell you to do this for ages. I'm also pretty glad you've decided to reach out to Elliott."

"Thanks, mate," Sullivan said. "Reg was pleased too. I had a brainstorm the morning after you all came over for tea. It was quite cathartic."

"Why? What happened?"

"Well, I got up early and went downstairs with David's photo in hand. I tell you, Daniel, I swear it almost talked to me. I got this brain snap about checking out the power behind the Commissioner and came up with Elliott. When I checked with the parliamentary accounts committee members about who was making the enquiries about my travel expenses, I found it was the Police Minister's office."

"And the only two people who could order the calls were the Minister and Elliott!"

"Exactly. Once I confirmed where the calls came from I

went and saw the leader and got the green light to expose the slime ball on Monday."

"Great news Terry. It also sounds as though David had a hand in it too, Kit will be pleased."

Sullivan thought for a moment.

"Daniel, I had the feeling David was in the room with me when I had the brainstorm. It's been pretty confusing since Kit found the photo for me and showed Betty those things only David and us would know."

"Mate, try living with it! Kit can sometimes be full of surprises, and he doesn't even know what he's done."

"What do you mean?"

"Well, he and Leah went over to see the mother-in-law on Saturday, and he told his grandmother things only she knew."

"Like what?"

"Kit was talking about his grandmother growing up and then asked her whether her grandfather had a pipe and used to nurse her. The answer was yes and even Leah didn't know that. He then described her doll and when Leah went to her mother's bedroom the damn thing was sitting on the bed. Kit had never seen it before. Just amazing."

Sullivan told Daniel how both he and Betty had little sleep the night the three couples got together for tea. He said both of them believed when David had died that was the end of him. Nothing could bring him back. However, Kit had opened a door to a realm that showed a ray of sunlight into a mindset that maybe there was a heaven, or a place people go when they die.

Daniel told Sullivan he had never said why Kit and Leah

had gone to visit Catherine, his mother-in-law. He told Sullivan the story of David helping Kit to identify his spirit guide and the internet search that was confirmed by the image Catherine had been given decades ago by her grandfather. Sullivan was flabbergasted.

"Daniel, I hope you're helping your son through all this ghost work he's doing," Sullivan said.

"Yes, next week he goes to a Medium we got introduced to recently, for some lessons on how to deal with what's happening to him."

"Good. Please tell him, the offer is still open for him to spend some time with Betty and me."

"I will. Good luck on the weekend with the Media calls I know you will get. If you need me, you know where to reach me."

"Thanks, Daniel."

The two men rang off. Daniel sat back in his high office chair and thought about what Sullivan said to him. Yes, it was good Sullivan was taking the fight to Ratcliffe and Elliott, but what would be the consequences. He remembered what Kit had said about why David had visited his son in the first place and a cold shiver ran down his spine. Daniel needed more information and Kit was the only one who could get it.

Sullivan replaced the phone and evaluated what Daniel said. The more he thought about the conversation, the more he wanted to see Kit again. Somehow his son had a pipeline into a knowledge base he couldn't tap into. Also, Kit brought about happiness in Betty that Sullivan had not seen in a long time. Sullivan checked his notes one more time and then faxed them to the Journalist writing the feature story for the Sunday paper. He then rang the reporter to ensure he understood the information was embargoed until Sunday and could not be used by any section of the newspaper or other agencies until then. Sullivan also confirmed his anonymity. All was now in place for a hectic Sunday. He rang his leader to tell him the story was now in play.

Kit arrived home from school feeling flushed. Leah was out for the afternoon doing some shopping so the Green house was empty when Kit arrived. He knew the feeling of a body temperature rise could only mean he was about to have a visit from David, or he was becoming ill. There were no signs of Kit being sick, just him feeling hot and flushed. The tingling started in the back of his neck and increased as he climbed the stairs to his bedroom. The tingling intensified beyond what he normally felt when David was around. He opened the door expecting to see David sitting on his bed but was shocked to see the slightly shimmering image of a woman standing near his desk. A feeling of awkwardness came over him as he stood looking at the apparition before him. The woman was aged in her fifties and held her two hands in front of her. She wore a long blue nightshirt and didn't mouth any words. Instead, Kit heard her voice in his head as she told him not to be afraid.

"My name is Ellen and I need your help," the spirit said.

"Hi, I'm Kit."

"I know."

"How do you know me?"

Ellen beckoned Kit to sit on his computer chair so the lad took off his backpack and placed it on the floor and sat on the chair, his eyes transfixed on the woman's image. She had soft features with dark brown wavy hair and was very elegant in her poise. Kit was transfixed by the beautiful shimmer representing the spirit he was communicating with. This was a scene being played out only for him and he was agog with the vision in front of him.

"Kit, you need to warn your father and Terry Sullivan that they are in great danger."

"Why? What's happening?"

"In a couple of days, a story will be published about the Police Commissioner which will make him very upset."

Kit thought about David's warning when he first came to see him too. David predicted both his and Kit's fathers may be murdered.

"What has this got to do with my father and Mr. Sullivan?"

"Your father works for Sullivan, and they are both trying to get rid of the Commissioner."

Kit felt anger rising inside him as he tried to work out where the woman was coming from. Was she warning him or trying to get him to stop something people, that is live people, do as part of their normal lives in this country.

"I don't know what you want me to do or why you are really here. Who are you?"

The woman looked down at the floor and then moved to Kit's bed and seemed to sit down.

"I am the Police Commissioner's wife Ellen and I know what he will do when the articles appear."

Kit was shocked. He had no idea what Sullivan was planning or any role his father had in the articles. He didn't work with his father, nor did he interfere with his dad's campaigns. Kit was just a schoolboy who happened to be visited by people who had crossed over to the other side.

"Did he kill you? Is that how you passed over?" Kit nervously asked Ellen.

"No Kit. I had cancer but died of a heart attack."

The teenager pushed himself back in the chair and sat more upright. He took in what the woman was saying.

"What do you want me to do?"

"I want you to tell your father and Sullivan to try and stop the articles from appearing. They'll know which ones."

"If I say I spoke to a spirit who told me to do this, they will only laugh. I need something more concrete to help convince them."

Ellen sat motionless for a moment as if in thought.

"Kit, ask Sullivan to check on Joe West who runs a secret police squad that answers only to my husband. These are the people involved."

Kit became perplexed as he heard the spirit of the Police Commissioner's wife tell him who his father's executioner could be. He went to ask another question but found he was staring at an empty space. The tingling on the back of his neck had subsided. Kit didn't know what to do. His father wouldn't be home for an hour and who knows, time could be of the essence here. Kit went downstairs to the kitchen telephone and rang his father at work.

"Hi Dad, do you have a minute?" Kit asked.

"Kit, can this wait, I'll be home in under an hour?" Daniel asked.

"No. It's urgent and I need to speak to you before mum comes home."

Daniel told his son to hold the phone while he closed his office door and then sat down with a notepad and pen.

"Alright mate," Daniel said in a very caring tone. "What's so urgent? Are you okay?"

"Dad, you know how I have told you David has come to visit me several times?" He paused. "I had a visit today from the Police Commissioner's wife, Ellen."

"What the …? She's been dead for a few years too," Daniel said, his focus suddenly sharpened. "What's going on Kit?"

"Do you remember I told you David said he came to me to try and save you and Mr. Sullivan …"

"Yes, from being murdered, I think you said."

"Dad, Ellen said you have to stop the articles being published this weekend as they are the event which could get you killed!"

Daniel went silent for a few moments. He was in shock.

"Dad, dad, are you there?" Kit screamed down the phone.

"Mate, I'm here. You just dropped a pretty big bombshell in my lap, that's all. Are you okay?"

"Dad I'm worried for you. I don't want to lose you," Kit said as he started to become emotional.

"Hey Kit, I'll be fine. You won't be losing me too soon. Come on now, things will be alright."

Daniel's mind started running at a million miles an hour and he had to force himself to stop and comfort Kit. His son had been through enough with the pool accident and the resultant change in him. He also became emotional quite easily.

"Kit, I take it your mother is not home?"

"No, that's why I wanted to ring you directly."

"I really appreciate what you are saying. Now tell me more about what this Ellen said to you."

Kit detailed the feeling he had when he climbed the stairs and the shimmering image of the woman who called herself Ellen waiting for him. When he mentioned her specific message about Joe West running a secret Police squad answerable only to the Police Commissioner, Daniel turned white. Daniel knew Kit could not concoct such a story with the detail he had just given him. He also knew his son did not know Ratcliffe and his operations.

"Kit, I want you to get changed and be ready for me. I'm coming home now to pick you up and we're going to see Mr. Sullivan. I'd like you to tell him in person what you just told me if that's okay?"

"Alright, but can't you tell him yourself?"

"Yes, but I think he needs to hear this from you."

"Alright. What about mum?"

"Leave her to me, I'll talk with her and square things for you and me to go out."

"Thanks, dad."

"Kit, thank you. I love you."

"I love you too, dad."

Daniel rang Sullivan and Reg Clementson and told them he had to have a very urgent meeting with both of them. The pair protested and said they had other things organised for the night. However, when Daniel pressed the point and said his and Sullivan's lives depended on the meeting all agreed to meet. Daniel rang Leah and found out she was food shopping and would be home within the hour. He told his wife Kit was upset over a spirit that had visited him and to not ask him for too much information if she came home before he did. Also, he was on his way home and would be meeting with Sullivan and Clementson within the hour and needed to take Kit.

Leah was stunned and wanted to know more about what spirit had visited Kit and what was said to make the meeting happen. Daniel said it was a woman who gave Kit a similar message to what David did about looking after himself and Sullivan, so they were going to start planning what to do. Leah trusted Daniel implicitly but what he said, and the speed of his actions, meant there was something more at stake. She also remembered her mother's reading of Kit's tea leaves the last weekend where she said the boy would have some sort of involvement with a woman who was not quite there. This had to be it, a female spirit. Her mother was right again.

Daniel arrived home within 40 minutes and found Kit waiting at the front door for him. He saw his son's moist red eyes and his heart started to melt. Daniel reached out and gave his son a strong hug.

"Hi mate, thank you for the call," Daniel said. "We'll beat this problem, you'll see."

Kit returned his father's hug and pushed his forehead onto his dad's shoulder. He loved his parents dearly and didn't want anything to happen to them.

"Come on, let's get cracking," Daniel said as he disengaged himself from Kit.

The pair got into Daniel's car and headed off. Both had moist eyes and sniffled a couple of times before they spoke.

"Where are we going?" Kit asked.

"We're going to Terry's place where we'll meet up with Reg as well."

"Okay. Does mum know where we'll be?"

"Yeah, I spoke to her straight after I spoke with you. She'll be home shortly."

"Kit don't be too concerned about things yet. Remember Mrs. Bishop told us we are on certain life paths, but these can be changed by events. I think we can change what may be in store for Terry and me. All we have to do is come up with a strategy to expose a few people."

"What about the two families – yours and Mr. Sullivan's? Don't forget us."

"We won't. Did Ellen mention anything about your mother and you or just me and Terry?"

"Just you and Mr. Sullivan."

"Okay, that makes it easier."

Daniel arrived at the front gates of the Sullivan residence and saw the security camera. Up ahead he saw both Reg and Terry's cars parked near the side of the house. Daniel gripped Kit's hand.

"Okay mate?"

"Yeah, dad. I'm fine."

"Just tell them the story as you told me, so they get a complete picture. We'll take it from there. Alright?"

"No probs Dad."

The moment Daniel and Kit started exiting the car the front door of the Sullivan residence opened and Terry started walking out to meet them, closely followed by Reg.

"Gents, thanks for coming over, I've just put the kettle on for a cuppa," Sullivan said.

He shook hands with Daniel and then put his arm around Kit's shoulders and gently squeezed him.

"Kit, I know this is a bit of an ordeal for you but I want you to know I really appreciate what you are doing," Sullivan said.

"Thanks, Mr. Sullivan. It wasn't my idea for any of this."

"I know, I know. However, we'll start fixing the problems now."

Reg also shook Kit and Daniel's hands and welcomed them. The four of them then went to the kitchen and sat down while Sullivan organised coffees all around.

"Where's Betty?" Daniel asked.

"She's gone to her sister's place for a few days and will be back on Monday," Sullivan said.

"Ahh, bring on the dancing girls," Clementson said as a form of light relief.

"Mmm, sounds good to me. What do you reckon Kit?" Daniel asked.

"Suits me," the teenager replied as a smile beamed across his face.

Sullivan finished making the coffees and placed a couple of trays of biscuits on the table. Kit checked his breathing and began to focus on what Ellen had said to him.

"Daniel, I've got to tell you I had a couple of meetings lined up tonight as preliminaries to a fundraiser for my electorate next month," Sullivan said. "I wouldn't have cancelled them for anything except you sounded so concerned."

"I was in a similar boat," Reg said. "I had arranged to meet some financial backers for my company. However, I couldn't ignore what you said, Daniel."

"Kit, take your time and tell Terry and Reg what you told me," Daniel said.

Kit took a sip of his coffee and looked directly at Sullivan.

"Do you remember when I was here for tea with mum and dad, and I told you David had come to see me a few times?"

"Yes, and it's something I will never forget," Sullivan said.

"Whenever he is around, I get a sort of tingling sensation in the back of my neck and then he would appear – mostly in my bedroom," Kit said.

The looks on the three adults became intense as they hung off every word Kit was now saying.

"This afternoon after school I was climbing the stairs to my bedroom, and I started getting a tingling sensation in my neck only it was more intense. I thought David had returned. However, when I opened my bedroom door, I saw a middle-aged woman standing there."

"Was this a real person?" Clementson asked.

"Mr. Clementson, she was real to me. Like David, she was a shimmering image. She initially just stood there with her hands in front of her."

"What did she say?" Sullivan asked as he looked at Clementson and frowned. Clementson raised his eyebrows and tilted his head.

"She never said anything. I heard her talk in my head."

Clementson frowned again and picked up a biscuit to eat. He seemed to have problems believing Kit. The lad picked up on the body language and clenched his teeth.

"Ellen gave me a sort of glimpse of the future. She said there will be a story published in a couple of days about the Police Commissioner that will make him very upset."

"Well, she's right there. The article …" Sullivan started to say before Daniel cut him off.

"Terry, give Kit a go. It's hard enough for him."

"Sorry Kit. You can see there's history about all this."

Kit nodded and then continued.

"I said to her I didn't know what she wanted me to do. She said she was the Police Commissioner's wife and she knows what her husband will do when the articles are published."

Kit sipped on his coffee again.

"I told her that if I told my dad and you I had been speaking to a spirit you'd only laugh …"

"Kit, no one's laughing," Sullivan said, jotting some notes.

"I told Ellen I needed something more concrete to convince you. That's when she asked that Mr. Sullivan check on Joe West who runs some kind of secret police squad that only answers to her husband. She said these are the people involved."

Clementson was dumbstruck and so was Sullivan. A few moments of silence fell in the kitchen while the three men took in what Kit had said. Kit drank some more coffee and reached for a biscuit.

"Terry, do you know this West guy at all?" Clementson asked as he opened a laptop.

"Hang on mate. Kit, did she say anything else?"

"Nothing more about the secret police squad. I asked her if the Commissioner had killed her and that's why she had passed over. She said she had died of …"

"Cancer. The woman died of cancer at their home, if I remember rightly," Clementson interrupted.

"No, that's not what she died of," Kit said.

The three men re-focused on Kit.

"She told me she had cancer but died of a heart attack."

"Well, that was never released to the Media. As far as we knew she died of cancer at home," Clementson said.

"Any more Kit?" Sullivan asked.

"No, that's it."

"Thanks, Kit, this must be distressing for you with spirits appearing out of nowhere warning your Dad and I are about to be bumped off," Sullivan said.

"Yes, you could say that."

"Don't worry mate, we'll come up with some sort of plan to counter this," Sullivan said. "When did you find out I was having some articles published about Ratcliffe?"

"When dad and I were driving here he told me you were planning to publish some sort of stories in the weekend papers. I don't know what."

"So, you did not know these articles or what's in them before Ellen appeared to you?"

"No, I've told you that. Mr. Sullivan I'm a teenager at school. I don't know what you and my dad or Mr. Clementson are working on. All I know is that I've had some unusual events happen lately and they seem connected to you all."

Daniel could see his son was getting irritated by the line of questioning and jumped in to help him.

"Guys, just for the record, what we three talk about stays between us. Kit is my son but is a schoolboy with another two years of high school before he finishes. Don't even consider that I say anything to Kit about our daily dealings. I don't."

Sullivan read the body signs and realised he had pushed Kit the wrong way.

"Kit I'm sorry. I didn't mean to sound offensive. The stuff you've been telling us about you would only have known if one of us told you. To hear that you have found out through a visiting spirit is quite compelling, I can tell you."

Kit looked at his dad and the other two men and nodded. "My pool accident has changed a lot of things for me, and I guess one of them is finding out things that don't concern me. It's not something I sought."

Daniel put his hand on his son's shoulder and gently squeezed it in a show of support and Kit seemed to lighten up.

"Jeez, Kit, you don't know it, but today you have given Terry the key to bringing down the Commissioner and Government in one fell swoop," Clementson said.

"What do you mean?" Kit asked.

"If the Police Commissioner has a secret squad operating under him then he's gone rogue, and no Government will support him. If the current Government stands by the Commissioner then it can be dismissed for going against the Parliament and having secret police squads."

The three men looked at each other wide-eyed and agreed. Clementson had a way of stating the obvious when no one else would. Clementson finished logging on to the internet on his laptop and called up his search engine. He typed in the name of Ellen Ratcliffe and went to the images section.

"Kit, do me a favour, will you? Have a look at these photos.

Do any of them look familiar?" he said, and turned the laptop around.

Kit's eyes widened when he saw photos of the woman who had visited him in his bedroom.

"That's her, only her hair was shorter, and she wore a long blue nightgown," Kit said.

"Thanks, mate," Clementson said as he showed Sullivan and Daniel the images. He got up and re-filled the kettle for more coffees.

Sullivan took the lead again and asked Kit if he'd like to watch a movie in his home theatre room.

"That's neat, Mr. Sullivan, thanks" Kit said.

"Grab a coffee re-fill and some biscuits and I'll show you how to turn the system on," Sullivan said.

Daniel got up and refilled everyone's coffee cups and pushed the biscuit plate to Kit who grabbed a couple to take with him. Sullivan then took Kit into his special cinema room and fired up his DVD player and monitor and showed him his collection of movies.

"The rest is up to you. There are no blue movies or overly graphic movies, so pick what you want," Sullivan said with a smile.

"Damn. Thanks, Mr. Sullivan," Kit said with an enveloping smile.

"Oh Kit, did your dad tell you my offer for you to stay here is still open to you?"

"No, but I haven't forgotten what you said at the barbecue. I've had exams all this week."

"How'd you go?"

"I think I passed most of them. Math is still the hardest for me, but I'll get there in the end."

Sullivan walked over to Kit and put his hand on his shoulder.

"Thanks for telling your dad about Ellen and I really appreciated what you said about David."

"Mr. Sullivan, you don't have to thank me. I was just passing on some messages from someone who truly loves you and Mrs. Sullivan."

Moisture formed in Sullivan's eyes, and he gently squeezed Kit's shoulders again as he left the room. Clementson had been searching on the web for any reference to Joe West in the police force. He couldn't find any.

"Well, guys what do you think of what Kit had to say?" Sullivan asked.

"Terry, Kit knew nothing of the articles you told me about. Also, I haven't mentioned Ratcliffe much at home and certainly nothing about his dead wife," Daniel said.

"I believe him, but it scares the hell out of me," Sullivan said. "When he talked about David at our dinner here, I was blown away by what Kit said and didn't quite believe him. But there was no way he knew about secret hand signals between Betty and David or his key ring surfboard. Now for him to come out with a visit by Ellen Ratcliffe and naming the head of a secret police squad the day I send articles to a newspaper is just … I don't know … amazing."

"Terry, I think you better call the Journalist and ask him to stop publication this weekend," Clementson said. "Then we need to decide whether to bring Graham Moon here and discuss tactics with him."

"If I stop publication, the Journalist will want to know why," Sullivan said.

"Tell him to hold off on publication this weekend and to put the story on total hold," Daniel said. "If you don't have a replacement story, maybe Moon does. Whatever you do, don't tip your hand about Ellen Ratcliffe or any secret squads."

"Okay, I'll ring the leader and ask him to come over."

Sullivan picked up the house phone and dialled his leader's private line. He explained he was having a meeting with Daniel and Clementson and that he had information that could bring on an early election. Moon tried to wiggle out of joining Sullivan until he was told the information he had almost had him killed. He also said he had to stop the publication of the article and needed another one to replace it. Moon agreed to join the three men for the meeting and that he would organise for a replacement story to be ready from one of the other Shadow Ministers.

Daniel picked up the plate of biscuits and took them into Kit to ensure he was alright. The lad was watching a science fiction movie with his shoes off and feet on a small coffee table.

"Thanks, Dad," Kit said.

"No worries, mate. We could be here for some time tonight so get comfortable," Daniel said.

"Lots of planning to do, huh?"

"Yeah. We've got Terry's boss coming over for a chat so he could be here for a while. Also, he may want to talk with you if that's okay?"

"Dad, I'm not an oddity of some kind, am I?"

"No. But you have been privy to some information none

of us could obtain. Now we have to work out what to do with it."

"Okay. What about tea? Have you told mum we'll be here for a while?"

"I'm just about to have a chat with her now. Enjoy the movies."

"Thanks."

Daniel returned to the kitchen to find Sullivan and Clementson deep in conversation about how they could try and trap Ratcliffe.

Chapter Twelve

It was not often the State Opposition Leader would drop everything to be with one of his Shadow Ministers. Time was too short, and an election was looming. However, the urgency in Sullivan's voice and knowing the background to what he was planning for the Parliament next week made it imperative he join him for this "urgent" meeting.

"Terry, I hope you have the kettle on," Moon said on his mobile phone as he was approaching the street where Sullivan lived.

"Boss, consider it done," Sullivan replied with a lilt in his voice.

"Okay mate, I'm a block away. See you soon."

Sullivan and Clementson went out to meet Moon while Daniel went in to see Kit.

"What's up dad?" Kit asked. "Is Mr. Sullivan's boss here?"

Daniel smiled. Sometimes he telegraphed his actions too easily to his son.

"Yeah mate. His name is Graham Moon. We'll brief him in the kitchen and then I'll come and get you and ask you to recount what happened this afternoon, if that's okay?"

"Dad, that's fine," Kit said. "I know you must do this. Don't worry, I'm fine."

“Thanks mate.”

Daniel walked out to the kitchen and greeted Moon. He was a bear of a man. He had a long face, and it was hard to see where the bottom of his chin ended, and his neck began. Moon was a heavy-set man who had a continuous battle with his waistline. His eyes were large like saucers, and he had bushy eyebrows. Moon could easily intimidate his political opponents in Parliament by his very stature.

“Daniel, it’s been a while,” Moon said, shaking is hand.

“Graham, it may have been a while since we met but you’ve been upper most in my mind today, I can tell you.”

“Yes, it seems your work with Terry is causing you some grief.”

“Not so much. However, I have my son Kit inside watching movies in Terry’s theatre room.”

“Is this the boy who fell in the pool and had to undergo head surgery?”

“Yes. Since then, he’s had a number of changes come over him. One of those helped bring us all together tonight.”

Moon was quizzical. He slightly closed his eyes, tilted his head and opened his mouth wider in an expression of asking what Daniel was saying, without uttering a word. His body language said it all. Daniel detailed some of the changes in Kit since the lad’s accident. He made a point of telling Moon he did not discuss his work with Kit at all. However, Kit had been able to tell him what he was working on and then dropped his bombshell today.

“Best I meet this remarkable young man,” Moon said as he slurped his coffee.

Daniel got up and went to the theatre room. Kit was already standing and had his shoes back on.

"Hi mate, Mr. Moon's here," Daniel said.

"I know I heard him arrive."

"Okay. Just tell him what you told us earlier, if that's okay?"

Kit nodded and walked with his father to the kitchen to meet Graham Moon. He was surprised at Moon's size but soon felt comfortable as he detailed what had happened when he arrived home from school. Sullivan and Clementson watched Moon closely as Kit detailed his story. The Opposition Leader was a strong judge of character and "believed" that Kit believed what he was saying.

"Thanks Kit," Moon said. "In my 20 years in politics that's the first time I've ever had a ghost story told to me by a teenager that could possibly influence the outcome of my political party."

Kit wasn't sure what Moon had really just said to him. While he was waiting for the man's arrival, he had put the movie on pause and sat quietly thinking about him. A tingling came over him and his neck felt funny. The image of an old woman came into his head, and he started receiving information from her. He decided to test the waters further with him and see if the image he had just seen in his head was "real".

"Mr. Moon, do you still visit your mother's grave?"

"Yes, everyone knows that," Moon said as he looked at each of the other men's faces and nodded. "I go to the cemetery the first Sunday of each month when I can. Why do you ask?"

"The answer you have been asking is no," Kit said matter-of-factly.

Moon now felt uncomfortable. He moved slightly in his chair. "What do you mean no? What answer are you talking about?"

"You asked your mother a question on your last visit and the answer is no."

"Terry, Daniel, how the hell would this boy know anything about my mother? Have you been briefing him about me?"

Daniel launched first.

"Graham, Kit shared something with us this afternoon he would have had no knowledge about ordinarily. He is a schoolboy who attends school every day. He doesn't work in my office or Terry's. Do you think it was easy for him to ring me at my work and tell me and then to have to relate the story twice more to adults he really has nothing to do with?" Daniel asked.

Before Terry could jump in to assist Kit the lad smiled and spoke out.

"Mr. Moon, your mother died of old age a couple of months ago, didn't she?" Kit asked.

"Yes, she was aged 85," Moon said with an irritated voice.

Kit looked him straight in the eye and continued.

"You asked her on your last visit whether you should quit politics. Her answer is no."

Moon was now taken back and embarrassed. Was this teenage boy a mind reader, a Medium or just crazy? Then again, he had never told anyone he had been thinking of quitting politics and taking up practicing law again. On his last visit to his mother's grave, he posed the question to her and sought her guidance. Now the answer was crystal clear.

"Kit, how would you know anything about that?" Moon asked.

Sullivan, Clementson and Daniel all seemed to lean towards Kit as he spoke.

"I sometimes have messages come into my head about things," Kit said. "When you were approaching the house, I had the image of an old woman come into my mind. She seemed to tell me the messages I just told you. It's up to you, I don't make up stories. Also, as dad said, I am a student with two years before I finish high school. I have nothing to do with my dad's business."

"Whoa Kit," Moon said, now clearly back peddling. "I didn't mean to accuse you in any way. Please appreciate that from where I sit, I have to ensure my team and I can withstand any probity by people in the government or community. Now what I have to do is find the evidence to substantiate what you've been told. After that I could be able to offer you a government job … well, if you needed one when you're old enough."

"And if you are still in power," Daniel added as he stood up and gave his son a hug. "Well done son, I'm proud of you."

Kit was trembling. He had never had to stand up to a group of adults before and justify himself the way he just did – especially those who could shape the next Government for the State. This would be a day he would long remember. He mentally thanked David and the woman who was giving him the messages about Moon.

"If you don't need me any more I'll go and busy myself in the theatre room," Kit said as he looked at Moon and Sullivan.

"Thanks mate, we all appreciate what you have said and done today. Well done," Sullivan said. "We'll organise some tea shortly, so I hope you're hungry?"

"Yep, I could eat a small horse."

"Good, I'll be in shortly to organise with you."

"Thanks, Mr. Sullivan."

Kit returned to the theatre room, kicked off his shoes and resumed his position on the large single leather chair and put his feet up on the coffee table. A large smile grew on his face, and he punched his fist in the air as a feeling of elation washed over him. He was right. The woman he saw in his mind's eye was Mrs. Moon and she had given him correct information. He wasn't just daydreaming.

"You went a bit hard on the boy didn't you Graham," Clementson said. "The poor kid was trembling when he came out here, I was watching his knees shake as he spoke to you."

Moon was usually the captain of his ship. He was normally quite in control of things happening around him and not many people could get the better of him. Then again, it wasn't every day he dealt with teenage boys – especially one who got the better of him. Also, it wasn't every day a teenage boy would give him messages from the grave – especially from his own mother. This was a day he would always remember.

"What's this you're thinking of quitting politics?" Daniel asked Moon.

"Well, it was just a thought I had last time I visited my mother's grave. The government may be in decay, but they could still be hard to shift from power. I guess I was just considering all options."

"So, Graham, how many people did you tell about the question you raised over your mother's grave?" Clementson asked.

Moon was now very embarrassed and turned a bright red.

"No one. It was a private thing between my mother and me."

"So, the boy was quite right? He saw something in his mind that he knew nothing of previously and confirmed the information came from your dead mother?"

Moon was very uncomfortable and took a few seconds before answering. "I've never dealt with Mediums or spirit conjurers before, so I was quite cynical to hear about Kit's prowess. However, what this teenager has said today has shaken my belief in the divide between the living and the dead. He never chose to be a conduit for those on the other side, but I'm glad he's on our team."

Daniel took his cue to speak up for Kit and bring the meeting back on track.

"Graham, now you know the sorts of things Leah and I have had to go through with Kit …" Daniel started to say.

"Well, I can tell you this Daniel, I've never had anyone tell me what I have said in my mind to a dead relative before. I'm still trying to take in how he knew," Moon said.

"And don't forget what Kit did for Betty and I in this very house with the finding of my long lost photo and giving us messages from David only we would understand," Sullivan said as he nodded.

Moon looked perplexed and asked Sullivan what he meant. Sullivan then recounted how Kit had delivered David's first message to he and his wife and helped him find a long lost cherished photo that had gone missing.

"Yes, that was a magical evening. I guess what we really need to do now is sort out the issues Kit has been able to bring to us," Daniel said.

"Well, the first thing he told us was Ratcliffe is hatching some sort of plot to have you and Terry murdered," Clementson said.

"Reg, we haven't seen any tangible evidence of that," Daniel said. "All we've had so far are some rough cops pulling me over and manhandling me in public and Terry being put through the wringer by the Fraud squad over his trip."

"Boys, what if Joe West was behind Daniel's collar by the cops?" Sullivan asked. "It could have been organised by this mystery cop."

"That is, if he exists," Moon chipped in. "We have been privileged to be given some extraordinary information by Kit. Our job is to prove it."

"Once we do, Parliament will never be the same," Sullivan said.

"Okay, we can stop our daydreaming and focus on what the issues are and how to handle them," Daniel said.

The men started working out tactics. This included putting a stop to the weekend's publication of the possible axing of departmental heads if the Opposition came to power and replacing it with something else; how to secretly investigate the mysterious Joe West – what agencies to call in to investigate Ratcliffe if they found West. Forty minutes went by as the men worked their phones and spoke to the group and took notes.

Kit quietly walked back into the kitchen, picked up the men's coffee cups and placed them on the sink. He then refilled the kettle. The men watched Kit but kept talking among themselves. When the kettle boiled Kit interrupted and asked who wanted a refill. A quick round of coffee orders followed with Kit making the men their brews and one for himself before walking back to the theatre room.

"That boy of yours is a gem," Clementson said. "I reckon he read my mind then as I was starting to hanker for a coffee or a beer."

"Hear, hear," Sullivan added in his best parliamentary tone.

Daniel smiled broadly and just nodded. Kit was a good son but wasn't necessarily organising the coffees because he thought the men were thirsty. He wanted another one.

"Gents, I think we need to think about ordering in some food so we can keep our teenage mind reader and the rest of us fed and on track."

Moon said he would organise pizzas and took the men's order. He then went to the theatre room and saw Kit watching a movie with his shoes off and his feet stretched out on a foot stool. Kit looked up as he saw a shadow of Moon approaching the doorway.

"Hi Kit, I'm going to organise some pizzas for everyone, so I hope you're still pretty hungry?" Moon asked.

Kit looked at Moon and smiled. He had a feeling Moon wanted to know something otherwise he would have sent Sullivan to do the menial work.

"Thanks, Mr. Moon. I'd love a hot and spicy pizza," Kit said. "Are you ordering any soft drink?"

"Well, I am now."

"Thanks. May I have a cola of some sort please?"

"No problems. By the way Kit, when you said you received messages from my mother did you have an image of her in your mind too?"

"Yes."

"How did she look?"

"Okay, you want it all," Kit said as he chose his words carefully. He concentrated on Moon's eyes and took a few seconds before answering. "Mr. Moon you buried her in a dark blue suit with a sort of red and white scarf around her neck."

Moon's eyes widened and his mouth opened as he heard Kit describe the last image he had of his mother in her coffin. The funeral arrangements for Moon's mother had been left up to him. He had decided he would bury his mother in her best suit as she was a woman of style and elegance. No one else knew what he had arranged as there was no viewing of the woman's body prior to burial. Moon put his right hand over his heart and started to breathe sharply and slumped to the floor. Kit believed Moon was having a heart attack and quickly called out to his father.

"Dad, dad, come quickly!" Kit yelled as he placed Moon in the recovery position on the floor.

Daniel and the other two men ran to the theatre room and were shocked to see Moon as pale as a sheet, eyes extended, hand over his heart and breathing sharply and lying on his side. Kit was at his side holding his hand and feeling his forehead.

"Graham, are you alright?" Sullivan said as he looked at Moon and then Kit.

Moon found it hard to talk at first and then slowly came around. His eyes focused, his breathing became more normal and colour returned to his face. He started to sit up and two of them helped him into a chair.

"Sorry guys. I had a bit of shock, that's all," Moon said as he looked at Kit and nodded.

Clementson went to the bathroom and brought Moon a moist face washer to help him refresh his face. Daniel returned to the kitchen and got the big man a glass of water. Sullivan knelt down at his leader's side and spoke softly.

"Are you alright mate?" Sullivan asked. "Do you want an ambulance?"

Moon refreshed his face and drank some water. Colour started returning to his face as his eyes narrowed and he focused on Kit.

"What happened Graham?" Clementson asked as he studied the big man on the chair.

"No ambulance. I'm fine now, thanks. I asked Kit what he wanted for tea. Then, I asked him if when he got the message from my mother, he also received some sort of image of her. Kit went on to describe exactly how I had her dressed for burial. No one except the undertaker and I knew. It just threw me, that's all. Sorry guys – I'll be alright in a minute," he panted.

"Graham, do you want me to get an ambulance?" Daniel asked.

"No mate. Don't do that. I'll be fine. It's like being winded in a football match – that's all."

A look of relief swept over Sullivan as he slowly stood up.

He took the face washer off his leader and helped him to his feet.

"Graham, I'll organise the pizzas while you get yourself sorted," Clementson said. He leaned forward and reached for the piece of paper Moon had been using to write down the pizza order. Moon gave him the paper and smiled.

"Thanks Reg. Don't forget some extra garlic bread for our young man over there," Moon said. "He's pretty hungry."

Moon walked over to Kit and shook his hand. He then placed his other arm on the boy's shoulder and gently squeezed.

"Kit, I had a lot of difficulty coming to grips with what you first said today about Ellen Ratcliffe," Moon said. "Now I understand you a lot better. Thanks mate."

Moon nodded and gave Kit a gentle slap on the shoulder before joining Sullivan and Daniel as they slowly walked back to the kitchen. Once Moon was settled, Daniel returned to the theatre room and looked at Kit. He smiled and then gave his son a big hug. Not a word was spoken between them, and Daniel returned to the kitchen. Kit resumed his seat and put his feet up to watch the rest of his movie. He felt his job for the day was now over. He had delivered his messages and the spirit world had helped with his credibility.

Graham Moon had a lot to think about. He was being given the key to a possible early election and the removal of a troublesome Police Commissioner through due legal process. First, he had to prove Ratcliffe was running a secret Police squad and second he had to prove West was behind Daniel's public intimidation. If Sullivan could prove Elliott was behind the fraud investigations by the Police, then the Opposition had the election in the bag. Moon went for a walk to Sullivan's backyard with his mobile phone and made a call to his brother-in-law Greg Cootes who worked with the State Police Internal Affairs as an investigator.

"Greg, it's Graham. How are you mate?" Moon asked. "I need a favour."

Moon outlined he had received information about the possible existence of a secret Police squad headed by a Joe West. He negated to say a teenage boy who said he saw an apparition of the dead Police Commissioner's wife had told him. Moon impressed on Cootes the urgency of the request and the secrecy that must surround it. Cootes agreed to make enquiries and to get back to him. Moon walked back into the house and had a smile on his face. He was happy now. A teenager had given him a message from his dead mother – the message he had hoped would come from her, but he didn't quite know how.

"How are the pizzas coming boys?" Moon asked as he walked back into the kitchen.

"On their way Graham," Clementson said. "With extra garlic bread and soft drink for our young friend inside."

"Excellent. Where are we up to Terry?"

"Graham, I've got my staffers working on Elliott and any orders from him to the accounts committee to investigate me," Sullivan said. "What about West?"

Moon studied each of the three men as they listened intently.

"I've placed a call and …"

Moon's mobile phone rang and he saw Coote's name on the caller ID.

"Speak of the devil," Moon said as he took the call and walked outside to the back yard. "Are you absolutely sure?" he asked Cootes.

"Yes," Cootes said and then detailed what he had learned from his enquiries.

"Mate your blood is worth bottling. Thanks for the work." Moon rang off and returned to the kitchen beaming.

"Graham, you look like the cat that just swallowed a mouse," Clementson said. "What"s the go?"

Moon sat down and sipped some of his water. The tension in the kitchen was electric.

"We may have him!" Moon exclaimed. "Apparently, West was in the same class as Ratcliffe at the Police Academy. He dropped out of sight when Ratcliffe became Deputy Commissioner and headed some special task force into major crime. The last few years he has had only one reporting line."

"I bet that was straight to Ratcliffe," Daniel said.

"Yes. Now we have to find out what he's been doing and whether he has been in charge of any secret group."

"How are you going to find out?" Sullivan asked.

"I think we need to spring a trap on our Commissioner and see what he does."

The doorbell rang and Sullivan quickly looked at a small monitor on the sink and saw the image of a pizza deliverer.

"Food's here," Sullivan said.

"Gents this is my shout," Moon said as he reached into his pocket and extracted his wallet. He pulled out some banknotes and gave them to Sullivan.

Clementson and Daniel cleared the table and put out some

placemats. Daniel then walked into the theatre room and told Kit.

"Eeha!" Kit said with excitement. "I'm famished Dad."

"I know what you mean. I could probably eat a small horse myself," Daniel said.

The pair made their way into the kitchen and found Sullivan with a stack of pizzas, garlic bread wrapped in foil and bottles of soft drink. The aroma was overpowering and welcoming to the five people now seated at the table.

Kit looked at his father until he got his attention.

"Dad, all sorted now?"

"I think so. We just need time to work for us now."

Kit nodded and picked up another piece of garlic bread. The pizzas were demolished pretty quickly and talk about tactics and procedures morphed into discussions about families and upcoming events. Daniel took the lead to wind the meeting up as the group had gone as far as they could without further assistance from people either in their workplaces or elsewhere. He was also lucky as he had Kit as an excuse to leave and head home. Throughout the meal, Moon had kept flicking his eyes in the teenager's direction to watch the lad as he quietly ate. Kit was well aware he was being watched by all the men but chose not to engage. He figured he had said things today they never would have expected and were still in some sort of shock at what he had said.

"Gents, it's time to love you and leave you," Daniel said as he stood up. "I better get Kit back home so he can finish his homework."

"Thanks Dad, a night off would be better," Kit said.

Daniel shook his head. Sullivan and Moon said they would see the Greens to their car and walked with them to the car park. Kit was first outside the house and only walked a few paces before he stopped. He felt his head and looked around. Daniel was watching Kit and saw his son's reaction.

"What's up Kit?" Daniel asked.

"Dad, remember when …" Kit started to say and stopped in mid-sentence.

He searched the tree line along Sullivan's fence with his eyes and then stopped. The lad beckoned his father closer and whispered into his ear. Daniel nodded and told Moon and Sullivan to go back inside.

"What's wrong Daniel? Is Kit, okay? Moon asked.

"I'll tell you in a few seconds," Daniel said as he pushed Moon back inside Sullivan's house.

Once Kit re-entered the house, he closed the door and faced the three men. His face was red, and he looked worried.

"Dad, you remember when we had the barbecue here, I told you I could feel the sensors in the back yard?"

Moon looked at Sullivan and then back at Kit quizzically.

"Yeah mate. You were able to pinpoint where they were positioned under the moss. Why? What's wrong?" Daniel asked his son.

"I had the feeling some sort of beam or sensor was being directed at us from the trees near the right-hand corner of the fence line."

"What the …?" Moon started to say.

"Graham, upstairs quickly, I have a telescope I use for star gazing," Sullivan said.

The three men started making their way upstairs when Clementson joined them wondering what had happened.

"Terry, what's going on? Has Kit found another photo for you?" Clementson asked.

"No Reg. He thinks some sort of beam was directed at us as we went to our cars so we're going to check it out," Daniel said between breaths as he pushed himself up the stairs.

Sullivan went to his bedroom and retrieved a telescope mounted on a tripod from a rear balcony.

"Guys come into David's room. It overlooks the car park and fence line Kit was talking about," Sullivan said.

The three other men and Kit followed him into David's room. Sullivan set the telescope up near the window and without disturbing the curtains quickly moved the telescope from left to right to scan the fence. He stopped and focused on a particular spot.

"Hell, Graham, have a look at this," Sullivan said. "Just before the joining of the two fence lines there are two guys in dark blue fatigues aiming what looks like a satellite dish and a camera at the cars."

Moon was visibly shaken and stepped up to the telescope to view the men for himself. He then had Daniel and Clementson view the men before asking Kit to have a look.

"Terry, do you have a camera with a long lens?" Moon asked. "I've had enough of this rubbish."

"I'm ahead of you Graham. My camera's in this wardrobe," Sullivan said as he slid the wardrobe door open and reached up to the top shelf. He withdrew a blue camera bag, took out his camera and changed lenses to put on the long range one.

Sullivan pushed the camera lens through the curtains and started taking a number of photos.

Moon walked out of the bedroom and called his brother-in law again.

"Greg, it's Graham," Moon said.

"Graham, I'm working on what you asked for earlier," Cootes said.

"Mate, I have a different problem," Moon said and then detailed what he had just seen.

"Holy hell Moony. It never rains with you, it pours. Okay, give me the address and I'll see if I can send one of my crews to investigate."

"Thanks Greg. I'll put you onto Terry Sullivan. He can explain better than I can."

Moon handed the phone to Sullivan and asked him to explain where the eavesdroppers were located.

"Who's that?" Sullivan asked after describing the adjoining street where he lived.

"He's a special contact who is on our side. Greg is one of the good guys I can depend on. Don't worry, I'll explain later."

Sullivan agreed, then described the address where the two people were operating. Each of the men in David's bedroom took turns to check out the telescope and see the two figures crouched near the fence. One had a small plastic looking oval shaped dish in his hands and the other a long lens camera.

"How did the photos come out?" Clementson asked.

"Pretty good. I can't clearly see their faces, but I think I've got the beginning of a word that could read Police," Sullivan said.

"Well done, Terry," Daniel said. "I hope they don't see your long lens with theirs."

Moon had been thinking for a few moments.

"Kit, you're a wonder. Thank you for telling us about these people. Did you have an image in your mind about the people and their sensors?" Moon asked.

"No. It's something I just feel when I'm near electrical impulses and this beam was pretty strong," the teenager said as he looked for some sort of understanding.

"We all appreciate what you did downstairs. I hope your pocket money gets a rise."

Moon looked at the nodding adults in the room before he spoke again. "Maybe we need to go back to the cars and talk around them for a while, so we keep their interest until the cavalry arrives," Moon said.

"Good idea," Clementson said. "Terry, we probably need a tour of the house with you explaining its history."

"Take Kit with you and I'll stay here and see if I can get a better photo as you walk around," Daniel said.

"Kit are you up for it?" Clementson asked.

"Yeah, no probs. Mr. Moon are you expecting a call back from your friend?"

"Why, Kit? Moon asked.

"If you're walking around out there and take a call, whoever the joker is with the dish may be able to record your call."

Moon reached into his pocket and pulled out his phone and gave it to Daniel.

"When the phone rings it will come up with a name on the face. If it is not Greg, please don't answer it."

“If it is Greg?”

“Step away from the window and take the call. Explain what we’re doing and take any messages.”

“No probs Graham.”

Sullivan looked at Kit and saw the lad looking around the room and smiling.

“Come on, it’s time for the grand tour,” Sullivan said as he stepped back to allow Moon and Clementson to exit first. “What were you smiling at?” Sullivan asked Kit.

“Well, the tables are somewhat turned. This is the second time I’ve been in David’s room, and I got to sit on his bed.”

“So?” Sullivan asked, trying to see the connection.

“So, when I have seen David, he’s been sitting on the edge of my bed in my bedroom.”

“Is he here now?”

“I don’t know. No, he’s not. I can usually feel his presence, but not now.”

“Okay, thanks. We better join the tour party.”

Kit waved to his father and then walked out of the bedroom and down the stairs to join the others, Sullivan was close behind.

“Well, this place has a lot of history apparently,” Sullivan said as he took the group over to the fountain. “This lovely water works for instance was brought back from England by the original owners who wanted a touch of Blighty in their front yard.”

Daniel watched the two figures watching the tour party and snapped several photos as they followed the group with their instruments. He checked with the telescope and saw both people had baseball hats on. One person had a moustache and square jaw and the other was clean shaven, with a more pointed jaw.

The tour party edged its way around the front of the house with Sullivan delighting in telling the history of his home but garnished with a lot of imagination. Several times Kit rubbed the back of his neck as he felt the invisible beam from the dish wash over him. Sullivan took the group around the fountain and back to the front door and then out to the front gates and returned to the cars. At no time did the tour group look directly at the two people recording their movements. Moon edged his way to the fender of his car so he could sit on it and take in what Sullivan was saying. He was starting to seethe as he tried to figure out who was behind the privacy invasion. The clock kept ticking and nearly thirty minutes had elapsed since the house tour began. Daniel joined the group with a tray full of drinks. He manoeuvred his body so his back was to the snoopers and gave Moon a note that read: "The good guys will be here in five minutes. We must stay here until then." Moon smiled and nodded. He asked Kit about school and what he was studying. Kit started detailing the subjects he was taking and what he thought of them.

Suddenly loud voices could be heard coming from the where the snoopers were positioned. The tour party quickly retreated inside the house and up to David's bedroom. Sullivan was first on the telescope.

"You little beauty!" Sullivan yelled as he punched the air. "The Cavalry is here! Four plain clothes men have got the other two people bailed up and are swapping details of sorts."

Moon retrieved his mobile phone from the window ledge. He checked Cootes had not rung back and then placed it in his pocket. A tap on the shoulder and Sullivan quickly moved aside for his leader to view the proceedings. Daniel had picked up the camera and taken a series of shots of the backyard commotion. Clementson was trying to view the proceedings by pulling the edge of the curtain back. He couldn't focus properly because of the distance and put his hand on Moon's shoulder.

"Okay, time for the old man to check out the scene," Clementson said.

Moon gave up the telescope and joined Sullivan at the window and peered through the curtains. Kit really couldn't fit around the window, so he sat back on David's bed and took in the scene. It was like watching a soap opera unfold before him only he had a part. Kit closed his eyes and concentrated on David. This was his spiritual friend's bedroom. The last place he rested before having his tragic car accident a decade ago. Kit's calm was broken with Moon's mobile phone ringing. The big man quickly reached into his pocket and saw his brother-in-law's name on the phone face.

"Yeah mate. What's happening?" Moon blurted out.

He nodded and muttered a few times.

"We really need to find out who they work for, why they were snooping on us and if they have a connection to West or Ratcliffe? Thanks Greg. I appreciate what you have done."

Moon slowly put his mobile phone in his pocket and pondered what Cootes had just told him.

"Well gents, it seems we could be getting somewhere,"

Moon said. "The pair was a male and female who said they worked for the State police in a special undercover squad. They'll be taken to Police Internal Affairs and questioned. Hopefully we'll know something later tonight."

"I think this calls for a drink," Sullivan said. "It's not every day the Opposition bags a cop."

"Or, the Police cop a bagging," Clementson said with his dry sense of humour.

The group returned to the kitchen and Sullivan passed around four beers from the fridge. He reached in again and pulled out a bottle of soft drink for Kit. The youth poured his drink into a glass while the others pulled the ring tabs from their cans. They all pushed them together in a salute.

"We may have just taken the war to Ratcliffe this afternoon," Moon said. "If that's the case and he was responsible for spying on us, then I'll be asking he step aside while an investigation is held into his clandestine activities."

"Hear, hear," the three other men shouted in unison.

Kit just laughed and drank his soft drink. This had been quite a day for him, and he was looking forward to its end. When Daniel finished his beer, he said his goodbyes and took Kit home. The others could carry on, but Daniel wanted Kit away from the drinking that he knew would ensue.

Chapter Thirteen

Daniel and Kit had a lot to talk about on their way home. This had been a day when proof of an afterlife came into very clear view for a group of people that had never had to think about it. Kit had been given messages from people on the other side that had proved to be accurate. This confirmed his standing among his father's peers as being genuine and an asset and he felt good about it.

"I'm glad you quickly helped Graham Moon this evening when he had his relapse," Daniel said.

"My first aid training paid off," Kit answered. "I initially thought he was having a heart attack or something which is why I called for you as I laid him on his side and placed him in the recovery position."

"Well, there are some things that go to the grave with people and obviously some that don't," Daniel said. "How did you know about Moon's mother?"

"I had an image in my mind of his mother laid out in her coffin," Kit said. "I saw Mrs. Moon as a spirit in my mind's eye standing up and she told me about what her son asked her on his last grave visit."

"Does any of this worry you?"

"What do you mean, Dad?"

"Seeing and hearing spirits and having them send messages to you."

"It did initially when I saw David for the first time. However, he generally looks like how I saw myself after my pool accident and floated above the operating table. Ellen was similar – so I know what we will look like after we die."

Kit's last words struck a major chord with Daniel as he searched his mind. Both he and Leah had not sat down and discussed in detail what Kit had seen, felt and experienced when he "died" on the operating table. The couple had been told by Dr Curry Kit believed he had experienced something odd during the operation and to be prepared for it. However, they never worked fully through it with Kit.

"Mate, I'm sorry. I guess your mum and I never really discussed with you what you experienced when you were operated on. We've never really had anything to do with people who have died and come back or have dead people contacting people in this world through them," Daniel said.

"So, you're saying I'm a sort of freak or something?"

"Whoa! No. Not at all. I'm saying your mum and I have never really discussed death and its effects before."

"Yeah well, it's pretty permanent!"

"Only for some, it seems."

They had a good laugh as they made light of Kit's operation and his flat lining of the heart monitor during his operation.

"Kit what was it like to come out of your body?"

Kit thought for a moment and realised his father was genuinely trying to engage him on something both his parents had avoided before. He looked at his dad and spoke slowly.

“My last memory before the accident was walking out to the pool and then slipping on Tara’s toy,” Kit said as he focused his mind on his life changing event. “There was a sort of void … when I had no feeling of anything. I guess this was when I was unconscious. The next thing I remember is a feeling of being pulled out from my feet, sort of like a vacuum cleaner tugging at me. I became free and was totally awake to what was happening around me. The only difference was I was floating above the operating table and could see and hear everything. I saw my body for the first time as the doctors used their instruments to probe my skull.”

Kit stopped and checked his breathing. He was becoming emotional as he thought back to the conversations surrounding Dr Curry.

“Are you okay mate?” Daniel asked as he reached across to Kit with his left hand and felt his shoulder.

“Yeah, thanks. When I think of how Dr Curry was hurrying to go to a function it makes me angry. The heart monitor started making noises and the moving pointer on screen that kept drawing a graph of my heart movements had stopped. I had died. The nurses kept pushing Dr Curry to continue with the electric paddles on my chest but he was ready to say I was dead after only a couple of attempts to re-start my heart so he could go to his damn function. I yelled to him I was alive and to keep trying but no one could hear me.”

Tears welled up in Kit’s eyes as he told his story in full. “If it wasn’t for the nurses pushing Dr Curry, I probably wouldn’t be here … no, that’s not quite right.”

“What do you mean?”

"The operation seemed to fade from my view. It was as if time stood still, and I was pushed into darkness. I could feel the presence of others around me but could not see them. Ahead of me was a pinhole of light that grew with amazing speed as my whole being, my spirit seemed to vibrate. Suddenly I was in an area that had the whitest of light. I have never seen anything so bright in my life before."

"Were you in heaven?"

"I'm not sure. It would be easy to say yes as I felt at home. It was like Christmas morning with you and mum as I felt I was in a place of total love – the purest of love. I met your parents, granddad and grandma and we all hugged."

Daniel choked back some tears as he heard how his son had met his dead parents.

"Two beings, like old men dressed as monks, appeared next to me, and talked to me with their minds. They showed me my life so far with all the times I had upset people and I saw how others felt when I had upset them. They also showed me all the good times I have had and when I had helped other people. I was told I had a mission to complete and that it was not my time to join them. They told me I had to go back. Dad, it was terrible as I wanted to be with you and mum, yet I felt so wonderful where I was. The next thing I felt a tugging at my side and a feeling of movement and vibration. My body came into view, and I saw and heard the nurses arguing with Dr Curry. I felt a bump as I re-entered my body and then I was breathing again."

Daniel had pulled over to listen to his son and had put his arm around his shoulders as he listened to his tale.

"What happened next?"

"I was back in some sort of void … probably unconscious for the operation again. I came to in the recovery area and saw Dr Curry. He became angry when I told him I had seen him trying to call my death early so he could go out."

"Did he believe you?"

"I think he did as I was pretty accurate in my descriptions. He actually went white when I told him what I saw and heard. Dad, let me tell you that although it is pretty great being with you and mum and I know I am surrounded by your love, wherever I went to in the place of light was so wonderful I want to return there. It's like I belong there as there was no feeling of hurt, just a feeling of being surrounded by love and total calm."

Daniel had been taken on an emotional roller coaster ride by Kit as he told his story. First, he was sad as his son detailed the pool accident. Anger soon took hold as Kit detailed the rush by Dr Curry to finish the operation and pronounce his son dead. Daniel became gobsmacked when Kit described his experiences of the afterlife and the meeting with his parents. This soon gave way to a feeling of wanting to hug his son and just hold him.

"Do you know why the monks sent you back to us?" Daniel finally said.

"All I know is the two older men said it was not my time yet and that I have a mission of sorts to complete. What the mission is I don't know."

"Well mate, you have certainly given me a lot to think about. Tell me, does David or Ellen differ in how you see them compared to what the old men did who took you on a life review?"

"No, and I guess that has been the constant reminder of things for me. Whenever I see David or Ellen a warm feeling comes over me."

"So how come they can't just tell you the answer to things like blah blah is set to murder your father this way on this particular date?"

"Dad, I don't know. Maybe they're not allowed to as we have free will and things could change quickly."

Daniel nodded and then re-started the car.

"Come on mate, we'd better get home to your mother."

"Ok. I bet she's asleep on the lounge."

"You're on."

The rest of the trip seemed to go quickly as the pair talked about other more urbane subjects. The father and son duo made their way through the front door of their house only to be met by a very wide-awake Leah dressed in her pyjamas sitting on a lounge chair watching TV.

"How did it all go?" Leah asked as Daniel gave her a kiss.

"Okay. We had a sort of pyrrhic victory tonight so I'm looking forward to see what the fallout will be, if any," Daniel said.

"What do you mean?" Leah asked as she switched off the TV and sat more upright.

"Well, we had a meeting with Reg and Terry and then Graham Moon came over to join in too."

"You brought in the big guns huh? It must have been pretty important to have both Kit and Graham Moon there?"

Kit smiled and walked over to his mother. He gave her a big hug and said good night to his parents.

"Oh no you don't," Leah said. "You can't leave me in suspense not knowing what the urgent meeting was all about and why the leader of the Opposition had to be brought in with my son there."

Kit looked at Daniel for support.

"It's okay honey, I'll explain it all to you now over a nice glass or two of port. Kit's had a big day and needs a lot of rest. Don't worry, you can be proud of him – he helped save the day."

"Thanks Dad. See you in the morning mum," the teenager said as he walked to the stairs leading to his bedroom.

"Leah, we have a lot to talk about and it will be better if Kit's not here," Daniel said as he walked to the drinks cabinet. He poured two ports, gave one to his wife and then sat next to her on the lounge.

"Thank you," Leah said as she took a small sip of port.

"Okay, where do I start? Oh yes. Kit's phone call to me at work."

Daniel went on to detail what had happened with Kit's visitation of Ellen; his phone call to him at work and the urgent meeting at Sullivan's place. He described how Kit had re-told the story of Ellen to the three men and then had to do it again to Graham Moon. Daniel took delight in explaining how Kit had proved he knew about Moon's mother and then gave the *piece de resistance* with the alert about being monitored. He re-filled the pair's glasses.

"On the way home, we had a heart to heart about things

and he opened up with me as to what happened the day he had his accident and what it was like to die," Daniel said. "It was spooky, and I think you really need to hear it."

"Daniel I'm already amazed at Kit and what he has done so far today what more could surprise me?" Leah asked.

"His description of how he died and where he went will rock your boat."

It didn't take Daniel long to launch into Kit's sequence of events of his accident, floating above the operating room and meeting his life reviewers. All the time Leah sat quietly, sipping her port and nodding.

"You know, it's more than time we organised Kit to have his lessons with Mrs. Bishop," Leah said. "I think she holds a key to his acceptance of things and his future development."

"Okay. Do you want to ring her tomorrow and get him started?"

"Yes. This way I can have a chat and find out what's in store for him."

"Okay, love. Let's go to bed. It's been a long day."

The next morning Kit was having breakfast when Leah walked into the kitchen. She walked up behind him and gave him a hug.

"I'm pretty proud of you, I want you to know," Leah said.

"How come?"

"Your Dad told me all the things you did yesterday. You certainly made us both proud."

"Thanks mum."

"I'll be talking with Mrs. Bishop today and organising your lessons with her."

Kit stopped eating his cereal and looked at his mum.

"That will be cool, thanks."

"Your dad told me last night about the busy afternoon and night you had. I was very proud of the way you helped."

"I did have some help from …"

"I know and that's why I'll be talking to Mrs. Bishop to help you cope properly with what's happening to you."

"Thanks mum. I know at times I can handle most things around me but like anyone my age I don't know it all and I'm keen to learn what I can."

"Okay. What are you doing today?"

"I've got some homework I need to finish then I want to go skate boarding, if that's okay?"

"No probs. I'll try and get an answer about Mrs. Bishop as soon as possible."

Kit gave his mum a hug and kiss and put his bowl and spoon into the dishwasher. He cleaned his teeth and then went into his room to complete his homework. The boy was happy. He just hoped that whoever was found snooping on his father and his friends yesterday at Terry Sullivan's house were "helping the police with their enquiries".

This was a term used by the Media when Police had caught a major suspect to a crime, and they were interviewing them.

Chapter Fourteen

Once Daniel had gone to work, Leah rang Mrs. Bishop. The pair talked for about twenty minutes and arranged for Kit to start his first Mediumship lessons with Mrs. Bishop the following Saturday morning.

"How do you teach someone to talk to the dead?" Leah asked. "Do these spirits pop into your head and you just think thoughts?"

Mrs. Bishop chuckled and realised she had to also teach Leah what Kit would be undergoing.

"Leah, there are six different skill sets I want to teach him. The first thing I will be doing with Kit is to show him how to be in control of himself through meditation where he will find his inner-self and learn how to calm himself mentally."

Leah thought of the image Mrs. Bishop was painting of her teaching practice and in her mind's eye saw Kit sitting on the ground cross-legged in the lotus position.

"Yes, this would be good for Kit," Leah said to Mrs. Bishop. "He is always on the go and the meditation would slow him down enough to take in what he is doing with his life."

Mrs. Bishop said she would then help Kit learn the art of psychometry where the teenager would learn to pick up and tune into the energies associated with man-made objects like people's jewellery.

"This sounds very much like what we think Gipsies do with people to help them read their minds," Leah said.

"No far from it," Mrs. Bishop re-joined. "If you think about what we do every day to take in an experience we feel it, see it, hear it, touch it, and even smell it. Psychometry is using our senses at a different level. We touch an object that belongs to someone and see if we can tune into the person. It's like these objects have a set of vibrations from the owner and we tune into the owner through the vibrations left in the object."

"So, these objects are like tiny radio transmitters or something?" Leah asked.

"Yes, in a way. They emit vibrations which I guess you could equate to radio waves and the Medium is able to pick up information about the owner from them."

Mrs. Bishop said she would then take Kit through the art of phrenology or reading the shape and bumps on a person's head. Leah found this skill hard to understand.

"A lot of the ancients believed the shape of our head is brought about by how our brains are formed," Mrs. Bishop said. "It's sort of to do with what a person believes and does not believe."

"No, I can't get this one," Leah said. "The shape has to do with how you were made and how you were born … not based on beliefs."

"Well, the various beliefs we have push the skull into shape and help form the bumps; flat spots, curves and character of the head," Mrs. Bishop said.

"I can't see how a baby could know anything, never mind a belief and therefore has its head shaped according to what it believes?" Leah persisted.

"Ah, but you see there is a catch. Our heads don't stop growing until we are adults so our beliefs can come into play any time along the way."

"Okay, you have me there."

Mrs. Bishop said the next skill Kit would enjoy would be tasseomancy where he would learn the art of tea leaf reading. Leah said this would thrill her own mother as she had read for Kit the week before. Mrs. Bishop said there were two more skills required for Kit. The first was dowsing or divining where a Medium can ascertain a quick yes or no answer to a vexing issue. The last was scrying which is one of the most ancient tools for interpreting the past or future from objects with a smooth surface like a crystal ball, crystals, water or even smoke. This last image had Leah laughing as she thought of Kit with a mantilla on his head crouched over a crystal ball trying to read someone's future. The image just didn't fit Kit.

Once Leah had finalised the timings with Mrs. Bishop, she rang her best friend Sarah Kaplan to tell her Kit was now on a new path of learning. Sarah was glad.

"He is obviously showing signs of doing things or having experienced something the rest of us haven't," Sarah said. "These lessons will hopefully focus his skills and allow him to control what comes into his life."

"Yes, I guess so," Leah said. "Daniel and I want to get him sorted and on track well before he starts the major study before leaving school."

"Well, then now is the best time and Niva won't disappoint you."

"Thanks for putting her in touch with us. She's an interesting woman and I think she does a lot of good with people, judging on the way she approached Daniel, Kit and me."

The two friends then spent the next half hour catching up and arranging their next meet.

Across the city, Daniel had been waiting for a call from Terry Sullivan. When it finally came, he wasn't surprised by its content.

"Hey Daniel, it's Terry," Sullivan said using his mobile phone. "We got some interesting results from last night and they seemed to have stirred a hornet's nest."

"Hi, Terry. So were our little friends beaming onto us next to your house attached to West or Ratcliffe?"

"It turns out the two cops were part of a special operations group who were allegedly tracking some high-profile underworld figures," Sullivan said with a laugh in his voice.

"I always knew members of Parliament were shady figures but is that the best they could come up with?" Daniel joked.

"Mate, Moon put the acid on Internal Affairs and told them he wanted to know why members of Parliament were having their conversations and movements recorded by the Police."

"Has Ratcliffe shown his hand yet?"

"That's interesting, as the two cops were tagged as working for a special group supervised by a …"

"Inspector West?"

"You guessed it. Internal Affairs is now investigating the squad they came from and the links from West to the Commissioner. Apparently West has been kept in the background of Police machinations over the last few years so he wouldn't gather a profile. The problem is his very actions could now give him a huge profile and that of his benefactor as we unravel the story and finger Ratcliffe for usurping Parliament – a charge that could bring instant dismissal or a very large Court case."

Daniel started chuckling. "I bet the midnight oil was burning in Ratcliffe's office on Friday night?"

"Yeah. My understanding is that Moon's call for Internal Affairs to check out our little friends caused Ratcliffe to cancel all appointments last night and today. He apparently has gone into a series of closed meetings with specialist staff."

"Specialist staff my eye! I'll lay odds the meetings were with his Chief of Staff, West and some of his other close advisors that are part of his special squads."

Sullivan thought for a moment. "Could be. We're trying to get information as to who attended but it is virtually impossible."

"Well, we have now brought the war to Ratcliffe's doorstep so the next move is up to him …"

"Not necessarily Daniel. We could up the ante and pass the information to the Independent Crime Commission and ask them to investigate. If this happens …"

"I know. Ratcliffe must stand aside until the investigation is complete," Daniel said with a laugh in his voice. "Terry, I know this is pretty serious business but our Commissioner seems to not stand even a ghost of a chance of surviving all this!"

"Thanks for the pun. I'm sure Kit would appreciate it. At this stage it's up to Moon now as to where we go with this, so we must wait and see."

"Okay."

The two men rang off. They both knew a new political game was now in play and if it wasn't for Kit, they would not have been appraised they were being monitored in the first place. Kit could be a new weapon in the political armoury of the party, but he would first have to agree to help and second, learn how to master the unknown so he was fully armed. The problem remained, Kit was a teenager and really was not interested in politics.

Chapter Fifteen

Kit had a long conversation with his parents about training with Mrs. Bishop. He saw the rationale behind the training and became quite eager to make a start. The way Kit saw it was that Mrs. Bishop had several skills no one else he knew had. These skills had helped her to master the ability to talk to those who had died and to predict the future. He also saw it as possibly a better way to contact David or Ellen – rather than the other way round. Daniel dropped Kit off at Mrs. Bishops' place and then returned home – he didn't want to be around and overshadow Kit in anyway.

"Are you going to have me sit in the lotus position with my feet crossed and my middle fingers touching my thumbs or something?" Kit asked Mrs. Bishop with a larrikin smile.

Mrs. Bishop smiled. Kit was keen to start, and she loved his good humour.

"You have a number of choices of how you participate in this first session," Mrs. Bishop said. "If you want to lie down, sit cross legged or even with your spine straight – it's all up to you. The bottom line is, I want you as comfortable as possible while I take you on a mental journey."

Kit nodded and decided to lie down on the carpeted lounge

room floor. He reached up to the lounge and grabbed a cushion to place under his head.

"Okay, I'm ready for my journey," Kit said and then beamed another smile.

Mrs. Bishop told Kit he was going on a guided visualisation – a journey where she would guide him mentally with suggestions, but he had to fill in the gaps with his mind. She lit some aromatic candles and darkened the room before turning on a compact disc player with quiet flute music. Mrs. Bishop explained how this technique of relaxation was only one of many to help relax the mind and body, so participants are more able to receive and control messages from the spirit world. The Medium explained how the meditations are used by businesspeople to destress and put their lives back in balance. Mrs. Bishop also said these types of sessions assisted with goal setting and refreshing the person mentally. She emphasised the sessions were only a beginning in how Mediums could speak with spirits.

"Alright Kit, I want you to close your eyes and let your mind help paint the canvas while I give you the directions," Mrs. Bishop said. "You are walking through a beautiful forest with lovely tall trees, pretty leaves, and shaped branches everywhere. You see how wonderful the forest is and this gives you a feeling of happiness. The path you are on leads to a lovely flowing stream, and you stop and take a drink …"

While Mrs. Bishop took Kit on his guided visualisation his heart rate dropped and his body and mind calmed. The teenager was taken through a scenario of wonderment as he went through the forest, open fields, and meandering hills.

Mrs. Bishop took Kit past some waterfalls and to the top of a hill that overlooked a valley and finally back to his starting point with a number of stops on the way.

"Where did you feel most comfortable?" Mrs. Bishop asked Kit as he sat up.

"I felt fantastic when I was on top of the hill overlooking the valley," the teenager said.

"Why?"

"I guess because it was so like heaven. It was like the place I went to after I died on the operating table."

Mrs. Bishop saw Kit was keen to talk about his near-death experience and started prompting him some more.

"You had gone to hospital after …"

"I fell in the pool after slipping on a toy and hitting my head on the corner of a table."

"Okay. So, you went to hospital and had to be operated on. What happened that took you to the valley area you just explored with me?"

Kit looked at Mrs. Bishop and thought through what had happened to him.

"It was similar to what heaven was like."

"Kit, what do you remember about going to heaven?"

The teenager's face had gone from looking playful to wistful as he began to remember what had happened to him.

"At some stage I was in the operating theatre. I remember being sucked out of my body and then realising I was floating above the people operating on me. I could hear and see everything that was going on but no one could see or hear me," Kit said as he became slightly anxious. "I could hear the nurses arguing with the doctor to keep trying to use the heart paddles to re-start my heart. The doctor just wanted to get away and call my time of death. The nurses argued with him and he finally continued again with the paddles. During the argument I found myself standing in what I believe was heaven."

"What was it like?" Mrs. Bishop said.

"I had this feeling of immense joy come over me. It was like I was in the safest place I could ever be and all I felt was love and calm. In the distance I saw my grandparents waving to me. This was odd as they had both died about a decade ago and here, they were waving to me and walking over to me. My grandfather hugged and kissed me and then my grandmother did the same. They were very excited to see me. The last time I saw them I was just starting school. They had died in a car accident which had made my father very sad for a long time as they were his parents. Here they were so happy and joyous, and this made me feel fantastic. As I kissed my grandparents a small crowd seemed to gather, and they all started clapping their hands on my back or hugging me and welcoming me."

"Can you describe the place?"

"It was like the beautiful top of the hill overlooking the valley you took me to. It was just amazing how bright the light was, yet there was no sun. All around me was white light like a fluorescent light but no shadows. Imagine being in the snow and seeing everyone with bright colour and light around them. The light was very intense but there was total calm and peace everywhere. Somewhere in the background were fantastic sets of choirs all singing different songs and I could understand each one. The colours of everything I saw were dazzling and so rich – much more intense than we see here on Earth. All the people who came to greet me kept saying how wonderful it was to see me. All I could feel were waves of joy and love just washing over me like gentle surf. It was fantastic. My grandparents had been stooped over and in pain the last time I saw them. Here they stood tall, looked younger and so happy. Time had no meaning where I was, so I don't know how long I was away from the operating table.

"I never saw God or anyone who looked like Jesus Christ, Buddha or any Saint I had seen in religious books. However, my time in heaven ended abruptly. Two men in long robes who looked like monks with hoods over their heads came up to me and told me it was not my time. They said I should go back as I had a mission to complete. They showed me how I had lived my life up to now including times when I had wronged people. This was weird because I became the other people, so I experienced what it was like when I acted wrongly with them. Dad said this was a life review of sorts. Before I could say goodbye to my grandparents, I was aware of my body and falling into it with a sort of thud."

Kit winced and shook his head.

"Did it hurt you to return to your body?" Mrs. Bishop asked.

"No, but all the wondrous beauty, love, and warmth I had just experienced seemed to end too soon. The next thing I remember was waking up in the recovery room and arguing with the doctor for trying to walk out on me."

"I bet he was shocked."

"You bet. I had him pinged from the moment I saw him. He

tried to squirm his way out of what I was saying but he knew I was right. I had been watching and listening to him in the operating room."

"Kit are you afraid of dying now?"

"No. Now I've been to where we all have to go, I know it will be wonderful. The only problem will be how I return there?"

Mrs. Bishop started laughing. "Hopefully through old age."

Kit stood up and Mrs. Bishop gave him a big hug. The teenager seemed to linger in the arms of the Medium before he relaxed his grip and stood in front of her.

"Do you want to have a break or a drink of tea or soft drink?

"No thanks. I'm okay. It just gets hard sometimes."

"Kit, what do you mean?

"Here I have the love of my parents and extended family and friends. The problem is it is nothing like I experienced in heaven! If I could go back right now I would, as long as mum and Dad came with me."

"How would you want to go back to heaven?"

Kit realised what he had said and then started shaking his head. "I didn't mean take my own life or anything. I don't know. It would be great if God just took the three of us to heaven as the joy would be so complete for me then."

"You know Kit, you and I share a similar bond."

"What do you mean?"

Mrs. Bishop smiled and put her right arm around his shoulders. "I have been there too. I know what it is like to be in heaven, and you described it to a tee. Even now, I can sometimes still hear some of the singing and music in my mind when I have quiet times. When I have a really hard day, I let my mind take me to where I met my dead brother and grandparents – that beautiful place we both call heaven."

Mrs. Bishop went to the kitchen to make a cup of tea and Kit followed her.

"Want a cuppa?"

"Yes please, I think I could do with one now."

Kit was entranced. "Why did you go to heaven? How did you die and come back?"

"I was in a car accident when I was about your age. I was a passenger in a friend's car, and he lost control of the car in the wet, went off the road and we hit a tree. I remember going to a similar place to what you described, and I too am longing to return. However, I was also told I have a mission to complete, and I am doing that as we speak."

Kit had been studying Mrs. Bishop and seemed to be hanging off every word she said. "Am I the mission?"

"Well, you are part of the mission. My role is to teach others and open their hearts and minds to what they can't see – that place where you and I have been and returned. Now tell me, did you see anyone on your trip you did with me just now?"

"Yes," Kit said as he winced. He hadn't told Mrs. Bishop he had seen David, yet she was asking. At no time during the guided visualisation did the Medium mention linking up with anyone else.

"Who was it?" Mrs. Bishop asked with a smile on her face.

"David."

"Good. Did you talk with him for long?"

"No. He just met me and said this would be a good place to

keep meeting when I wanted to see him, otherwise he would meet with me where he could."

"Ah, now you see Kit, you must work out how to go back there when you want to. Don't you?"

"Yes, but wouldn't that be through meditating and thinking my way through a similar journey you sent me on mentally until I catch up with David?"

"Well yes, however, it takes practice and more practice. The most important thing you must remember is to be calm, breathe slowly and deeply. Your mind will then help do the rest."

The whistle on the kettle started to blow as steam shot out of the spout. Mrs. Bishop poured the boiling water into a teapot while Kit organised two cups and saucers. The teenager was slow in his actions as he mulled over what his mentor had told him. He knew Mrs. Bishop was special but never guessed she had also undergone a near death experience. Her insight into the other realm was like his, almost.

"Mrs. Bishop, before you had your accident and died, could you see dead people and speak with them?"

"As a little girl I used to see spirits in my house and often became quite scared," the Medium said as she passed Kit a cup of tea. "I didn't know what they wanted or how to handle them. Unlike your parents, mine didn't know anyone who knew a Medium I could talk with or be schooled by. I would try to block out the sights of spirits and the voices I sometimes heard in my head."

"That must have been very hard for you?"

"In a way it was a similar experience to you in that I would also get thoughts in my head that weren't my own."

"How did you know they weren't yours?"

"I would have thoughts about subjects and time periods I knew nothing of. They weren't connected to my daily routine of life or with anyone I physically knew – therefore I learnt I was being sent messages and thoughts by spirits."

Kit sipped his tea and munched on a biscuit while he pondered what Mrs. Bishop had just said and thought about Thomas. "So how did you take control of what was happening to you?"

Mrs. Bishop cupped her tea in both hands and investigated the rising steam from the brew.

"When I had my accident, the paramedics said I had died on the spot as they could not find any pulse or breathing from me. They worked on me for a while before I regained my breathing and my heart started. In between, I felt I was in a dark space and my body started resonating to a high pitch – like what you described. It then moved towards a slit of light at tremendous speed and that's when I believe I entered heaven. In this extraordinarily brightly lit area, I met relatives and friends I hadn't seen for a long time and then realised why – they had all died. After talking with them and being hugged by them a man in a sort of monk's habit with a hood took me aside and said it was not my time to be there. Who knows, it could have been one of the two men you met in robes? This monk then told me what I told you earlier that my role on Earth is to teach others and open their hearts and minds to what they can't see and help prepare them for their journey."

"Wow," Kit said. "I wasn't given a message like that. I was

basically told it was not my time and I had to go back. The next thing I remember was falling into my body and then being asleep before I woke up in the recovery room. So how did you become a Medium?"

Mrs. Bishop looked carefully at Kit's eyes and saw the wonderment he had as the teenager sipped his tea. "During my recovery phase at the hospital I told the nursing staff of my experiences after I crashed. I was put in touch with a group of other patients who had undergone near death experiences. The tutor for the hospital group was a Medium and I became very good friends with her."

"Did she teach you to become a Medium?"

"Yes, I guess so. She helped me to take control of my gifts and open my mind to how to deal with spirits and what I had experienced in heaven. Now, enough of me. I want you to think of a question you want answered, anything at all. Lift your cup and lay your napkin over your saucer."

Kit did as he was told and started to smile. His lesson in tasseomancy had begun. "Are you going to teach me how to read tea leaves today as well?"

"No, not fully. This will be one of your other lessons we'll go through later. Think of it as a quick teaser. Now leave a bit of tea in the bottom of the cup and swish it gently around the cup. Turn the cup upside on the napkin and twist it around clockwise three times."

Kit started laughing. "This sounds like a magic formula to a spell by Merlin the magician or something."

Mrs. Bishop started laughing with Kit. "Yes, you could say that. Others think we are dabbling in the dark arts but the image of Merlin is nice. I like that. Now pick up your cup and let's see if your question was answered."

The Medium moved her chair closer to Kit and investigated the cup as the boy tried to make heads or tails of the various clumps of tea leaves stuck to his cup. She pointed to the various shapes that made letters, images of objects, animals and even geometric shapes like circles and triangles.

"Each of these shapes has some sort of meaning but not all is clear to the viewer," Mrs. Bishop said. "When you look into the cup is there any feeling you receive about your question or is there a particular shape that means anything to you?"

"I thought you could read the leaves?"

"Yes, I can. However, mostly it is up to the person whose cup it is to read their own leaves and intuitively feel any messages they may see."

"Like what? All I can see are little groups of leaves on the side and bottom of the cup."

"Okay, let me help you," Mrs. Bishop said she peered closer into Kit's cup. "Have you had anything to do with cameras recently?"

"Yes."

"Good. See what looks like a square leaf on a tripod?"

"Ah, yes I do."

"So, what happened? Have you been taking photos of the family or playing with your father's movie camera?"

Kit laughed. "No. I was visiting his client's home and had a very strange feeling come over me."

"Did you feel David was trying to contact you?"

"No, but that wouldn't have surprised me as it was his father we were visiting. My Dad and I walked outside the house to leave when I felt a beam of something washing over me. I told my dad, and we went back inside and checked it out from a top floor bedroom window. Behind the next-door neighbour's fence were a couple of people filming and voice recording us with a satellite type dish."

"Kit, what happened?"

"David's father's boss was also at the house, and he rang the Police who found the two people were from a special Police Unit. Now they are being investigated."

"Wow. There's never a dull moment with you, is there? Is everything okay now?"

"All is fine. Apparently, the Police behind the fence had the wrong address to film and record."

Mrs. Bishop used the end of her teaspoon to point to a small row of checkered tea leaves and said it was the connection with the camera. She then pointed to what seemed like a top hat and cane and then looked slightly above him.

"Have you heard much from Thomas lately?"

"No, but the hat reminds me of what he is supposed to wear."

"Yes, he does, and he twirls his cane when he knows you are talking about him."

"Is he here now?"

"Yes. Thomas is assigned to you and will be with you while ever you remain on this Earth."

"I'd like to see him too."

Mrs. Bishop smiled. "Kit, usually the only times you ever meet your spirit guides are at your birth and your death. You have been lucky to have had a very active spirit guide who has helped awaken some special gifts in you."

"Yes, I suppose so. After all, it's not everyone that has an image of their guide."

"No, so enjoy. Now back to the matters in hand."

Kit raised his cup in salute and chuckled. He then lowered it again and began looking at the leaves and their patterns in earnest.

Chapter Sixteen

Todd Ratcliffe had progressively become unwell over the past month. The Police Commissioner had started to lose his edge as he began worrying about his failed attempts to set-up Terry Sullivan and his team and achieve his aims. Ratcliffe called his best friend from his Academy days to his office.

"Sir, good morning," Inspector Joe West said as he reached for his friend's right hand.

"Joe, it's good to see you. Please grab a seat. Tell me how your special filming went all pear-shape?"

"We've got no idea. My team and I have gone over the tape a few times and can't work out what triggered the group's awareness we were even there."

"Do you know whether Sullivan had any sensors or cameras directed at you?

"No, not that we could tell. He has cameras in the grounds that would cover his front yard and entrance but nothing high enough to see into his neighbour's yards where my officers were positioned."

"Joe, I find that extraordinary. I had a tip off from one of the Sunday papers that Sullivan was going to do a number on me and then he replaced his story with one from Moon. This paints the picture of him being spooked for some reason."

"Todd, maybe he had second thoughts …"

"Yes, but the question is who spooked him."

"Mmm, I think we need to analyse the tape further and see if there were any body language changes in those on film that show they knew something was happening. You know, someone looking at where your men were positioned or a curt and possibly evasive conversation with heads turned in your direction."

Inspector West hesitated for a moment as if trying to work through a thought. "You know, there were a few moments when Daniel Green's son leant in close to talk to his father."

"What happened then?"

"Maybe that's the strange thing. The kid seems to have had some sort of conversation with his father and then they all went back inside the house."

"That's it, Joe. The kid … what's his name?"

"Kit."

"Yes, Kit, must have been alerted somehow to your team's presence. I think I'd be looking at how he knew you were there. You may have to have a closer look at Kit and see if he is a problem to us."

"Todd, we're talking about a young teenage boy still in high school," West said. "If I remember right from the film, we took he wasn't wearing any special vests or kit that would conceal the gear necessary to detect us. He's just an ordinary boy."

"Alright, Joe. You can see we need to look at everything we can and evaluate it. This uncovering of our team was uncanny, and we must find out how it was done."

Joe West was a man who had done the bidding of his

classmate and friend Todd Ratcliffe for a number of years. He had investigated and worked with some of the worst criminals and Police in the State but had never been ordered to "investigate" a teenage boy – especially someone who was not on the Police radar for having done anything wrong. West's investigation usually meant bailing up the target and seeing how they reacted under Police scrutiny; checking the Police files to see if the individual had come under any notice before and bullying them to see if they made any mistakes.

The two men spoke together for the next half an hour and tried to work out a strategy for the Internal Affairs investigation that had started since West's men had been found snooping on Sullivan and his team. West then left the Commissioner's office and made his way back to a former industrial area where he and his team of five Police had their offices.

"Team, we have a special job to do," West said as he looked uneasily at his officers. "I have it direct from the Commissioner that we are to target a 14-year-old boy and his family to see why we were compromised at Sullivan's place."

"Is the kid a geek or gizmo tech head?" Senior Constable Matt Gaze asked.

"No, I don't think so," West said as he started to smile with the image Gaze had just drawn for him. "If you remember, when Sullivan and the others came out of the politician's house, they were all talking together. Kit Green, the son of Daniel Green, leant forward to have a word with his father and then the group retreated into the house. Something spooked the kid about us, and we must find out what."

"Boss, the kid wasn't wearing any special equipment – at

least nothing we could pick up. Also, I saw nothing on the tape about him that was untoward so why pick on the boy?"

West became impatient with Gaze. He knew Gaze was right but he had to follow through on what Ratcliffe had ordered. "Ratcliffe wants him checked out so see what you can find out about him."

"Alright boss."

Gaze spoke with a couple of his other Police officers to map out how to check on Kit Green. First, the Officers interrogated the Police computer system to see if Kit had come under notice by the law. They drew their first blank. A call was made to the Inspector in charge of the local Police station near Kit's home to see if he had come under any notice and been given any warnings that may not have been recorded. Another blank. One of the officers started trawling social network sites on the internet to see if Kit was actively engaged in chat rooms and if so, to determine his Internet Service Provider (ISP) address. Another blank.

"This kid seems pretty clean," Constable Brian Crouch said. "If we go to his school, word will leak out pretty quick we're after him for something."

"Crouchy, don't go any further until I see the boss," Gaze said. "I think he'll want us to use our radio van tonight and go phishing."

The look on the other three Police Officers said it all. Each one winced as they realised, they could be used to help set up a clean skin teenage boy who had done nothing wrong.

Chapter Seventeen

Kit felt uneasy all day. He had a gut feeling he was about to have a fight with someone but couldn't work out why or who – there had been no trouble between he and anyone else at school. He found it hard to concentrate in his last lesson of the day as the queasiness set in. When the bell rang to signal the end of the period, he packed his bag and slowly walked out of the classroom and along the corridors leading to the outside world. Kit looked among the throng of students and saw a large looming shape heading his way. Craig Hooper, the school bully from his form, walked towards him. Their eyes met in a steely gaze and Kit stiffened himself ready to do battle with the teenager who had the size, shape, and gait of a gorilla. Hooper disengaged his stare at Kit and talked with one of his stooges as the two boys passed each other.

Well, it wasn't Hooper, Kit said to himself. *Then who could it be?*

He made his way to the bus stop and joined another small crowd of students all eager to get home. Kit spoke and laughed with a few of his friends and then boarded the bus. The ride home was uneventful too until he started walking up the path leading to his home. His neck began to tingle, and images of David started to come into his mind. Kit looked around but saw no one. The teenager made his way into the house and the kitchen to get some afternoon tea.

A note on the fridge read: *"Kit, afternoon tea is in the fridge. Love Mum."* Kit opened the fridge door and before he could reach in the tingling on his neck started again. He closed the door and turned around. Standing in front of him was David.

"I was wondering when I'd see you," Kit said, smiling.

David's body form was almost see-though. A slight shimmer shone around his form as he returned his smile.

"I have felt you around most of today," Kit said. "I also felt I was going to have a fight with someone. What's going on?"

David's lips never moved. His arms slowly moved as he used his mind to communicate with Kit.

"Mate, Ratcliffe and West's Police team are trying to see if you are as crooked as they are," David said.

"Me? I'm not the one who's a crook. It's them."

David nodded and looked at Kit's feet.

"What are they doing? Is there anything I can do to catch them out?"

David smiled and gave Kit the thumbs up. "The police have a special car that checks on people using the internet. Keep a lookout for it."

"David, what sort of car is it?"

"You'll know it as it is black."

David left as quickly as he arrived and the tingling on Kit's neck subsided. The teenager stood rooted to the kitchen floor as he thought about what had happened. He walked over to the phone and rang his father.

"Kit, what's wrong mate?" Daniel asked.

"Dad, I need to see you pretty soon something's going on."

"I'm pretty flat out at the moment. Can this wait until I get home?

"No, and I can't talk about it on the phone."

"Can you give me hint?

"My friend came to see me this afternoon.

"You mean …"

"Yes, and we have to talk pretty soon."

"Alright mate. See you soon."

Daniel went to Reg Clementon's office rather than ring him. Something in the way Kit was talking gave him the impression this was safer than making a phone call. The two men talked for a few minutes before Daniel left to drive home. Daniel was glad the election was in sight and Ratcliffe and his friends would be dealt with one way or another. The moment he pulled his car up outside his home Kit came out of the front door and walked towards him. The teenager sat in the passenger seat and closed the door.

"Are you okay?" Daniel asked.

"Yes and no. Can we drive around the block please."

Daniel started the car and drove off. He waited for Kit to start the conversation.

"Dad, David came to see me this afternoon. It was pretty weird," the teenager said. "I kept thinking all day I was going to have a fight with someone at school. You know, when you think you're in trouble and your heart seems to jump around a bit."

"Yeah, I can relate to that."

"Well, when I got home David came to me and said Ratcliffe

and West were checking on me to see if I was as crooked as them …"

Daniel gripped the steering wheel hard and pulled over. "What else did he say?"

"He said they would be sending some Police in a black car to see what internet sites I was using. Dad, I haven't been on any sex sites or crime sites. I haven't done anything wrong like cyber bullying. This is not fair."

Daniel put his hand on his son's shoulder. "Don't worry mate, we'll get them. So why didn't you want to tell me about any details on the phone? You really worried me."

"Sorry. When David said the Police would be in a black car, all I could think about was they would be tracking our calls."

"You're right mate. It's time we had a talk to Graham Moon so we can bring this nonsense to a close."

Daniel drove to the nearby shopping centre and both he and Kit went to a public telephone. Daniel rang Terry Sullivan, Reg Clementson and then Graham Moon and detailed what Kit had said. He was amazed at how each of the men took his call – especially as he was talking about information passed to Kit by the spirit of a dead teenager. Moon said he would take charge and asked for Daniel to take Kit home and ring him from Leah's mobile phone if there was any sighting of the Police. Moon then contacted his brother-in-law Sergeant Greg Cootes who had helped at Sullivan's place. The trap was set. All that was needed now were the internet police and the good guys.

Greg Cootes was a thin man in his forties with a balding scalp and close-set eyes. He had been spoiling for a fight with Ratcliffe for a while because of several Internal Affairs investigations that implicated the Commissioner but could not be proved conclusively. Cootes did his own check on Kit on his Police computer after discussions with Moon. He too found Kit was clean as far as the law was concerned. His team had warned off West about any illegal activities surrounding the Greens, Sullivans, Clementsons and Moon following their "accidental" taping of conversations at Sullivan's place. Now it looked like he had West where he wanted him.

Daniel was rung by Moon and told to stay indoors and to use the internet to access information about the State Parliament. He was told to stay online until Moon gave him the all-clear. Daniel organised his laptop and followed Moon's instructions by accessing the State Parliament website. He told his son to do the same and then made some phone calls.

Kit got changed out of his uniform and decided to play some quite music in his bedroom. He pulled the pillow off his bed and lay on the floor where he began to relax and start his own guided visualisation. Kit was keen to see David again or even Ellen, the Commissioner's dead wife, to try and find out more of what he could expect to happen.

The teenager's mind began to slow down to the rhythm of the music. He mentally started to re-trace the steps he did with Mrs. Bishop on his first guided visualisation as he wandered through the forest; across the streams and up to the hill where he met David. Kit's breathing slowed and for the casual observer, he looked dead. In fact, Kit was having a great time taking in the sights and the beauty of the place he was visiting. He walked up the soft grassy hill and sat down to take in the view. Calmness and serenity enveloped the lad as he absorbed the surroundings he helped create in his mind. A slight rustling of the grass told Kit he was no longer alone on the hill.

"I was hoping you'd come," Kit said to David, without turning around.

David put his hand on Kit's shoulder and squeezed gently before sitting down. "I'm glad you came here so we could actually talk."

"Yes, it makes a difference to hearing you in my mind and only partially seeing you," Kit replied before shaking hands with David.

The two teenagers talked for some time with David explaining possibilities of what Kit could expect from the Police and when. Kit then changed tact and tried to draw David on what happened to him when he died.

"This all becomes pretty hard to explain," David said. "You know what it is like to die so I don't need to tell you about that. As far as what happens next depends on how you died and whether you need to complete any further learning."

"So if you die early or haven't learnt whatever it is you are supposed to learn, do you go to some sort of teaching by the angels or something?"

"Kit, we're all angels. When I died, I found myself in what is called the healing halls. These are giant areas of pure calm and low coloured light where my spirit recovered from the shock of dying in the car wreck with the injuries I received."

"Were you there long?"

"No. But remember, there is no time in heaven, only here on Earth."

"What happened next?"

"Do you remember the hooded men who sent you back here after you died on the operating table?"

"Yes."

"Well after I came out of the healing hall I was sent to a sort of giant library where my life review books were retrieved by a hooded person like what you described – dressed like a Monk. When this Monk got my books a couple of spirits called the elders, who were also dressed like Monks, took me through them."

"Is this final judgement we hear so much about in church?" Kit said with a quizzical look on his face.

"Not quite. I was taken through my life and saw what it was like to deal with me from other peoples' perspectives."

"It's confrontational. I had a similar type of review before being sent back to Earth, so I know where you are coming from."

"Kit, you must appreciate you may have already gone through this several times so far after living other lives. You'll find out when you do your full life review. Remember the feeling you had when you first died?"

"Yes, it was an overpowering feeling I was surrounded by the purest of love."

"Well, that feeling never leaves you when you die. Nor does it leave you as you do your review or afterwards when you join your friends and family who have passed over. So do not be afraid."

Kit turned to David to ask him some more, but his friend told him he had to leave. The boys stood up and David waved as he started walking down the hill and began to disappear. Kit had so many questions on his mind about death but was now feeling more at ease for when he next "died". He slowly made his way back through the forest and across the stream to his starting point.

Back in his bedroom, the teenager's hands moved as he breathed deeply and seem to awaken from a sleep. He opened his eyes and began to smile. His mission for this part of the journey was complete and he felt calm – no matter what happened. Kit got up and refreshed his computer screen and then sat near his window where he could see the street below and waited.

Chapter Eighteen

The black unmarked Police car made its way to the street where the Greens lived. The car was bristling with electronic gadgets including cameras and devices to assist with vehicle number plate recognition. The devices that captured information of number plates of vehicles helped Police identify suspects when they were pulled over for questioning. Some Police cars have three cameras mounted on their roofs. These are linked to a computer installed in the front dashboard of the car which in turn is linked to a Police database of unregistered, stolen, or suspect vehicles. The electronic gadgetry can scan a handful of number plates a second or up to 1500 a day. Two small aerials were also mounted on the rear parcel shelf of the car. In the front driver's area, instead of what could be one GPS screen atop the centre console, there were two. One was a monitor for the roof mounted cameras and the second was a special scanner and decoder of internet signals which were fed into a laptop on the front passenger side.

"Okay, I have Daniel Green's car on the left. His registration checks out," Constable Crouch said. "So that's his place alright."

"Brian, switch on the scanner so we can go phishing," Senior Constable Gaze said.

"Okay boss."

Gaze drove slowly up the small cul-de-sac and followed the curve of the road as it formed a half-circle and then pulled over two houses away from the Green's.

"Hey, you're not going to believe this," Crouch said.

"What?"

"I count eight houses in this cul-de-sac and six of them are accessing the State Parliament website. This is unbelievable!"

"You've got to be kidding. Check the scanner again."

Crouch tapped his screen and then confirmed all the leads were in place behind the scanner. A shiver went up his spine and his eyes bulged as they saw web address after web address with the same coding.

"Boss, hang on I'm getting two other websites being looked at."

"Don't keep me in suspense. Which ones? Porn? Games? Gambling. I'll lay odds they're porn sites."

"This doesn't add up. I think we better get out of here," Crouch said with a noticeable change in his voice.

"Why?"

"The other two sites are our State Police sites. Something is wrong here. This would have to be …."

Before Crouch could finish his sentence two marked State Police cars and one Federal Police car drove into the street. One State Police car blocked the entrance to the street by turning his car side-on and put on his flashing lights to bar any vehicle from entering or leaving. Four armed uniformed Police wearing flak jackets and brandishing handguns entered the cul-de-sac from the turnaround point where a walkway to the next street was situated and headed towards the rear of the unmarked Police car. Two State and two Federal Police officers, also wearing flak jackets with pistols in their hands, alighted from their cars and ran towards the unmarked Police car. A State Police Officer with a TV type camera on his right shoulder followed the action as his confreres bailed up Crouch and Gaze who were ordered from their car and made to lie face down on the grass verge.

One of the State Police who arrived on foot from the walkway, leant into the unmarked black Police car and turned off its camera before nodding to his boss. Residents started coming out of their houses to watch the action and take photos of all the activity. Daniel yelled to Kit and Leah to join him on their front porch where they watched Gaze and Crouch being pat searched while they lay face down on the grass.

"You know Leah, those two blokes on the ground look awfully like the cops who pulled me over and made me lie on the grass," Daniel said as a huge smile came across his face.

Leah put her arm around her husband's waist and started smiling. "Well, it looks like they got their comeuppance."

Daniel went to say something to Kit but noticed his son taking photos of the Police action and held back.

Kit looked at his father and smiled. "I think this evens the score."

"No, we're one up," Daniel said. "Remember, after they nabbed me you were instrumental in having West's people nabbed at Terry's place. Now the ball is back in Ratcliffe's court."

"Yeah, you're right, but our journey is not over yet."

Daniel turned to Kit and saw his son with a whimsical look on his face. "You know something don't you?"

Kit chuckled. "Yes. While I was resting upstairs, I practiced my guided visualisation and met David."

"Your what? Oh yeah. What did he say?"

"Dad, I don't want to talk about it here," Kit said as he nodded his head towards the Police action a few doors away from his home.

"Sorry mate. I understand."

Daniel watched as neighbours edged their way closer to the unmarked car to try and hear what was being said. Uniformed Police stopped the neighbours getting too close but not before one of them took a few photos of the inside of the car and its electronic array. Daniel's mobile phone started vibrating in his pocket. He pulled out his phone and saw Graham Moon's photo ID as the caller.

"Hi mate," Daniel said.

"I understand you have some high drama happening in your street," Moon said with a mocking tone.

"How the hell do you …"

"Daniel look up to the laneway entrance and you'll see a lone person with a mobile phone to his ear."

"Yes, is he a cop too?"

"No, he's one of my staffers who has kept me informed on what's happening. Very shortly you should … ah here they come now."

"What? Who?"

Daniel looked at the entrance to his street and saw what looked like an unmarked Police car and a TV outside broadcast van arrive. A newspaper photographer: Journalist and a TV videographer alighted from their respective vehicles and started filming and taking photos of the Police scrum up the road.

"I take it you had the news crews on standby, Graham?" Daniel asked.

"Yeah. You could say West tipped his hand which allowed us to capture the moment. When this has cleared from your street, we need to meet so I can talk with you, Terry and Reg."

"Okay mate. I'll talk with you soon."

Leah looked at Daniel, smiled and nodded. She tightened the grip around her husband's waist.

"Well, this will be something our neighbours and us will be talking about for some time."

"Yeah love … you can bet on that."

Kit ventured out his front gate to take photos of the two police officers on the ground. When he started getting too close a uniformed officer directed him to stand back and go back to his house. The lad wanted to argue about the indignity his father had to go through in public, so how come it was different for these two Police … but he changed his mind. He went for a walk towards the laneway and saw a young man aged in his twenties taking photos of the scene with a mobile phone camera.

"Hi, get any good shots?" Kit asked.

"Yeah, I got them being handcuffed and beginning to lie on the ground."

"Good stuff. My name's Kit, I live a few houses down the road."

A smile came over the young man as he eyed Kit. "Hello Kit Green, I'm Barney Haggarty. I work for Graham Moon."

Kit was initially stunned as he heard a stranger mention his name. However, when he heard Graham Moon's name mentioned the teenager relaxed and shook Haggarty's hand.

"Nice to meet you. How did you know about this little piece of action?"

"You could say we were tipped off, but I'll let my boss explain it to your father," Haggarty said as he continued to watch the Police action.

"Any chance of a copy of some of the photos you've taken here?"

"On one condition, Kit. You send me a copy of yours."

"Done."

The two exchanged e-mail addresses and shook hands again before Kit headed back to his home. He knew his father wanted to talk with him some more about Commissioner Ratcliffe. Leah and Daniel had already retreated into their lounge room away from the view of any Media cameras. Within a few moments of Kit walking into his front yard the two Police officers on the ground were stood up and taken to a Federal Police car with Kit capturing the moment on his camera. The State Police car guarding the entrance to Kit's Street moved off and parked correctly at the kerb allowing the Federal Police car to leave. A State Police officer drove the unmarked black car away and was quickly flanked by the remaining Police cars, leaving only the Media crews working the houses in the street to see who would speak up about what had happened.

Daniel had a very good rapport with his neighbours and

every so often they would hold street barbecues that would last hours. Once he received a call from Moon about the approaching undercover Police crew, he quickly phoned his neighbours and helped set up the "sting" where each of the neighbours were logged into the Parliament or the Police websites. He also cautioned his neighbours about speaking to the Media in case they also became victims. The Media crews went knocking on the front door of each house in the cul-de-sac without success. The neighbours had closed ranks and told the Media they needed to talk to the Police for information.

When the Media first arrived on site an officer from the State Police said a statement would be issued later from Police Headquarters. He would not be filmed saying it. Once the houses in Kit's street had been door knocked by the TV film crew and they did a stand-up piece to camera, they left.

"Here you go Dad," Kit said as he gave his father a photo printed on A4 paper from his computer.

Daniel smirked and then laughed as he looked closely at Kit's photo.

"Well done, Kit. This photo is worth its weight in gold. You've got a photo a lot of Media would love to have – the moment of arrest. A cop arrested by a cop. Nice shot son."

"I've got some more coming from Barney, so I'll send you a file."

"Who's Barney?"

"Barney Haggarty – he works for Graham Moon."

It was Leah's turn to laugh as she looked at both of her boys.

"Like father, like son. Where did you meet him, Kit?"

"He was standing at the laneway entrance taking photos. I went there after being shooed away by the cops from the main action. I started to introduce myself and he finished the introduction and said he worked for Mr. Moon. We decided to swap photos."

Daniel shook his head and smiled.

"That's my boy. How sure are you this Barney works for Mr. Moon?"

"Because his e-mail was the state office in Parliament which was the same as Mr. Moon's."

"Okay. No probs. Just ensuring he wasn't another rogue cop. Now, what else is coming our way?"

Kit hesitated a moment before answering his father as he thought of the best way to say the answer. Daniel and Leah looked intensely at Kit but waited for their son to answer. The lad sat on a lounge chair, got comfortable and then looked at his parents.

"Before the cops were arrested outside our home I did some meditation in my bedroom – you know, like Mrs. Bishop taught me."

"Was this some sort of trip in your mind where you meet up with your spirit friends?" Leah asked.

Kit laughed. "Yes, sort of. I have to calm myself right down and then take myself on a sort of trip using my mind."

"Okay. What happened," Daniel asked with a tinge of anxiety in his voice.

"I met up with David at a hill overlooking the lushest of valleys and we seemed to have talked for hours. I guess, it was only a few minutes."

"Did David have much to say?" Daniel asked.

"Yeah. He told me what was about to happen with the cops outside. I guess it was like you being told by Mr. Moon to organise the neighbours with their internet links."

"Did he tell you about any threats involving me?"

Kit looked hard at his dad as he evaluated what he was about to say.

"Oh yeah, he said Ratcliffe will still try and come after you and for you to be wary of strangers around you."

"Did he give any other details about Ratcliffe?"

"No."

"Thanks Kit. I'll keep a sharp eye out. Now I better ring Graham and see what the latest is with these cops."

Daniel went to his back verandah and used his mobile phone to ring Graham Moon. He wanted to know whether any move had been made against West or Ratcliffe. He dialled Moon's number. Within seconds Moon's deep voice came through the phone.

"Daniel we've certainly stirred up a hornet's nest."

"Hi mate. How so?"

"Once the State cops were arrested and news leaked out, State Police Headquarters went into damage control. The Internal Affairs people went looking for West, but he can't be found. Now the attention will turn to Ratcliffe to see what he knew about the illegal tapping into your internet and who ordered it."

"Graham, thanks to your warning call it gave me enough time to organise the web surfing efforts of my neighbours. They were all delighted to help, especially after how I was 'mistakenly arrested' in peak hour traffic and forced to lie on the grass while I was handcuffed and searched. Several of them actually saw the event but never realised it was me."

"Sometimes revenge is sweet. Daniel, I'll keep you updated. I'd suggest you ring Terry and see if he needs anything."

"Okay, thanks mate."

Daniel rang Terry Sullivan to see what he knew of events involving West's men. The two talked for a couple of minutes and arranged for Daniel to go to Sullivan's place to do some work. Leah handed Daniel a cup of tea and said he had time to drink it before rushing off. Daniel agreed and joined Leah and Kit in the kitchen, sitting at the breakfast bar and sipping his hot brew. Within a few minutes he started to get up and Kit reached forward to grab his cup and saucer to take it to the sink with his own.

"Thanks Kit. Leah, I should be home in a few hours."

"Okay love. See you soon."

Daniel picked up his laptop and made his way through the house to his car and drove off to meet Sullivan. Kit placed his father's cup upside down on the saucer and turned it three times clockwise before picking it up. Leah watched silently. Kit tilted his father's cup in a couple of different directions. His face was a portrait of study as he gazed into the cup and looked at the various combinations of tea leaves. He nodded, pursed his lips and then returned the cup to the saucer before looking ahead into middle space.

"Well … does your father win the lottery?"

"No mum," Kit said as his face relaxed into a smile. "But I think he may be getting a new job."

"What makes you think that?"

"Just the way the leaves form what looks like a briefcase. Here have a look." Kit picked up his father's cup and showed his mother the unmistakable shape of a briefcase. He then rinsed the three cups under the kitchen sink.

"Well, I hope he enjoys it."

"It will be interesting to see what happens."

Kit was feeling uneasy and went back to his bedroom. He thought more of what he saw in his father's cup. Among the leaves Kit believed he also saw the shape of a handgun and the chequered band associated with Police. He checked his e-mails and found that Barney Haggarty had sent him several photos of the Police activity outside his home. Kit sent Barney a copy of the photos he had taken. He then picked up his mobile phone and sent his father a text message asking if he could stay at the Sullivans this weekend coming. Daniel had not long arrived at Sullivan's place when his mobile phone vibrated.

"So, you want Reg and I to work with you this Saturday to complete the Media work regarding who your party wants at the helm of each of the Departments if you win Government?" Daniel asked as he looked at his phone but spoke to Terry Sullivan.

"Well, we could ..."

Daniel put his hand up to cut Sullivan off as he looked at the message on his mobile phone and smiled.

"Would you like a young house guest this weekend?"

Sullivan narrowed his eyes and turned his head slightly as he took in what Daniel was saying.

"Who are you offering?"

"The text message was from Kit asking if he could be allowed to stay here this weekend."

"That's pretty uncanny. We hadn't even finished discussing you and Reg coming to work on Saturday at my office and your son asks to stay here. I know Betty would be really pleased to have Kit here, but I couldn't spend much time with him on Saturday as the three of us will have a bit of work to get through."

"Up to you mate. Do you want me to turn him off?"

"No. It would be great to have him here from Friday night. This way I can spend more time with him before you return on Saturday. Betty can play housemother for the day before the three of us do something, whatever, on Sunday."

A huge smile came over Sullivan as he mulled over what he had just said. Kit's stay wasn't going to be on the most convenient of weekends – but then again, what weekend is for a politician when an election is looming? Daniel noticed Sullivan lose concentration as he talked to his client about the various issues surrounding West and his snooping Police officers. The more Daniel tried to get into details, the more easily Sullivan became distracted. Daniel knew the Sullivans were really keen to have Kit stay at their home for a weekend, but he didn't know Kit wanted to stay until he received his son's text message. He also thought it was quite funny to see Sullivan so distracted as he tried to discuss the ramifications and fallout from the arrest of the Police who tried to snoop on him. The two men worked out Media strategies in relation to the arrests and if West was found.

"Daniel, I think that's as far as we can go until something

happens," Sullivan said as he reached into his refrigerator for two cold beers.

"I think we're organised," Daniel said with a large smile.

"What? What's up?"

"I haven't seen you so nervous in a long while and it has nothing to do with the Police. Does it?" Daniel said.

Sullivan squirmed and bit his upper lip as he glanced up at the top of the refrigerator at the photo of him and David fishing.

"Ever since Betty and I met Kit and he showed us David's greeting and found my favourite photo, we have been looking forward to having him stay over. The kid's a force to be reckoned with but a lovable character we'd like to spoil, that is if his mum and dad can spare him for two days?"

"I'll speak with Leah. I can't see a problem as it will give us all a break and I know Kit has been looking forward to being here with you. Ever since his pool accident, it seems all roads have led Kit to here."

"What do you mean?"

"Well since the accident and his near-death experience, the boy has undergone several changes. We all saw some of those at our dinner here and then when the first two of West's people were caught trying to snoop on us in the adjoining backyard. Now that two more of West's people have been arrested Kit wants to return here and stay for a weekend."

"I think you are reading too much into it."

"He's uncanny at times. I guess that's the issue. No parent could ask for a better son."

"Well, Betty and I thought the same about David and after a

decade of letting go we find ourselves drawn emotionally back to the son who was killed in a car crash. Your son is pivotal here, which is one of the reasons why we would like him to stay with us."

Daniel looked at Sullivan and guessed the time was right to give him an update.

"One of the things a Medium we know has been doing with Kit is what is called guided visualisations."

"What the hell is that?"

"Imagine lying or sitting down in your most comfortable position. In your mind's eye taking a journey wherever you feel comfortable and then resting somewhere there is a beautiful spot to observe. Now imagine at this spot you meet up with your spirit friend or even David."

"What a load of poppycock!"

"Okay, but Kit will tell you this is what he has done to meet up with David twice and to be told certain things that were about to happen."

Sullivan almost choked on his beer. He was about to speak but stopped, closed his mouth, and thought for a few moments.

"Doesn't David just appear to Kit and talk with him – you know like you see in the movies?"

"Terry, this is the conversation you will need to have with Kit. David has apparently appeared a couple of times to Kit in his bedroom. And also now a couple of times in his guided visualisations."

"This will be an interesting weekend."

"Mate, look for when Kit starts rubbing his neck and then going vacant in his expression."

"Why?"

"This is when he has felt spirits about to talk to him and then he has a conversation with them as if they were real people standing in front of him."

"I remember what he did to Graham Moon. That was scary – knowing exactly what his mother was buried in and what he had privately asked her at her graveside. Those I'll never forget. When Kit told Graham that story, I had shivers running up my back."

"Well, open it further. I'll bet none of the three couples that shared a barbecue with you recently slept much after Kit demonstrated his signs from David to you or helped you find your lost photo. I know Leah and I were asking a lot of questions to mid-morning."

Sullivan started to have moist eyes and shook his head slowly.

"You know Daniel, Betty and I had no real belief in the afterlife or a God until our barbecue. What Kit showed Betty and I that night and then subsequently with Graham Moon and the first cops found snooping, was positively breathtaking. Betty and I have now reconciled there is an afterlife where we all go when we die. Also, that there is a God, otherwise your beautiful son couldn't communicate with David and show us mere mortals that Angels do exist."

"Thanks Terry. Please remember Kit is just a teenage boy trying to expand his mind and body. He has a lot of learning to do."

"I know, but he has helped raise so many questions for me about life and death."

"Maybe you need to meet Niva Bishop, the Medium Kit has been working with to develop his talents and help him understand what has happened to him."

"That would be great Daniel. Once the election is out of the way, I'd like nothing better than to sit down with this woman and expand my mind about life and death."

"I'll organise. Okay, I'd better be getting back so I can arrange with Leah for you to have your guest tomorrow night for this weekend."

Terry put his beer down and gave Daniel a big hug. He hung onto him tightly for a few moments. Daniel returned the hug and then released his political client. He looked intently and silently at Sullivan's eyes and nodded.

"Thanks mate, I needed that," Sullivan said.

"I know. You have changed and it's for the better."

Daniel drove home with more questions in his mind than when he arrived. Most of them involved Kit and the effect he had had on people since his near-death experience. The rest were about West and Ratcliffe and where the current Internal Affairs probe would lead the Opposition and Government.

Chapter Nineteen

Some loyalties were hard to shake. Inspector Joe West was thankful of this when he had a quick phone call from one of his former protégés now working in Internal Affairs on Friday morning. The call alerted him his offsiders had been arrested and there was a warrant out for his arrest. West was a balding man who built strong loyalties with the people who worked for him. He had a stout build and a moustache, but a crooked smile. The left side of his mouth didn't seem to open as far as the right-hand side when he smiled. He had trained his officers to always have a getaway bag handy at home in case they were called at the last minute to go on jobs anywhere in the State. The bag contained a change of civilian clothes; toiletries, coffee, long lasting milk, a mug, filled water bottle, toilet paper and some money. Once West received the call from his former protégé he quickly went home, changed clothes, picked up his passport, getaway bag and caught a taxi to the airport. Within two hours he was jetting out on his way to Indonesia where no treaty existed to return people through extradition. A number of times West had gone on holidays to a southern island archipelago in Indonesia. On his last trip he bought a small bungalow there. His decision to flee so quickly caught the Federal Police by surprise as they had not notified airports of West's warrant and the Inspector slipped their net.

West had been a bully at school and ended up being the "bovver boy" of Ratcliffe when his classmate became Police Commissioner. Ratcliffe had kept West's outfit out of reach of the Government with most Police not even knowing it existed. Terry Sullivan and a young boy called Kit Green had changed all that. He only found out about Kit after his first two officers were caught snooping at an adjoining property to Sullivan's. The only thing West could point to that gave his officers up was a quiet conversation Kit was filmed having with his father and Graham Moon when they left Sullivan's house. West knew something had spooked the boy but he didn't know what or how he somehow knew the group was being taped through advanced electronic gadgetry. He wanted the boy's secret – if in fact he had one. West was further humiliated when he sent two officers around to the Green's street to try and capture what they were downloading off the web. When West was told all the neighbours were either viewing the Parliament's website or that of his police force, he knew Daniel had to be involved but couldn't put his finger on how so many people were tipped off. West remained puzzled and perplexed over the situation.

Two unmarked Police cars glided to a stop outside the two-story mansion of Todd Ratcliffe in the Friday afternoon sun. Two men in suits and carrying clipboards alighted from the first vehicle while two uniformed Police stepped out of the second car. The uniformed Police wore flak jackets and were armed with Glock pistols. These officers stayed near the cars and watched the entrance to Ratcliffe's house. The other two made their way up the path and verandah leading to the front door. Chief Inspector David Caughey was a tall man. He had a long face and mouse-grey coloured hair but was very fit and agile. Sergeant Greg Cootes was stocky and shorter but just as agile and fit as his boss. Caughey rang the doorbell and stepped back. He wasn't sure if the reception he was about to receive from the State's Police Commissioner would be genteel.

Ratcliffe opened the door and looked at the two men standing before him for a few seconds. There was a look of fright in the Commissioner's eyes as he stared the two officers up and down and saw the two uniformed officers in his front yard.

"Commissioner, I'm Chief Inspector David Caughey and this is Sergeant Greg Cootes. We're from Police Internal Affairs and we need to discuss some matters with you."

Caughey paused while Ratcliffe took in what was happening before he answered.

"Gents come in, we can go into the living room," Ratcliffe said as he held the door open for the two visitors. He then walked ahead of them down his hallway and into his expansive living room.

"I believe you know my lawyer, Jeff Maxwell – he used to be the department's senior lawyer before returning to private practice," Ratcliffe said with a sneer.

The three other men shook hands and then sat down on a lounge and lounge chairs.

"Mr. Ratcliffe, we need to discuss with you some events concerning Inspector Graham West and some civilians including a Daniel Green, Reg Clementson and the State Member for Banksia Cove, Terry Sullivan."

The interview lasted more than an hour with Caughey and Cootes leaving with a feeling they were the ones who had been ambushed. Ratcliffe was on notice he could be stood down if the Internal Affairs investigation moved to him.

"Todd, at this stage you don't have much to worry about as West must have flown the coop or Caughey would have had him by now," Maxwell said.

"That mongrel West! I know he didn't set me up but if Internal Affairs can't find him, he's left me holding the bag. It's virtually the same thing."

"Mate we must ensure if there is any fall out that West becomes the scapegoat. If there is even a scintilla of evidence you have been involved, the Premier will direct you to step aside while you are investigated. Then, if the enquiry finds you guilty, you could actually face jail time."

"I think the Premier will ask me to step aside now while Internal Affairs does its bit."

Ratcliffe had gone an ashen white colour in the face. He was enraged that West's activity had led Internal Affairs to him. The Commissioner also knew he would be watched, and his phone monitored. He picked up a glass ashtray and hurled it to the floor smashing it into a thousand pieces. He formed fists with his hands and brought them up to his waist while his stare went vacant. This was not the sort of exit the Commissioner had wanted. Maxwell got out of his chair and put his arm on his friend's shoulder. Ratcliffe snapped his head in Maxwell's direction and snorted.

"Todd, calm down mate, we can sort this."

Ratcliffe lowered his fists and nodded. He had made his mind up as to what to do and who should pay for his ignominy. Sullivan would pay the ultimate price and his Public Affairs guru Green would share the same fate for the way he turned the community against him and had two of West's Officers arrested.

"Jeff thanks. I'm fine now. It's just that this was never meant to happen. West was doing his own work, but it has spilled over to me and now I'm the one who is the criminal."

"It was lucky I dropped in today with your superannuation papers. It seemed to shake up Caughey and Cootes that I was here."

"Yes, they must have thought I knew something was going to happen and had you here waiting … well, better they think that."

"Okay Todd, I'll get these papers sorted for you. If there are any developments regarding West, let me know and I'll represent you."

"Thanks Jeff, I appreciate that."

Ratcliffe saw Maxwell out and returned to his lounge room. He saw the slivers of glass sparkling in the light on the floor where the ashtray was smashed. Ratcliffe stood motionless for a few moments looking at the glass and then into empty space. He had to put a stop to Sullivan and Green. If he organised someone else to murder the politician and his offsider the chances were the job could be botched. This was a job he had to do himself. The Commissioner went to his drinks cabinet and poured himself a whiskey, put some ice cubes into the glass and took a sip. He walked outside to his wife's rose garden while he sipped his drink and thought about Ellen.

Ratcliffe had killed two criminals in the line of duty when he was a younger cop. Two men in their 30s had robbed a convenience store and held the store owner hostage. Ratcliffe and his partner were the first Police on the scene after the store's silent alarm had been tripped. While Ratcliffe went to the rear of the store his partner went to the front to try and calm the situation.

The store owner was being held in a half-nelson wrestling hold by one of the robbers and had a handgun held to his head. The robber was demanding the combination to the store's safe to get the weekend's takings and the store owner was starting to have a fit because of the shock of what was happening and the belief he would be killed. The second robber looked up from the shop's aisles and saw a lone cop about to enter the store and panicked. He moved backwards and tripped on some packing sending him towards the floor. In his fall he accidentally squeezed off a shot from his handgun which hit the ceiling. Ratcliffe had manoeuvred into the rear of the store and was an aisle away from the robber who fell when he heard a shot. He quickly ran to where the fallen robber was and saw the man pointing his handgun at him. Ratcliffe fired two shots that killed the man instantly. The second robber pushed the shop keeper away and raised his weapon towards Ratcliffe. It was the last move he made. Ratcliffe fell to the floor and on the way down pumped two bullets into the robber's head. The force of the shots flung the man back into the shop's front window smashing it into a thousand pieces of glass and leaving the man half in the store and half out facing upwards. He had two bullet holes in his forehead. The shopkeeper went into an epileptic fit on the floor and foamed at the mouth, banging and thrashing around until an ambulance arrived.

Ratcliffe was decorated for saving the life of the shopkeeper and this helped accelerate his climb up the Police ranks. The day's events in the store never left Ratcliffe – especially how easy it was for a fit, trained person to kill two criminals. As he strolled around his garden and touched the roses his wife so dearly loved, he contemplated how he would solve the conundrum of Sullivan and Green. Ratcliffe had known since the last State Government election how poor the Government's ratings were in the community. The Government had been in power for 16 years and was tired. There had been a resurgence of popularity in the Opposition which meant he and several other Departmental heads faced the axe so the Opposition could appoint who it liked to work with. Commissioner Todd Ratcliffe wasn't one of them. Ratcliffe bent down to smell the scent of a rose and went to pull the flower towards him to sniff it when he gripped a thorn. He quickly let the flower go but it was too late. The thorn had pierced his thumb and a drop of blood appeared at the puncture point. The image of his dead wife came into his head when his thumb was pricked.

"Damn you, Ellen. I know what I'm doing," Ratcliffe said as he stood up and sucked the blood from his thumb. He then walked into his house and to his bathroom where he applied a small adhesive bandage strip to his thumb. Ratcliffe returned to his lounge room, swept up the glass from the ashtray and then rummaged through several files on his desk.

"Ah, here it is," Ratcliffe thought as he pulled open a file with a report on West's officers being caught snooping on Sullivan and his associates. He had read the report once before but wanted to refresh his memory. West said his team couldn't explain how they were found out. A review of the film taken of Sullivan, Moon, Reg, Daniel, and Kit in the car park revealed no one pointing to the team. The only incidental movement was Kit leaning in to talk to his father and then the group going back inside the house for a few minutes.

"So what spooked the boy, that's the real issue," Ratcliffe said out aloud.

The only thing he could think of was any glinting of light on the front of the cameras the teenager may have seen in the spaces between the fence palings. He wrote down some notes and went to his bedroom where he changed into dark clothes. Ratcliffe went to his walk-in wardrobe and pulled up the edge of carpet near a wall which allowed it to be eased away from the floor. He tugged on a recessed lug and lifted up a lid. Like his confrere West, he too kept a getaway bag. Old habits were hard to break. He opened his bag and rummaged through it to check for his handgun and a metal cylinder. First, he checked the weapon was empty then slowly he wound the cylinder onto the end of the gun's barrel. He found two full magazines of bullets and loaded one into the gun. The second, he put in his pocket. He was now ready to silence Sullivan once and for all. If he got Green too, it would be a bonus. The pair's demise would put a hold on any change of Departmental head, including him, until the Opposition sorted itself out and elected a new Shadow Minister to take over. The delay would allow him to get the dirt on the replacement and try and set him up so Ratcliffe had him in his pocket – not the other way around.

Ratcliffe sat quietly in his lounge room and studied the files on his coffee table waiting for night fall. In the subdued light he could easily have been mistaken for a black costumed hero from a bygone era minus the flat squat hat, mask, and sword. He was almost ready to go.

Leah agreed for Kit to spend the weekend with the Sullivans and had bought Kit a new action DVD so he could watch it with the Sullivans in their theatrette. The Greens' plan for the weekend was simple – Daniel was to drop Kit off on Friday night so the lad could spend time with the Sullivans, and he could take Leah out to dinner. On Saturday morning Daniel would team up with Reg and Terry for a few hours to iron out the last of the Opposition's Media campaign. Daniel didn't think this meeting would last too long as Sullivan would be keen to get home and spend time with Kit before he was picked up late on Sunday.

"Looking forward to the weekend Kit?" Leah asked as her son came rushing in through the front door after spending the day at school.

"Sure am. It'll be good to get to know David's parents and spend some time with them," the teenager said as he rubbed his neck. "What time is Dad dropping me off?"

"Your father will be home within the hour, so you'll need your bag packed and be ready to go then."

"Okay, the bag's pretty much packed. I just need a towel and some toiletries."

"Don't worry about a towel. I'm sure the Sullivans will have plenty of them. I've got something for you to share with the Sullivans tonight or tomorrow night."

Kit walked over to his mother, and she gave him the DVD she bought that day.

"Oh, great mum. I hope the Sullivans like action stuff."

"I'd be pretty sure they would like anything you like this weekend."

Kit broke out in a large cheesy smile and gave his mother a kiss.

"Thank you."

"No probs. You better get changed now."

"Okay."

Kit turned and started climbing up the stairs with the DVD in one hand, his other hand rubbing his neck. His smile turned to a grimace as he looked up at the top of the stairs. Initially he thought David may have been waiting for him in his bedroom because of the tingling on his neck. However, this tingling was more urgent and demanding. The teenager rushed up the stairs and flung open his bedroom door. There was no one there. He closed the door, took off his backpack and sat on his bed to think about what was happening. Within a few moments the shimmering image of a middle-aged woman with long hair stood before him and his tingling stopped.

"Hello Ellen," Kit said as the tingling on his neck subsided.

"Hello Kit."

"I take it something is about to happen involving my dad?" Kit asked as he sat up.

"Yes," Ellen said as her shimmer became stronger. "The

Commissioner will make his move tonight against your father and you must be brave."

Kit had been lounging on his bed but sat bolt upright when Ellen delivered her message.

"Can you tell me what the Commissioner is going to do and how I can help avoid it?"

"You must confront him. Only then will he back down."

"I'm supposed to be going to the Sullivan's this weekend. Is this where the Commissioner will turn up?"

"Yes, tonight."

"Is he going to kill my father or Mr. Sullivan?"

"Kit, the Commissioner is very angry about Sullivan's work so you must talk him out of his actions."

"What can I say that will stop a Police Commissioner from trying to kill my father?"

"Tell him you know he pricked his thumb in my rose garden today and blamed me for it. Also tell him you know about the ashtray – this will get his attention."

"What happened with the ash tray?"

"He smashed it on the floor of his lounge room today after Police Internal Affairs had been to see him."

"Is there a message I can give him from you that only he knows about?"

"Yes – tell him our daughter is with me."

"What do you mean? What daughter?"

"He will know."

Ellen's shimmer began to fade and within seconds she was gone. Kit was scared as this was the showdown with Ratcliffe foretold by both David and Ellen. The lives of both Sullivan and his father could hang in the balance if he didn't act properly and decisively. He sat back on his bed for a moment and tried to calm himself. Kit smiled when he remembered what David had said to him the last time, he met him on the hill. The teenager sprang up, got changed into casual clothes and packed his toiletries bag into his overnight bag, along with his action DVD. He sat on his computer chair and began to smell coal burning. The clip clop sounds of horses pulling carriages also came into his mind and he knew Thomas was letting him know he was around.

"Thank you, my spirit guide. I knew I could rely on you," Kit said nervously to Thomas. "So, now I know where the event is going to happen and roughly when. I need to tell Dad and forewarn him without letting mum know, otherwise she will panic and try and stop Dad and I going."

Kit took his overnight bag downstairs to wait for his father. He mentally re-traced the last guided visualisation he did where he met up with David on the hill. The teenager believed this conversation was the second half of how to save his father and Sullivan.

Leah noticed nervousness about Kit, and she misinterpreted this as her son concerned with staying with the Sullivans. Kit loved his mother and did not want to worry her about what he and his father must do. He sat on the front porch and waited for his father to arrive. Within a short while Daniel rounded the corner into the cul-de-sac in the family car and tooted his horn as he saw Kit sitting on the porch.

"That's my boy – ready early and keen to go," Daniel said to himself.

Kit went back inside the house and kissed his mother goodbye and gave her a strong hug.

"Have a great time Kit," Leah said. "Relax and just be yourself."

"I will thanks. Have a great time with Dad this weekend."

"We'll miss you."

"I'll miss you too."

Kit then picked up his bag and ran down the stairs to his father's car. Daniel got out of the car and waved to Leah.

"I won't be long – see you soon," Daniel said as he waved again to Leah and got back in the car. He looked at Kit and a strange feeling came over him.

"You know something, don't you?"

"Yes, and we need to go back to that public phone you used before to ring Mr. Moon."

Daniel nodded and a serious look came over his face as he drove away slowly. He drove the car around the cul-de-sac and the pair waved again as they went past their home and saw Leah on the porch.

"Okay mate what's going on," Daniel said in a very controlled voice.

Kit was nervous and his eyes were moist as he thought about what he was going to say.

"Dad, Ellen came to see me when I got home from school today and told me the Commissioner will be at the Sullivan's tonight."

"Bastard! Won't that man ever learn? What else did she say?"

"She gave me a message to give him and said I had to be the one to face him."

"I don't think so. If he's out to kill Terry or me, there's no way you will be involved. In fact, I should just call Terry now and call off this weekend for you and organise some protection for us both."

"Dad don't do it, please. I know you find it very hard for me to be telling you I see and speak to the spirits of dead people. I also know you find it hard to cope with the actions of the Commissioner and his bad cops."

"Kit, I don't want to lose you or have you lose me. Hell, your mother, and I fought hard enough to have you and then look after you following your accident. We fought to keep you on this Earth."

"Dad, I know, and I love you and mum very much. Maybe this will be a rite of passage for me," Kit said with a noticeable tremble in his voice. "David told me this will all work out."

"When did you see him? Did he come to you today as well?"

"No. When I last saw him in my guided visualisation, we had a long talk and he told me how tonight would roughly play out."

"Roughly? That's all your all-knowing spirit friend could say?"

"Dad, if we don't stop him at the Sullivan's the Commissioner will come to our place. Is this what you want?"

Daniel bit on his bottom lip and thought through everything Kit had said. His mind raced as he fought for a solution. He saw a public telephone on the side of the road and pulled over.

"Alright, we will play it the way David and Ellen have seen it, but I want some added protection. I'll just make a few calls."

Daniel got out of the car and made several phone calls. He was animated in his actions but very controlled. Within eight minutes he headed back to his vehicle and a nervous son.

"Okay mate we're organised," Daniel said as he put his arm on Kit's shoulder and gave a gentle squeeze.

"What do you mean?"

"Mrs. Sullivan will be having dinner at our home tonight with your mum. Mr. Sullivan and I will have dinner at his place."

"Won't the women be upset about this as their plans have been turned upside down?"

"Yes and no. If all goes to plan, we'll organise something special for them very shortly."

"Did you ring Mr. Moon so he could get some Police?"

"Yes – I spoke with Graham, and he's sorted. Let's go and have tea with Mr. Sullivan and get prepared."

"Alright. I trust whatever you have just organised, Dad."

Daniel looked at Kit and saw his son calming his breathing and focus. He wished he had started some calming sessions with Mrs. Bishop as his heart was racing and his mind was in overdrive. He was ready for a fight and had to protect his son at all costs. The last thing he wanted was for Ratcliffe to go to his home and for Leah to be involved. The fallout could be catastrophic. The drive to the Sullivans took around 30 minutes, yet in Daniel's mind it took hours. He drove through the open gates leading to the Sullivan house and pulled into the visitor's car space. Before Daniel and Kit could alight from the car Terry Sullivan had exited his front door to meet them.

“Hi gents,” Sullivan said as he did a small look around.

“Hi Terry.”

“G’day Mr. Sullivan.”

Sullivan shook hands with Daniel and then went to the passenger side of the car where Kit was retrieving his overnight bag. A huge smile came over Sullivan as he shook hands with Kit and gave him a hug.

“It’s great to see you both – especially you young man. Come on through.”

Sullivan showed his guests into his home and closed the door. He took them into his kitchen.

“Kit, do you want to put your bag in David’s … I mean your room?”

“No probs. Thanks Mr. Sullivan.”

“Terry this will be a hard night,” Daniel said as he sat on one of the breakfast bar stools.

“I know and I’m sorry I have dragged both you and Kit into this. Ratcliffe’s removal must happen as the man is nothing but a crook.”

“Any word on West?”

“No. He seems to have either vanished or just gone to ground somewhere out of reach. The Feds have put a warrant out for his arrest and alerted all airlines, airports and shipping ports. We’ll get him.”

“Let’s hope so. He has a tale to tell.”

“The arrest of his officers outside your home was poetic justice. I wish I could have been there.”

“Well, it was a sight to behold when the good guys came bursting up the street and bottled-up West’s men so they couldn't escape. It gave me a renewed feeling of faith in the justice system."

Kit made his way to David's room and put his bag down on the bed and looked around.

"Well, I hope you are right," Kit said aloud. "I don't mind telling you I'm scared. However, as Mrs. Bishop has taught me, I have faith in you and the universe, and I stand ready."

He walked back downstairs and re-joined his father and Sullivan. The two men were organising cups of coffee.

"Kit, would you like a coffee or a soft drink?" Sullivan asked'

"I think I could go a soft drink if that's okay Mr. Sullivan."

"Yeah mate. In the fridge there's several cans – take your choice."

"Thanks."

Kit grabbed a can of drink and joined the two men at the breakfast bar. He saw the nervousness in the faces of both men.

"I'm glad you could make it this weekend Kit. It will be good to have a young person in the house again."

"Thank you."

"Alright team, we'd better plan our tactics as to how we will face Ratcliffe and what we'll do."

Kit looked around the kitchen and noticed the security cameras watching the front gate, front and rear yards were all working.

"Good to see you've got the cameras all working," Kit said as he motioned to the camera monitors on a bench.

"After you were last here, Betty and I decided to ensure all the cameras were working. I guess we made it in time."

"Do they record as well as monitor?"

"Yes. They all have a timeline running on them and now record 24/7."

Kit looked around the kitchen and saw several stuffed toys including a teddy bear on shelves. His eyes zoomed in on the bear and Sullivan smiled. He was about to say something, and Sullivan shook his head slightly. Kit understood and said nothing. Daniel sipped his coffee and checked out the monitors. He was still worried as to how this night would play out.

"Have you heard back from Graham and what he has organised?" Daniel asked.

"Yes. Several Federal Police and State Internal Affairs Police have taken up or will shortly take up positions in yards around this house except where we saw West's men."

"The cops are forming a channel for Ratcliffe, so he has a clear run to the house from where the cops were with the listening devices. Once he enters my grounds, they should pounce on him."

"What if he gets through the net and comes into the house?" Kit asked, a slight nervousness showing in his voice.

"Well, in that case you must stay out of things and leave it to your father and me to handle him. If he does elude the good guys, try and go outside where the Police can see you."

"Okay will do. What are mum and Mrs. Sullivan doing?"

It was Daniel's time to jump in.

"Mr. Sullivan has arranged for your mum and Mrs. Sullivan to go to the movies, so they'll be fine."

Kit nodded and said he had something for Sullivan in his bag. He went back upstairs to David's room and rummaged in his bag for the DVD. Just as he was about to leave, he felt a strange twinge up his neck and into his head. He mentally asked if David, Ellen, or Thomas were in the room with him and had no reply. Kit looked around the room and saw he was aligned with the centre of David's bedroom window. He then recognised the twinge as the similar one he felt in the backyard of the Sullivan's when he felt the electronic sensors. Kit went to the doorway; turned off the light and closed the door. He then went to the window and looked through it from the side. The view was good as he could see a number of the neighbour's yards. Kit calculated where he had been standing and then looked in the opposite direction out the window. He only saw shadows in the yards and was about to withdraw when one of the shadows glinted. Someone had been looking at him through a scope and moved. Kit went out of the bedroom and down the stairs to where the two men were sitting.

"Get what you wanted?" Daniel asked.

"Yeah, but I just had a weird experience."

"What happened?"

"I was standing in the middle of the bedroom when I felt a twinge or slight pain in my neck. The last time I felt this was the time we were all here for the barbecue and I found the sensors in the backyard."

"It was probably one of the good guys checking on who is in the house," Sullivan said with a grin.

"Well, I turned off the light, closed the door and peeked out the window from the side of the curtain. At first I saw nothing – then something glinted as a person moved."

"Are you sure it was a person and not a domestic pet with dog tags or something," Daniel asked his son.

"The feeling I had was a sensor being aimed at me – no dogs can do that."

Sullivan checked the monitors. "More than likely Kit it was one of the good guys checking to see who was in the house. Remember, these people don't know about your affliction to electronic beams. Now, what did your mum organise for you to bring here?"

"Mum bought a special DVD for me to watch with you and Mrs. Sullivan."

"Great mate, what is it?" Sullivan asked as he checked the monitors again.

"It's an action movie about …"

Before the teenager could answer the question, the kitchen door opened from the rear yard and a tall man in dark clothes and holding a handgun with a silencer attached entered and closed the door. Kit's heart jumped a few beats. Both his father and Sullivan went white when they saw the Police Commissioner in front of them dressed in black and armed.

"Gents don't be alarmed. I thought I'd drop in for a chat," Ratcliffe said as he scanned the room and saw Kit with the men. "Ahh, this is a privilege Kit to have you here too. I understand you helped in the arrest of West's men here recently."

"I don't know what you mean," Kit said as he scanned Ratcliffe and saw the dressing on his thumb.

"Leave the boy out of this," Daniel said as he started walking towards Ratcliffe.

"Green don't be a hero. I'll shoot you in front of Kit within a heartbeat. Now sit down. You too, Sullivan. Kit how did you do it?"

"Do what?"

"How did you know West had people listening and watching you from next door?"

"I had some help."

"Kit don't say anything," Daniel implored.

"One more sound from you and I'll demonstrate the power of this handgun."

"Commissioner, how's your thumb?" Kit asked.

Ratcliffe suddenly became off guard and tried to analyse what Kit would know about his thumb.

"What do you mean?"

"You pricked your thumb in your wife's rose garden this afternoon, didn't you?"

"What? How would you know? Were you there?"

"No. But I know you blamed your wife Ellen when you pricked your thumb."

Ratcliffe's eyes suddenly went wide, and a noticeable tremble could be seen taking hold of the Commissioner.

"I, I don't know what you mean. Who's this Ellen?" Ratcliffe said as he tried to rattle Kit.

"She's the lady you married and who you said died of cancer but had actually had a heart attack."

Sullivan and Daniel looked at each other and then back at Ratcliffe and Kit.

"I've no idea what you're talking about. Okay Sullivan, enough of this rubbish. Why were you trying to …"

Before he could finish Kit piped up again and kept the

attention on him. "I suppose you don't remember throwing a glass ashtray in your house today and smashing it into hundreds of pieces either!" Kit seemed to be on fire as he took control.

"What the … ? How would you know anything? What are you a psychic or something? Now back up and shut your trap or you'll die along with your father. I have some business with your father and his boss."

"I know you buried Ellen in a long blue night dress."

Ratcliffe had now become really rattled as to what Kit was saying. His gun began to wave slightly from side to side as he took in what the lad was saying.

"Mr. Ratcliffe, I know a man from the Minister's office has helped you and West in trying to set up and frame my father and Mr. Sullivan."

Ratcliffe went white. He never expected to be told the things Kit was coming out with. How the hell did this teenage boy know about him pricking his thumb, the ashtray or Elliott. He went to speak when Kit started again with the clincher.

"Mr. Ratcliffe you loved your wife a lot at one stage and you two had a child."

"We what? No one would know anything about that. So shut up!"

"I know the child was a girl and she is dead. She is with your wife Ellen as we speak."

Ratcliffe dropped his gun and clutched his heart as he looked at Kit and then the two men. He fell to the floor and started foaming slightly at the mouth. Within seconds four Police officers dressed in ballistic vests and helmets stormed into the kitchen from the front and rear doors. All had their guns drawn. One went over to Ratcliffe's handgun and kicked it away. Another radioed in the Commissioner was down and an ambulance was needed. Sullivan and Daniel stepped away from the breakfast bar and both hugged Kit who was now crying and visibly upset.

"I killed him. I killed him. I didn't mean to but he was going to shoot you both," Kit sobbed.

"Kit, Kit it's okay. What you said just now had a bigger impact than any bullet ever would," Daniel said as he kissed his son on the forehead. "I'm so proud of you. You did what only the brave dare. Well done."

"Kit, you beat the crooked mongrel with a litany of words which were far more powerful than anything he could have done to us. I think we have a lot to talk about this weekend."

Federal Police agents began swarming into the kitchen and started talking to Sullivan who said Ratcliffe had bailed them up and must have suffered a heart attack in the process. A State Police Officer crouched down and started giving heart compressions to the Commissioner while another used a pencil to pick up his gun and put it into a large plastic bag which he tagged for evidence.

"Mr. Sullivan I'm Federal Police agent Sergeant Len Quirk. We'll need a statement from the three of you," he said.

"Yes, no problems, but it will have to wait until Monday."

"Why is that?"

"This is a very special weekend, and the young boy and I will be spending it together with my wife."

"Alright sir. I'll arrange with Chief Inspector Caughey for you to see him first thing Monday morning at his office."

"No, mine. Parliament sits again next week and my time will be very short."

"Okay sir, I think I can arrange that."

Sullivan, Daniel, and Kit watched as two Ambulance paramedics arrived with a gurney and a defibrillator to try and shock start Ratcliffe's heart. Within a few minutes the Commissioner was breathing properly and was strapped into the gurney and whisked to a private hospital where he was guarded by State Internal Affairs Police.

A Police photographer took photos of the Commissioner as he was being taken away. He then took photos of where he had been lying. Other Police dusted down the rear door to take fingerprint samples. A State Police Officer asked for the recorded discs of the outside cameras. Sullivan gave them a single CD and replaced it with a new one in his monitoring system and re-started it. While this was going on Daniel took Kit into the lounge room and sat on the lounge with him.

"You were very brave out there tonight, Kit. I'm very proud of you," Daniel said as he hugged his son.

"Dad I didn't want to lose you. Sometimes when I spoke tonight it was as if someone else was speaking through me."

"What do you mean?"

"A number of times I had a voice in my head telling me what to say and when."

"Was it David?"

"No. It was Ellen. She was here tonight."

Daniel was dumbstruck. The Police Commissioner's dead wife had played a part in her husband's eventual downfall.

"Did she tell you about the rose and the ashtray too?"

"Yes. However, I think the piece that got him was the information about his daughter."

"Yeah, that's something the Police will have to look into and also how Ellen died."

Sullivan came into the lounge room carrying two beers and a soft drink. He was followed by State Police Detective Joshua Toohill.

"Team, I think we deserve something to drink after what we have just been through," Sullivan said. "Kit you were absolutely marvellous out there. I know both your mum and Betty will be very proud of you too when they find out what happened here. Who'd ever thought it would end this way? I'm surprised the cops didn't catch Ratcliffe before he made it to the house."

"I can answer that for you Mr. Sullivan," Detective Toohill said. "The Commissioner had arrived here before we were in place however one of our vehicle registration checking cars found his wife's car parked up the road."

"Ellen's car? But she's been dead for some time," Daniel said.

"Well, he kept the car registered in her name so when he wanted to drive anywhere, he wasn't in a car specifically registered to him. Anyway, we went looking for him with night scopes and finally found him standing in your kitchen. I'd be really interested in hearing what conversation took place."

"We'll give you a full statement on Monday in my Parliamentary office."

"Alright. I have notified Chief Inspector Caughey and he has agreed to this."

The detective then left. Kit looked at Sullivan and asked whether he was going to tell the Police about the bear.

"What bear?" Daniel asked.

Sullivan started smiling and laughed as he looked directly at Kit.

"In the kitchen Betty and I have a few stuffed children's teddy bears. One of them is wired up with a camera and microphone to record anything that goes on in the kitchen. I guess it's like a nanny-cam."

"So, you mean everything that took place tonight in the kitchen has been recorded?"

"Yes. I knew Kit knew when he looked directly at the bear and then me. I didn't want to say anything to you in case you let it slip to Ratcliffe it was there. It is our back up plan."

"And we were the guinea pigs – thanks Terry."

"If tonight went badly or Ratcliffe was able to say something false, we have it all on tape."

"Ok. Well done. There's nothing like being surrounded by spies."

All three laughed. Kit then looked down at his lap. Daniel noticed what his son did and gently lifted his boy's chin up.

"Alright, you must be busting to telling us now. Did you know it was all going to end this way?" Daniel asked.

"Yes. It was a major possibility."

"What were the others?"

"Ratcliffe still had free will and could have chosen to shoot you and Mr. Sullivan before the Police arrived."

"What about you?"

"That's the hazy part as I still have a mission to complete so I was not in the picture."

"Do you know what your mission is? Has David or Ellen told you?"

"Yes. I thought it was just to live an ordinary life as you and mum would expect. However, I asked both David Ellen if they could tell me what my mission is – both said I was to help other young people who are near death not to be afraid of dying. I'm supposed to also help others connect with those who have passed over."

"You mean become a Medium or something?"

"Yes, I think so. Mrs. Bishop has only helped me develop a couple of special traits so far, so I have a lot of learning to do."

Daniel and Sullivan looked at each other and then back at Kit. The boy seemed twixt heaven and Earth as he was receiving messages from the grave about how to live his life on this planet.

"What's all this about Kit?"

Kit looked at Sullivan and went and sat on the arm of the lounge chair he was in. He put his arm on his shoulder and watched his face.

"It was David who told me about how tonight could play out."

"What? When? How would he know?"

"Mr. Sullivan, we have a lot to talk about this weekend. David saw me in my last guided visualisation and in my meditations. We talked at length about tonight and the various possibilities. He was very worried for you and was keen for me to be with you this weekend – that's why I asked to stay here this week."

"So, you knew Ratcliffe was coming here tonight and was going to possibly kill me or your father."

"Yes, that's why I told Dad in the car about the visit I had this afternoon in my bedroom from Ellen. She was the one who told me about the roses, the ashtray, and her daughter. How else would I know? I was at school all day."

Sullivan put his hand up to Kit's and pressed against it. His eyes became moist and his voice slightly croaky.

"You and David make a wonderful team. It's like having two sons. Thank you. Daniel thank you also as I know you could have been blown away tonight."

The three talked for another 30 minutes before Daniel said it was time to go.

"Do you still want to meet in the morning?"

"No mate. I have more pressing business – sort of family matters to attend to," Sullivan said as he pressed Kit's hand again.

"Okay, I'll ring Reg and let him know what's happened and he can work a statement with Police Media about tonight. I'll also ring Graham and tell him everything is in order for the Government to pick a new Commissioner."

"Thanks Daniel. Come on mate, we better see your dad off or he'll never leave."

Kit started laughing and stood up. He put his hands on the shoulders of both men and pressed hard. Automatically, both men responded and did the same to Kit.

The smell of coal fires and smog started to waft up Kit's nostrils. He heard the distant clip clop of horse drawn carriages and realised Thomas was sending him a message of 'well done'.

Kit nodded and mentally thanked his spirit guide. An intermittent tingle also went up Kit's spine and neck and he knew David and Ellen were with him.

Epilogue

Within an hour of Daniel arriving home Leah was dropped off by Betty Sullivan. Leah saw Daniel sitting in the lounge room with a bottle of whiskey opened on the coffee table and him drinking a half glass. She could see from the drawn expression on Daniel's face something had happened.

"Enjoy tea with Terry and Kit?"

"No, we never got to eat anything. We had too much happen tonight to worry about food."

"Serves you right. Giving up a date with a lovely woman on such a nice night and at such short notice!"

Leah looked at Daniel and realised he wasn't in a good humour. She sat down next to him and put her arm around him. Daniel lay back in his wife's arms and started sobbing. It had been a very hard and long night and his son, and two spirits had brought about an ending to a story the way no one would have imagined. Daniel calmed and then started telling Leah what happened as it unfolded and why he had to call off their special dinner date. After ten minutes Daniel was done. Leah had started crying as she realised their son had played such a huge part in the downfall of the State's crooked Police Commissioner. She was also concerned about how her husband

and son could have been killed by Ratcliffe if it wasn't for Kit verbally taking him on.

Daniel and Leah eventually calmed and went to bed. They wanted Kit around more than anything right now, but they had made a deal with their son and the Sullivans. *Damn*, they thought.

Once Daniel and the Police left, Sullivan took Kit back inside the house and organised a late-night pizza delivery with garlic bread and ice cream. He hadn't played being a dad for a decade and loved every minute of it. Betty arrived home to find the kitchen in a mess and the two males sitting on the floor of the lounge room eating pizza and talking. She joined them and chuckled as she saw how animated and alive her husband was when talking with Kit. Sullivan then detailed what had happened in their kitchen and why the special night out for the three of them had to be cancelled. Betty was flummoxed. She found it very hard to understand how Kit did what he did and the role David played in the whole affair.

The next day Sullivan arranged with Betty and Kit to escape and stay at an inner-city hotel for the next two days and night to avoid the Media. State Police had been ordered to stand guard outside the Sullivan's house as it was still a crime scene. The hotel escape allowed the Sullivans to take Kit on a harbour cruise, to dinner at the city's tallest building and to the movies on Sunday.

On Monday, Daniel, Sullivan, and Moon were visited by Chief Inspector Caughey and Sergeant Cootes as they took a statement about the Friday night incident. Ratcliffe had suffered a major heart attack and lingered between life and death until Tuesday morning when his heart stopped beating for the last time.

Sullivan detailed to the Parliament later that day what had happened in his kitchen. He said during the attack Ratcliffe had clutched his heart and had a heart attack from which he never recovered and had died early that day. No mention was made of any spirits helping Kit and warning the two families of impending doom. The State Premier appointed an Assistant Police Commissioner to the top cop position until the election was over, and a new Commissioner would be appointed.

Kit continued with his lessons from Mrs. Bishop and eventually became a Medium in his own right. Daniel helped Kit realise his dream of working with groups of people who had undergone near death experiences by contacting several local hospitals and having his son join the groups. Kit not only became a group member but a healer for those who became worried about their experiences.

He listened more to Thomas his spirit guide and visited David through guided visualisations and in his head. A couple of times he also met Ellen Ratcliffe and her daughter on the same grassy hill where he chatted with David. His mission on Earth was not complete.

Acknowledgements

Finding Thomas was written after an extraordinary series of events that proved to me there is life after death. I finished writing the Scott Morrow adventure trilogy – *Only The Brave Dare; Canyon,* and *A Rite Of Passage* – and was keen to explore the afterlife.

I grew up with a maternal grandmother and mother who at times were very fey and could often say what would happen to my brothers, sisters, and me before it happened. Several times I remember my grandmother and mother reading my tea leaves and trying to ascertain what meanings lay within. Later, when my two sisters reached adulthood, they both became tarot card readers and are very good at their readings of things past and current and future events.

In the process of writing *Finding Thomas*, my two brothers, Peter and Mark died eight weeks apart. I had booked in to see some Mediums as part of my research for this book and the visits started taking place several weeks after my second brother died. The Mediums knew nothing about my family yet were able to tell me how my brothers met their fates in detail. Also, they were able to say the spirits of my parents had come through and when they gave some definitive information only,

I would know I truly accepted the fate of us all when we leave this earthly plane.

I also interviewed several people as part of research for *Finding Thomas* who told me they had experienced near-death experiences. Each had a different tale to tell but all had a similar experience about leaving their body and being turned back from the next realm by relatives or figures dressed similarly to monks. Thank you for telling me your stories.

A big thank you to my wife Yvonne; my sisters Liane and Nerida, Robert Hodge, Ron Curry, Sue Jones, and Ian Winters, for their tireless work in helping to edit *Finding Thomas* – I truly appreciate your efforts and guidance.

Postscript: *In the editing phase of this book, I revisited a medium called Janet who had earlier told me about the fates of my brothers. On the first visit, I asked Janet, "Who is my spirit guide?" She said we only ever meet them when we are born and when we die. Not in between. On my second visit, I asked her again about who my spirit guide is. Janet told me a name and gave me some information. She said my guide was born in England and moved to Canada where he joined a band of Indians. When I returned home, I interrogated a web search engine and found the person Janet mentioned. He had a series of connections within his life that mirrored mine even though he had been born in the 1800s. In a sense, I unwittingly became Kit Green and found my own Thomas.*

About the Author

Christopher J. Holcroft is the author of six books. His background is in communications, media training, complex public information planning and implementation, and journalism.

He was a member of the Australian Army Reserve for more than 43 years. His overseas deployments have included Bougainville (1999), East Timor (2001), and Iraq (2006). He is now a Commander in the Australian Navy Cadets as Director of Communication and Media

For more than 36 years, Christopher has been involved in scouting, including Venturer Scout Units in both Victoria and NSW. Christopher was presented the Silver Wattle Award by Scouts Australia in August 2008 for his outstanding service to Scouting. He was later awarded the Silver Koala in 2016 for his distinguished service.

Christopher holds a Masters degree in Organisational Communication from Charles Sturt University and a Bachelor of Arts degree from the University of Technology, Sydney, where he majored in Journalism and Communications Technology. He is also a Justice of the Peace.

He is married to Yvonne and the couple has three sons. They live in NSW and enjoy outdoor recreational activities including camping, abseiling and scuba diving.

www.ingramcontent.com/pod-product-compliance
Lightning Source LLC
Chambersburg PA
CBHW031611240626
47153CB00002B/716

9780645570571